PRAISE FOR
REA FREY

IN EVERY LIFE

"Devastating, thought-provoking, and hopeful, Rea Frey plays deftly in the tantalizing world of 'what if . . .' *In Every Life* is a gem!"

—Emma Grey, author of *The Last Love Note*

"Frey broke my heart into a million pieces, then tenderly put it back together with her deeply moving message that sometimes the truest way we can love someone is by letting them go."

—Kate Robb, author of *This Spells Love*

"Seamlessly weaving together three timelines of 'What is,' 'What was,' and 'What if,' Rea Frey's *In Every Life* is an incredibly relatable story for every woman who has ever faced an impossible situation and wondered what if she had made a different choice. Perfect for fans of Taylor Jenkins Reid's *Maybe in Another Life* and the film *Sliding Doors*, Harper's journey is an exquisite reminder that there are no coincidences and that life unfolds exactly as it is meant to."

—Sara Goodman Confino, bestselling author of *Don't Forget to Write*

"In this heartfelt, poignant novel, Rea Frey has crafted a stirring narrative that grips the heart, uplifts the spirit, and takes the reader on a journey of life-changing events that shapes the characters while dabbling in the idea of how their worlds would shift if they altered one moment in their past."

—Jennifer Moorman, bestselling author

THE OTHER YEAR

"Tenderly observed and heartfelt. Raw and emotional. *The Other Year* is sure to strike a chord with readers everywhere."

—Josie Silver, *New York Times* bestselling author

"In this world-altering women's fiction novel, single mother Kate Baker looks away for a single moment, only to lose sight of her daughter in the ocean. As a result, her world splits into two separate realities: one where she gets to keep being a mother and the other where she doesn't. The message is clear: love your people. A tear-jerker with heart."

—Brenda Novak, *New York Times* bestselling author

"A clever and beautiful novel—the ultimate 'what if' book. The emotional pull of Frey's words made me cry on many occasions, and the last line broke me. What a read!"

—Cesca Major, bestselling author of *Maybe Next Time*

IN
EVERY
LIFE

IN EVERY LIFE

A NOVEL

REA FREY

HARPER MUSE

Published by Harper Muse, an imprint of HarperCollins Focus LLC.

Library of Congress Cataloging-in-Publication Data

Names: Frey, Rea author, author.
Title: In every life : a novel / Rea Frey.
Description: [Nashville] : Harper Muse, 2024. | Summary: "What happens when a husband's dying wish is for his wife to find a new love. . . before he's even gone?"—Provided by publisher.
Identifiers: LCCN 2024009270 (print) | LCCN 2024009271 (ebook) | ISBN 9781400243136 (paperback) | ISBN 9781400243143 (epub) | ISBN 9781400243341
Subjects: LCGFT: Romance fiction. | Novels.
Classification: LCC PS3606.R4885 I5 2024 (print) | LCC PS3606.R4885 (ebook) | DDC 813/.6—dc23/eng/20240301
LC record available at https://lccn.loc.gov/2024009270
LC ebook record available at https://lccn.loc.gov/2024009271

Printed in the United States of America

24 25 26 27 28 LBC 5 4 3 2 1

For Joe and Anna—welcome to the other side

In the end, we learn that to love
and let go can be the same thing.

—Jack Kornfield

A Note from the Author

When I was nineteen, I was a freshman in college and a competitive boxer. I was studying creative writing and journalism at Columbia, while also gearing up for my very first boxing competition. Days before I was set to compete, I got hit during sparring class and began to get a thumping headache behind my left eye. Thinking I was just overtraining, I went in for a CT scan and ended up receiving the startling news that there was a three-and-a-half-inch mass on the left parietal lobe of my brain. As if that wasn't scary enough, it was on the verge of hemorrhaging, which meant, if I got hit in the head *just one more time*, I was dead.

Essentially, boxing saved my life.

To say my world changed overnight is a drastic understatement. In a millisecond, I had to give up the sport I loved in order to get brain surgery during spring break. Since the location of the mass was so rare, the neurosurgeon was unsure how it would all go. (I was literally instructed to say goodbye to my family before they wheeled me back to operate.)

During surgery, they discovered my skull was as thin as an eggshell and had compressed my brain completely flat on the left side. They removed my fragile skull, cut out the mass, and screwed in four titanium plates with sixteen screws for extra reinforcement. Forty-two staples later, I was waking up in the ICU. The thing I remember most during that twilight surgery haze is my neurosurgeon making a comment about how much smaller women's brains are than men's. (Cue eye roll.)

Luckily, the mass was benign. It was actually classified as an arachnoid cyst, which they think had been there since birth and grew over time from physical activity. Because my neurosurgeon was such a boxing fan, however, I was back in the ring just months later, which led me to write my first novel (that had both boxing and brain surgery in it—go figure). That close brush with death made me look at everything differently.

And it also led me to writing novels.

It sent me down a path of healing too. What had caused that arachnoid cyst in the first place? What would I do if it came back? What traumas had I been carrying that I wasn't aware of? What energy was stuck? What was I not willing to face or uncover? Could I have managed to shrink the cyst without being operated on?

In Western culture, it's so easy to diagnose and treat with a pill or surgery. But we so rarely get to the *root* of our diseases or discomforts, and with one in two people diagnosed with cancer in their lifetime, it's clear that our medical system is failing us, our food isn't nourishing us, and our lifestyles aren't supporting our nervous systems or our overall health.

We are sick, and we've forgotten we have the capacity to heal.

This book was born for many reasons: one, because I have my own journey of self-healing and I wanted to share some of that through my characters, Harper and Ben. Two, because I love the what-if questions. I love when we wonder what if the grass is greener, what if we picked the wrong partner, or what if our lives would have turned out differently if we had chosen another path? I love the harder questions too: How can we face the finiteness of our own human bodies? How can we make the most of our time here? How can we love better and harder and pay attention to what truly matters? How can we be certain we are living the "right" life? I also love oracle decks and manifestation and the moon and crystals and neuroscience and quantum physics and spirituality and healing, and I wanted to wrap it all up in a single story.

I hope you love spending time with Harper, Ben, Liam, Wren, Jenna, and the other characters as much as I do. As always, thank you for reading . . . I know there are so many books you can choose from. Thank you for choosing mine.

Prologue

I'm a wife.

I stare at my exhausted but happy reflection in the bathroom mirror and try on the unfamiliar word: *wife*. I'm a wife! Ben and I got married yesterday, and now we are in Hawaii for our honeymoon.

I can hear him humming a song he wrote for the latest Marvel movie soundtrack while he unpacks our suitcase.

"Wifey?" he calls affectionately from the bedroom.

I flip off the light and step into the suite's living room, nearly gasping once again at the startling oceanfront view. "Yes, husband?"

"Do we think a Speedo is appropriate for the beach?" He dangles a tiny strip of fabric that he wears for triathlons from his index finger.

"Oh, most definitely."

He laughs as I enter the bedroom and sling my arms around his shoulders, feeling the heft of him. Though we've been together only two years, we've packed so much into our relationship, it feels like we've always been together. After seven adventure races, five triathlons, one ultramarathon, and visiting four countries, we've set a blistering pace for what we want, which is really just one wild, adventurous life. Somehow, getting married seems like the biggest adventure of all.

"Three things," I say to him now.

"You, me, this," he replies instantly. He stares deeply into my eyes, and I run my fingers through his thick hair.

It's a game we play. At any given moment, we must name what we are grateful for in a world that sometimes leaves us grasping to find something good.

"Your turn."

My entire being radiates with a happiness greater than my body can contain. I know it's not a small thing—to start a life with someone—especially in this day and age. But with Ben it doesn't feel like a risk. It feels like coming home. I think about what I'm grateful for: we both love our jobs, have a good friend group, are healthy and happy, just booked several upcoming trips, bought a new condo, and have our entire lives ahead of us. I'm not sure I can narrow it down to just three.

"Our wedding, this suite, and definitely that Speedo," I say, eyeing the slime-green bathing suit balled in a tiny wad on the king bed. "Maybe not in that order."

He kisses the joke right from my lips. I melt into him, wondering what it will be like to kiss Ben like this for the next fifty years. "I love you, Harper," he whispers in my ear after he finally pulls back.

"I love you too." I snuggle into a hug.

After a lingering moment, he slaps my butt and turns away. "I made dinner reservations," he says. "Five o'clock. Hotel restaurant. Senior citizen hour, baby!"

"You know me so well." I love eating dinner early. When I was growing up, dinner was always on the table by five, and the habit stuck. As a high school art teacher, I'm done with work well before dinner and I love to cook. Ben's work as a film composer, on the other hand, often keeps him trapped in his studio late into the night. When he can, he eats early with me.

Before I can ask him to model that Speedo, all the color drains from his face as he places a hand on his stomach.

"Hey. You okay?"

He swallows and closes his eyes. "I just got really nauseous for some reason. Oh man." He grips his stomach harder.

"Here, sit down." I lead him to the bed and rub his back. I try to remember what we ate on the plane. Chicken, maybe? As I think about it, though, I realize Ben has been complaining about his lower back and stomach for the last few weeks. I assumed he was overtraining.

Something like panic traverses my skin as I look at him, pale and suddenly sweating. Ben never gets sick.

"I need to go to the bathroom," he says. The door shuts, and I can hear him retch into the toilet.

"I'll call down and get you a ginger ale." My fingers shake as I stab the button for room service.

"How can I help you, Mrs. Foster?"

My eyes well with tears at hearing Ben's last name, which is now my last name. Harper Swanson Foster. My new identity. I tell the woman what we need and hang up. I sit on the edge of the bed and try to rationalize what's happening. It's probably nothing. Just something he ate. But there's a deeper feeling, some sense of *knowing*, that I can't shake. What if it's not just something he ate? What if it's serious?

Ben emerges a few minutes later, clutching his stomach. "Wow. I haven't thrown up in years. I think I'm dehydrated."

3

"Why don't you rest for a little while? See if it passes?"

Before I can grab him water or a cool rag for his head, his knees buckle and his eyes roll back in his head. Everything slows like someone has pressed Pause on my life. I can't move. I can't speak. Instead, I only gasp as my strong, healthy husband crumples to the floor with a sickening thud. His head bounces violently against the carpet.

I'm too stunned to catch him.

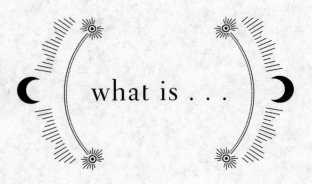

what is . . .

1

I'm going to be a widow.

That word—*widow*—still catches me off guard. It seems like a word reserved for someone who has lived a long life—someone with kids, grandkids, and decades of memories. Someone who is closer to the end of their journey, not the beginning.

Ben says something I don't hear. His hair is growing back, highlighting green eyes laced with flecks of gold. I focus on his thick black lashes, the cleft in his chin, the way his eyes crinkle when he's looking only at me. It seems like yesterday that we got married and had our whole lives ahead of us. What I wouldn't give to go back.

"What did you say?"

"I said, I have a crazy idea."

I fumble for a response. "Define crazy." I nurse my beer and stab another tortilla chip into the guacamole before shoving a fat glob into my mouth. It's Taco Tuesday, but Ben's plate sits untouched, his once sturdy body hollowed out and sucked dry from doctors, chemo, endless treatments, and flimsy hope in sterile hospital rooms. Still, there's a glimmer of mischief in his eyes that tells me he's up to something.

Though we're in pajamas, in our condo, in the middle of the city, with some terrible reality show blaring in the background, it feels like what he's about to say is important and I should listen. I cross my legs and feel a little lightheaded from the beer.

Ben places his warm, large hands around mine, his skin pale where it had once been browned from the sun. The chemo made him sensitive to the sun (and a million other things), so even though he's stopped treatment, he has to be careful. "I want you to just listen first. Listen to what I have to say before you say no."

I laugh. "How do you know I'm going to say no?"

He drags his thumb back and forth over the skin of my hand until it burns. "Because this idea, while totally *brilliant*, is also really, really crazy."

"Out with it, Foster." I feel a giggle bubbling up my throat in anticipation. This is the most normal conversation we've had in weeks.

"Okay." He takes a shaky breath and rubs a hand across his stubbly head. "I want you to find someone else . . . before I go."

The giggle I've been suppressing bursts from my throat until I feel hysterical. He doesn't respond, doesn't laugh in return. "No," I say, squinting at him. "What is it, really?"

He levels me with a look, and I swallow.

"You can't be serious." I glance at my watch, a present from Ben for my last birthday. He had it engraved to say, *You're the only woman who makes me forget about time.* The hysteria turns to outrage, and I shift, spilling tortilla chips onto our comfy fort of pillows and quilts. "What is this really about?" I rack my brain. Has *he* met someone else? Is he tired of me? Is this some lame attempt at distracting me from what we both know is coming?

After our honeymoon, we took Ben to get tests, and then an oncologist delivered words you never want to hear. Ben has stage four advanced pancreatic cancer . . . the type of cancer that often doesn't present symptoms until it's far too late. The tumors were too big to remove and had already spread to his lymph nodes and liver. The chemo couldn't shrink the masses enough to even attempt surgery. So, despite all the treatments that made him feel sicker than the cancer, here we are, facing the end.

"Harp." He pats the stack of pillows on the floor, our lazy pallet for food because Ben gets too exhausted sitting upright at the table and is more comfortable on the ground. Sometimes he falls asleep mid-bite or curls up in my lap, and I stroke his short hair while he naps for hours. And then I cry, trying not to drip tears and snot onto his cheeks.

I move closer to him and cross my arms. "Explain."

"I've been thinking a lot about this. I know you are an independent, capable woman who most certainly does *not* need a man, but I want to do this for you." He looks deeply into my eyes until I want to scream. "I want you to be okay when I'm gone."

"Well, I'm *not* going to be okay," I say. "You're dying."

That word is an affront. Ben is one of the most vibrant humans I know. The man you want beside you in a physical emergency. The friend you ask to help move furniture. The guy who goes for a thirty-mile bike ride and then plays a pickup basketball game with friends. How can he be dying?

"But you're not, Harper. I want you to live your life." He threads his fingers through mine and searches my eyes while tears fill his own. "I want you to find love again."

My nostrils flare, and I rip my hand free, gathering my long, auburn hair into a bun and securing it with a rubber band from my wrist. "Have we met? I don't want anyone else but you. I barely like people. That's why I waited almost thirty-five years to get married in the first place. You know this."

"This is precisely my point. We both know you won't ever find someone if I don't find him for you." He produces a composition notebook he's been hiding under one of the pillows and flips it open, stabbing the page. At the top, it says, "Master Plan: Find Harper Someone to Love Before I Go."

Tears spring to my eyes as I see the numbered points beneath it.

1. *Get Harper to agree to my crazy idea.*
2. *Once she is done telling me I'm an idiot, explain crazy idea.*
3. *Come up with a time line for crazy idea.*
4. *Find dates for Harper.*
5. *Find dates for Harper who don't make her want to gag.*
6. *Find dates for Harper who aren't sociopaths, psychopaths, or just lame.*
7. *Find the one for Harper who can make her laugh and take care of her the way she has taken care of me.*
8. *Remind her that I will be watching from beyond the grave . . . so she better not love him too much.*

"Ben . . ." Tears stream down my face faster than I can flick them away.

"Look, if the situation were reversed, you'd do the same for me," he says. "Right?"

I bark out a laugh. "Absolutely *not*. I'd want you to love me and only me and be miserable for the rest of your long life." I grin through my tears, because we both know that isn't true.

"Just think about it, okay? That's all I ask." He reaches for my hand again, and I let his fingers entwine with mine, fingers that have held mine as our whole big, shiny plan for our lives has been decimated by the dreaded *C* word. These are the hands I held while saying vows, fingers I've kissed through chemo and doctors' visits and making love.

I can't tell him I'll think about it, because there's nothing to think about. I want to scream. I want to tell him this is not okay. I want to explain that our love story, in my mind, is still unfolding, so no, Ben, I am most definitely *not* open to finding someone else.

As my outrage gains momentum, just to spite him, I vow, right here and now, never to love another man as long as I live.

Sensing I don't want to talk anymore, he turns back to his plate of food and tentatively takes a bite. My heart aches, as it so often does, in seeing his lack of appetite, not just for food but for life. That hunger used to define him, define *us*.

How can someone so excited by life suddenly be on the tail end of it? It doesn't seem fair. I bite back my pain. No pity party today. Instead, I tuck back into my tacos, though my appetite is gone.

"Three things," Ben says softly now.

I lower my plate and look at him. "I'm not in the mood."

"Too bad."

"Fine." I adjust to look at him. "Tacos, tacos, and more tacos."

He laughs. "Fair enough."

"You?" I ask.

"Tacos, of course." He ticks them off on his fingers. "Being here with you. And meeting your new future boyfriend." He nudges me with his shoulder.

In response, I smack him lightly on the arm.

"Careful," he says. "I'm fragile."

Though he's joking, I feel like crying. "No, Ben," I say, turning back to my food. "You're not."

2

It's been two days since Ben issued the challenge of finding me someone else to love, and I hope by my pretending he didn't say it, he will let it drop.

But Ben is someone who needs a project. As if losing his fight with cancer isn't all-consuming enough, he wants to ensure I fall in love while he's still here. I haven't even tried to explain all the reasons that will never work, how it isn't physically possible to fall in love with someone while you're still madly in love with someone else. That it will probably be years before I feel even an iota of normal, and the last thing on my mind is finding a new husband.

I make coffee, leave Ben a note, and head out for work. Today is the last day of school before summer. While I wanted to take a leave of absence at the start of Ben's diagnosis, he insisted I keep working so I could have some semblance of a normal routine.

"Kids put life into perspective," he often says.

To which I always reply, "Have you ever met a teenager?"

Truthfully, I adore my students. They give me a sense of purpose and have kept me motivated this past year while Ben endured treatment.

I take the elevator to the main floor of our building, say good morning to our doorman, Randy, and step outside. It's a perfect Chattanooga day, not a cloud in the sky. I lift my coffee to my lips and take a big gulp, indulging in a fleeting moment of joy. This happens sometimes. I can appreciate the smallest things—a chirping bird, the glistening water of the Tennessee River, the majesty of the Appalachian Mountains—and then I feel bad, as if I can't be sad about Ben *and* happy about life. Ben insists these moments are the moments that matter most, because he finds beauty everywhere now too. Before cancer, we were both moving so fast, working hard and making future plans, and now that's all been wiped away. It's been one of the most surprising effects of his diagnosis, how we are both finding glimpses of beauty in the grief.

"Hey, hey." Jenna falls into step beside me, and I realize I passed the front of her building without even slowing for her to join.

"Sorry." I stop, turn, and give her a hug. She smells like flowers. "Lost in thought."

"Gee, I wonder why."

We both laugh, because if I don't laugh, I will cry. Jenna has been with us during the entire ordeal and is one of the few people who doesn't treat Ben with pity. She still jokes around, busts Ben's balls, and tells him to get it together when she stops by and he's too sick to get out of bed.

"So did you know?" I ask. I don't even say what I'm referring to, because if she does know, I'll be able to tell.

"I know nothing." Her cheeks redden as she tucks her wild, curly hair behind her ears. Jenna teaches French, knows five languages, has a gorgeous partner, Wren, and two hairless cats. She's sharp as a tack, and her answer tells me everything I need to know.

"Wait," I say. "When did he come up with this stupid plan?"

She shrugs. "You know Ben. He needs something else to focus on besides . . ." The truth hangs between us. "I told him it was ridiculous, but when has he ever listened to me?"

"Good point." I laugh.

"Well, if you think this idea is insane, just wait until you talk to him and Wren." Wren owns the Terrington art gallery downtown. For years, she's encouraged me to take my craft more seriously, though I always claim I don't have enough time. At first, it was because of work, then it was because of Ben.

I stop her. "What do you mean?"

"It's not my place to say."

"Really, Jenna? You're just going to dangle that carrot?"

"Yep."

At the high school's entrance, I hold the door open for her as a crush of students barrel inside before the morning bell.

"Have a good day!"

I roll my eyes as she heads off to her classroom. What are Wren and Ben up to? I stand in the foyer and listen to the chatter around me as I make my way to my classroom.

My seniors stripped their work from the walls earlier this week. Before they flood in for first period, I stare at the husk of this room, which has contained so much creativity this year.

The walls are studded with putty and nothing more. The room seems cold and bland without their wild, colorful, abstract creations clogging up every available surface. Though I claim not to have favorites, my seniors are easily that, mainly because they remind me of what's possible in the world.

They pile in now, excited about the last day of school. I let them grab their supplies and tell them we are doing one last project, which is free choice.

Once they settle down and find their rhythm, I close my eyes for a moment and hear the quick swish of brushes and graffiti pens being shaken and pressed to fresh canvases. There's the *tap, tap, tap* of bristles in water, the long, smooth strokes of thick acrylic, mingled with a stray cough or sneeze. When the kids are locked in and focused, not distracted by their phones or each other, the energy swells. I absorb the vibration of it now, that strong creative force of being in the groove while time disappears.

Though I teach art, I pretty much gave up on my own dreams because my one big shot didn't happen in New York. An image flashes through my mind that stops me cold: of me, the gallery, of *him* . . . but I promptly swipe it away, like always. That is the past. I know now, more than ever, that there is no point in playing the what-if game.

Classes whip by, one after another, and before I know it, it's the end of the day. I gather my supplies and rush through the hallways, waving at kids, wishing them a good summer, and absorbing all the raucous sounds of young teenage life. Seniors whoop through the halls, excited to be free from this place for good, with its metal detectors, security guards, and active shooter drills. School, like so much of the world, has become such an unpredictable place.

At the teachers' lounge door, I feel the familiar curl of excitement at the promise of summer. No matter how old I get, it's still my favorite season. But the moment I think about it, I remember what could happen this summer. This might be the summer I lose Ben. This might be the summer my whole life changes. This might be the summer I become a widow.

Before I can let those thoughts go, Jenna yanks me inside the lounge and starts chatting my ear off. The emotions from the day leak out of me slowly, like a gently pricked balloon. I am tired. I want to see Ben. Instead, I plaster on a smile and spend time with my colleagues.

But my brain keeps drifting away. When I leave here for the summer, I am stepping into an unfamiliar world in more ways than one.

Though I am excited for the break from work, I also know that what I'm facing with Ben will no longer be a hypothetical anymore. I won't have work to scurry off to. I won't be able to morph into Harper the teacher and bury my problems for seven hours every day.

Instead, I will face it head-on—this new reality of losing my favorite person.

The big question isn't *if* anymore . . . it's when.

3

Instead of getting drinks with everyone after work, I rush home to be with Ben.

I know I will have a life full of after-work drinks, dinners, and parties ahead of me, and he does not. Thankfully, no one gives me a hard time when I skip out.

"Hey, hey." I step inside our condo and immediately smell vomit. "Ben?" I rush to the bedroom. The covers have been shoved back, rumpled, as if in a rush, and there's a wisp of viscous bile on the floor. I follow the sluglike trail to the bathroom, where I find Ben, head deep in the toilet bowl. He raises one hand limply.

"Hey, babe."

I kneel beside him, feel his cheeks to see if they're warm, and rub his back in gentle circles. "Why didn't you call me?"

He swipes a hand across his mouth and sits back. The fatigue on his face is about so much more than getting sick right now. It's been a year of not feeling well, of being so engrossed in every symptom, *every* second of the day, because a simple cold could morph into an infection and kill him faster than the cancer. For a man who rarely, if ever, got sick before his diagnosis, this is a cruel way to spend his final months of life, and I wish there was something more I could do to make him feel better.

But there is, a voice reminds me. *His idiotic idea.* "Is it something you ate?"

He nods. "Probably. I was feeling pretty good and might have gone a bit overboard with lunch. I'm okay, though. Feeling better already." He places a hand on his stomach and sighs.

I press the back of my palm to his forehead now that he's sitting upright. He doesn't feel warm, and I instantly relax. The fact that he was feeling better this morning is a good thing. He's still learning his limits with what he can eat, however. Though his doctor suggested palliative care, he doesn't feel ready yet. And because he's not doing any treatment now, he's pretty much on his own.

He closes his eyes. "How was your last day?"

"It was sweet." I want to pounce and ask him about what Jenna said, but I need to make sure he's not going to be sick again.

"Good, I'm glad." His eyes stay closed as he offers a small smile.

The toilet water runs between us, bubbling and then settling as I contemplate how to ask him about Jenna without seeming insensitive to how he's physically feeling. But I know myself; if I don't get it off my chest soon, it will drive me crazy.

"When did you tell Jenna and Wren about your big idea?"

His eyes snap open and he shifts to look at me. "So she told you."

"What I really want to know is what she was talking about when she said you and Wren had something to tell me?"

"Oh. That." He winces. He exhales and then closes his eyes again. "Wren and I were chatting and thought it would be an interesting idea for you to pursue your art for a while."

19

"What does that mean?"

"Like, maybe quit your job and try to make it as an artist?"

I wait for the punch line, but there is none. "Oh, sure," I say as I adjust my back against the tub. "I'll quit a job I love, lose my health insurance *and* benefits to chase some pipe dream. Seems totally rational." He's hit a nerve, and we can both tell.

Ben knows most things about my life, but he doesn't know how hard I fell on my face in my twenties after trying to do just what he's suggesting. It's a time in my life I don't like to revisit . . . for more reasons than one.

"Look, if I'd decided to teach music instead of going after my dream, how would my life have turned out?"

"But it worked out for you," I insist. "You got your lucky break. I didn't. And I happen to love my job."

"Do you?"

"What, because teaching art can't be enough for me? I can't be happy with what I'm doing? I'm supposed to want more?"

"When you're as talented as you are? Yes."

"What's that supposed to mean?" This is the second time in as many days that he's pressing buttons, and I want to know why.

"It means that you're hiding!" His voice bellows in our tiny bathroom. "You're in a comfort zone. You're not really happy!"

Both of us sit in stunned silence. Ben rarely raises his voice, and never at me. I place a hand on his arm. "Ben, where in the world is all this coming from? Needling me about my job? Wanting me to find someone else?"

He looks at me with tears in his eyes. "Because I cannot leave this world without knowing you're okay." His voice has dropped to a whisper. "I want you to have your dreams. I want you to spend your life with someone. I want you to have everything, Harper."

My tears match his. "Don't you see that I already do?" Even with the inevitable end looming in front of us, I wouldn't trade a single day of being with him for anything.

"Ugh." He exhales and draws his knees to his chest. "I'm sorry. I'm an idiot. I'm just panicking."

"You're not an idiot. Well, on second thought . . ." I nudge him and that gets a small smile. "Look, Ben. I get it. I do. Everything feels like it's out of your control. But you can't control the outcome of *my* life too. That's for me to figure out, okay?"

Instead of responding, we sit in silence, something that is happening more and more the sicker he gets. It makes me realize how quick we are to fill the quiet in everyday life, how we jump over each other to talk without really listening. I've learned more about my husband from the silences between us than any meaningful conversation. I used to avoid them, afraid of what I might find there, but now I welcome them because it forces both of us to face our feelings.

"I just want you to consider it," Ben finally says.

"Which part? Finding someone else or pursuing art?"

He smirks. "Well, both, ideally, but maybe we could start with art?"

"We'll see." I don't tell him that ship has sailed—that after a brief stint of going all in, it was clear I was meant to teach, not paint. Plus, even if I wanted to pursue art, the world is a very different place than it used to be. I'm not an Instagram influencer or a TikTok star, for one.

He rolls his head toward me and smiles, his eyes crinkling in that exact way I love. "It's a start." He gingerly caresses my cheek, then grips the edge of the tub as he struggles to stand. I help him, and once we are upright, he pulls me into a hug. The outline of his bony ribs jabs my palms beneath his shirt. My fingers dance over them, counting them under my breath. It seems like yesterday I was holding him in our honeymoon suite, my arms caressing well-developed muscles. Now I feel I could break his bones if I squeeze too hard.

"Do you feel up for a short walk around the block? Maybe get some fresh air?" When we first met, we'd take our bikes and ride the long, winding road up Lookout Mountain. Drivers would honk in admiration as their cars chugged upward to visit Rock City, while we cranked our way up the punishing incline. At the top, we'd have a beer and stare at the astonishing view as the mountain breeze cooled us. Now he gets winded walking from room to room.

"Maybe in a little bit. I think I'm going to rest awhile."

"Okay. I'll make us some soup for later." I kiss his forehead and tuck him into bed, turning off the light as I leave. I stand in our condo, which was once so full of life but now grows quieter and darker each day. I know the end is coming; I can feel it in my bones, and despite all of our talks and preparations, I am not ready to say goodbye. In many ways, we are still getting to know each other. How can it already be over?

I swipe the tears that come and decide to go on a quick walk by myself while he's resting. Maybe I'll even walk down to my studio, like Ben suggested. Air it out. It's been a while. I slip on my shoes, take the elevator down, and step outside.

The Chattanooga heat warms my face as the mountain wind ruffles my hair. We live right by the pedestrian bridge, and people are out riding their bikes, walking their dogs, holding hands. No matter how dismal it gets in our condo, when I step outside, I am faced with the fact that life constantly moves on, that there will be life after Ben, even if I don't want it.

I step onto the bridge and smile at other pedestrians. I pause at one of the blue benches overlooking the water and sit.

Ben constantly tells me how stoic I've been through all of this, but what I don't tell him is that I am absolutely terrified. Besides my grandparents, I've never lost anyone close to me, especially not a lover. And Ben is so much more than just my partner; he's in my marrow. He's part of me. I can't imagine a day without him, much less a lifetime.

What if I do end up all alone?

I close my eyes and begin to cry, wiping my eyes behind my sunglasses as I stare at the glittering water and the pulse of life all around. Down below, people are sprawled on colorful blankets in the park, a few kids going round and round on the carousel. I probably need to find a support group soon, open myself up to other people who are going through the same thing. I let the emotions pass, then stand and continue across the bridge.

I think about when we first met, which was less than three years ago. Everything seemed so easy then, the world at our fingertips. I truly believed that anything was possible and that our lives were just getting started. It boggles my mind how much we've been through in such a short time.

But as I've learned, today is all that matters. I'll continue to take life one day at a time until Ben has no more time left.

4

When I return from my walk, Ben is up, sitting on the couch with a journal, a bit of color back in his face.

"Good nap?" I ask, dropping my keys and sunglasses in the bowl.

"If by good, you mean I didn't puke in my sleep, then it was great." He grins, and my heart seizes.

"How will I live without your terrible jokes?"

"Oh, I've left you about five hundred Post-it Notes in odd places. You'll see."

I flinch as I imagine roaming from room to room once he's gone, plucking sweet notes from hidden places. My eyes instantly fill with tears again. Banishing the image, I lean in from behind the couch to give him a soft kiss and slide my hands around his neck and chest.

I eye the pen in his hand. "Making another master plan?"

He winces. "Sort of." There's a look on his face I can't quite discern.

I crawl over the back of the couch and scoot in beside him, my knee touching his. "Care to elaborate?"

"You know the latest score I did for the Bond movie?"

I nod.

"Well, I was doing an interview, and the journalist got wind of my . . . struggles, and he asked if he could interview me."

"So now you're keeping a journal of your innermost thoughts to share with him?" I tease.

"No, more like questions." He clears his throat. "He has a whole body of work on alternative therapies for cancer patients, which I thought was cool."

My gut clenches at the mention of alternative therapies. In the last few months, Ben has tried almost everything he can get his hands on, but it seems nothing's worked. "What would the interview be about? Your music? Or your health?"

"Maybe both." He taps his pen to the page. "This journalist . . . He wants to do a feature on me for the *New York Times*."

I nod again. Ben has been written up in major outlets over the years, though few of them have been so personal in nature. "Well, that's great, isn't it?"

He reddens, which is unusual, as his go-to colors as of late are either ashen or pale. "Depends on how you define great. *I* think it's great."

I cross my arms. "What have you done?"

He shifts to look into my eyes, and I cave once his gaze connects with mine. There are whole worlds in those eyes, and I never stand a chance once he locks in. "I may have told him about my crazy idea."

I don't even have to ask *which* crazy idea, because there is only one. Something akin to annoyance taps my shoulder, but I ignore it for Ben's sake. "What exactly did you tell him?"

"I told him that I wanted you to find love again."

My nostrils flare as I wait. "And?"

"And then he had the brilliant idea to, um, write about it." His eyes flick away from mine and back to the page. "To interview you too."

I laugh and lightly shove his shoulder. "You are just so full of amazing ideas lately, Ben, it's hysterical." I hop off the couch and attempt to keep my voice light. "I'm sure that's when you told him that your wife would never, in a million years, entertain this insane idea, so boo-hoo for him and his readers." I don't know this journalist, but already I dislike him immensely.

To detract from my annoyance, I busy my hands with pouring a Topo Chico over ice and hacking a lime into wedges. I squeeze the juice into the glass and drink down the fizzy water in one long, greedy gulp. My throat burns. I feel desperate. Desperate for Ben to let go of this ridiculous idea. Desperate for us to have one normal day where we can just be together without wishing for a miracle to descend from the heavens and spare us both the inevitable grief and pain of when he's going to collapse right in front of me. This knowing that the end is coming but not knowing *when* is the real disease.

"So is that a no?" He cranes around to look at me. His eyes are pleading, and I can't for the life of me understand why this is so important to him.

"Yes, that is a no, Ben. I really want you to drop it, okay?"

He opens his mouth, then snaps it shut and nods. "Okay. I'll tell him it's off the table. The article can just be about me."

A loaded silence blooms between us. We are not a couple with tension; we've been to the bowels of hell. We've faced a cancer diagnosis. We've been cautiously hopeful, then come crashing back down when the doctors said that Ben will die, and soon. *There's nothing we can do* is one of my least favorite phrases ever, and as it throttles through my brain now, I suddenly understand why Ben wants this so very badly: because it is something he can do for me.

But I can't. Even when I search the deepest parts of myself, even when I understand why he would be doing it, I know, without a doubt, that my heart belongs to Ben.

I sidle up beside him again and tap his knee with my own. "How about our bucket list? Do you feel up to resuming it now that I'm off for the summer?" Ben revised his bucket list when he received news that none of his treatment efforts worked. Instead of big things, like riding an elephant or jumping out of a plane, it's now full of smaller experiences, like helping a stranger in need or conquering a fear.

He looks like he's about to say something but doesn't. Instead, he snaps the journal shut and tosses it on the coffee table with the pen. "Yeah," he says. "I guess we should, shouldn't we?"

I grip his hands and force him to look at me. "Look, I love you so much for wanting to make sure I'm going to be okay, but you're it for me, Ben. I've never loved anyone the way I love you, and I never will again. That's just a fact. Okay? But that doesn't mean I don't appreciate the gesture. And," I add, just to lighten the mood, "if the universe wants me to be with someone else, then I'm sure some hot guy will fall from the sky." That gets a grin. "But until then, can we drop it?"

He processes what I'm saying and finally sighs. "Yeah." He hoists himself off the couch with as much effort as a heavily pregnant woman and grimaces as he stands. His entire body aches, all the way to his bones. I'm not sure he can even make it around the block, much less embark on a bucket list adventure. But I know Ben well enough to know that he understands his own limits.

"How about I start dinner?"

"Sure. I'm going to take a shower." His voice is flat and small, and I feel terrible for bursting his bubble.

As I chop vegetables and heat the broth, I think about my new-found freedom this summer. A heavy, dark cloud trails that excitement. Of course it does. But I have to start organizing my life for what comes *after*. Who I will be *after*. How I will spend my days *after*.

I glance around our tiny, comfortable condo and wipe a few tears that have carved wonky lines down my cheeks. We were so excited when we bought this condo; it symbolized our new marriage and a fresh start. Instead, it's been a container for bad news, endless tears, and illness.

A few minutes later, Ben emerges in some version of the same outfit he always wears: loose-fitting pants and a T-shirt. I turn the soup to low and grab his shoulders. "Hey, you."

"Hey." He stares into my eyes, but they are dim, sad.

"Let's go for a walk. Get some ice cream?"

There's a hint of a smile as he points at the stove. "But you're making soup."

"So? We're adults, aren't we? Who says we can't have dessert before soup?"

"If you'd told me I would be pushing forty, eating all soft foods, I wouldn't have believed you."

"If you'd told me I'd have to talk the lit and fit Ben Foster into going on a walk around the block to get ice cream, I wouldn't have believed you."

There. The spark ignites, and he goes to retrieve his shoes. When he stands after tying the laces, he smiles. "Race you there?"

"Only if you use those dorky speed-walking arms." I mimic a speed walker, and he erupts into a genuine laugh.

"You can do that . . . on the other side of the street. While I'm winning."

It used to be the joke between us, how he was so obsessed with winning the obstacle course race where we first met that he literally knocked me over and didn't look back. At the time, I'd been doing Tough Mudders for a year and traveled to Chattanooga for the race. If I hadn't caught up to Ben that day, we could have lost out on the chance to get to know each other. Luckily, because of *my* hyper-competitive streak, we were literally thrown together at the finish line, right as I passed him to win. And now here we are, at another finish line.

"See you there, loser." I racewalk out our door to the elevator, hips swiveling, arms pumping.

He calls from the doorway, unable to run to catch up.

"Yeah?" I turn, and there are tears in his eyes as I jog back to him. "You okay?"

I scan his body to be sure. Instead, he crushes me in a firm hug and digs his fingernails into my back.

"I'm so in love with you, Harper." He cries softly into my neck, and I hold him as tears slide silently down my cheeks and drench the neck of his shirt. I'm transported back to the bliss of those early days of falling in love. We didn't waste time playing games as we might have in our twenties, but it was still exciting. We were two people who had been waiting for the right person, refusing to settle. And then there he was, literally knocking me off my feet. Once we began to date, everything crackled with possibility. Everything was an adventure. Everything, after so much time, finally made sense.

"I love you too. So much." I've never meant the words more. I squeeze him back, though not as hard as I'd like.

Finally, he pulls away and smooths the tears from my cheeks. "Also, you should never come back to check on the person who's trying to beat you," he whispers. Then, to my shock and delight, he races past me toward the elevator, faster than I've seen him move in months.

He stabs the elevator button. It opens, and he steps on. He peeks his head out, his tear-streaked face raw and beautiful. "You coming?"

I nod and swallow my grief. It grows like a pit inside me, bigger and heavier by the day. "I'm right behind you."

5

The next morning, I tell Ben I'm going to run a few errands.

He blows me a kiss goodbye, as he is busy composing for a friend's independent film. When treatment got too intense, he transitioned to work from his at-home studio, but he has never slowed down. Work keeps him going, gives him a purpose, an outlet.

As I walk down the street, I think about what he said about me giving art another shot. It's not like I don't *want* to know what would happen if I went all in. I just haven't made time for it. Deciding to forgo the market, I turn right and head toward my art studio instead.

While I come here sometimes to think, it's been a while since I've created anything. When I let myself into my sacred space, however, I audibly exhale. The loft sits on the top floor of an old, converted textile mill. Years ago, I got it at a steal and luckily have a landlord who keeps his promise of rent control. My body releases all of its tension as I spot my line of acrylics and step gingerly onto the giant tarp, eyes roaming over half-finished canvases.

Though Ben doesn't know it, before this final prognosis, I'd started a series about his life. His mother was kind enough to send me all sorts of photos, and I'd begun to capture him in his simplest moments as a child: sitting, standing, walking, reading, and later, moving, composing, racing. I haven't ventured into the cancer series yet, mainly because it's still too close to home. Maybe that's why I've been avoiding coming here altogether. It's just too hard.

I clean my brushes and organize the space, pausing on a portrait of Ben standing on the beach, sun setting behind him, arms thrust wide. It's my favorite picture because on that trip, we'd talked about our lives: all the places we'd go, all the things we'd see. We were going to live our lives to the absolute fullest, not settle into a domestic rut like so many couples we know. But then life slapped us in the face, and here we are.

I check the time, decide there's nowhere I really have to be, and crank up some good music. Dipping my brush against my palette, I tune out the depressing commentary of what could have been. Already I've spent so much time trying to get back to what Ben and I once were, but also dreading what we will become . . . what *I* will become.

Today I vow to stay right here with my art I've long neglected, to hopefully find some sort of flow. As I work, I keep my mind focused on the task at hand, and before I know it, it's lunch. I break and stretch, judging my work in front of me. I want it to convey all the best parts of our lives together, tiny details I would normally never share with the world. I want to capture those moments. I want to capture Ben.

Less than three years, under normal circumstances, is not enough time to really know someone, especially when a chunk of that time has been spent battling death. But I know Ben more than I've ever known anyone, because we have faced the darkest, hardest part of being human.

I make some notes for the current pieces, then decide to pack up for the day. When I get to the pedestrian bridge, I freeze. Ben is standing there, waving. He looks well, the sun shining on his face.

"Hey, you." I give him a kiss. "What are you doing here?"

"I hoped you might have gone to your studio, which, from the looks of you, you did." He motions to the paint under my fingernails. "And I figured today is a beautiful day for a bucket list adventure."

"Ah, it is, isn't it?" My heart flutters as I consider what he's come up with. I mentally scan our most recent list, but before I can think of what it could be, he interrupts.

"It's a new one," he says. "Follow me."

He takes my hand and leads me back toward my studio. We take a right on Walnut Street and stop near a tattoo shop. I turn to him, floored.

"Tattoos? Can you even get a tattoo?"

While he was in treatment, he couldn't do anything that would risk excess bleeding, but I'm not sure what the restrictions are now. "I can," he says. "And so can you."

I nod. I've never gotten a tattoo, though I've definitely thought about it over the years. Before Ben's diagnosis, I put it off and said I would do it someday. Now that we're here, I have no idea what I want to get. We go inside, and he says we have a one-thirty appointment.

"Wow, confident, are we?" After handing over our driver's licenses and filling out paperwork, with words like *infection* and *death* turning my stomach, we are led back to a small space with a black table covered with the same crinkly paper they use at doctors' offices. The artist introduces himself, and Ben turns to me.

"So, I've given this a lot of thought because, frankly, you are going to have to live with this much longer than I am." He smiles. "You know I'm not into symbols or zodiac signs—"

"Thank God," I interject, immediately relieved that I won't have a yin and yang symbol tattooed on my butt.

"Instead, I thought about words. How important words have been to us throughout our entire relationship. How, when I was too sick to speak, we could look at each other and say one simple phrase that would bring us back to each other."

I swallow the gently forming lump in my throat because I know just what words he's referring to. He grips my hands loosely and whispers, "I see you."

"I see you," I say.

Suddenly I know it's the perfect tattoo. Those words take me back to a million what-if moments, when Ben was so sick that he no longer resembled the man I knew, and I didn't know how to help him. He would always look at me and simply say, "I see you." *I see your fears. I see your love. I see your uncertainty. I see you.*

And I would say it back: "I see you." *I see you beyond your diagnosis. I see your soul. I see your spirit. I see your love. I see you healthy. I see you healed.*

The tattoo artist clears his throat, and I laugh, squeezing Ben's arm. "Crying in a tattoo parlor is *so* not cool, Benjamin," I joke.

For the next forty minutes, we get the words tattooed on the inside of our wrists. Ben's is in small uppercase letters that I write for him, and I opt for his cursive script. This way we will carry a piece of each other with us, no matter what.

When we leave, I have a boost of adrenaline at doing something so wildly spontaneous, like we used to. "Feel up for something else?"

I ask. I don't want to push it, especially if he's tired, but to my surprise, he smiles.

"Lead the way," he says.

"Follow me." I wiggle my eyebrows.

We walk toward Coolidge Park, which is packed with kids since summer has just begun. As I approach the carousel, he laughs.

"Seriously? You want to ride the carousel?"

I nod. "I haven't ridden one since I was little, and I want to ride one with you."

"From tattoos to carousels," he says. "A day in the life."

"That should be the title of your memoir." I stick out my tongue at him as I pay for our tickets and tell him to pick an animal to ride. We choose seahorses side by side, and Ben groans as he hoists himself up and clings to the pole.

"We're the oldest people here," he whispers.

"Because adults are boring," I say. We've spent so much time talking about how we simply stop playing as we get older, how we stop wanting to do the things we used to when we were kids. No coloring. No playing games. No carousels. At this moment, we are resurrecting that childlike excitement. At least I am. When I glance at Ben, he seems embarrassed, but I know he's in good spirits.

We go around and around, and I check to make sure he's not getting nauseous. Instead, he's already struck up a conversation with a little boy beside him who is scared and searching for his mother. He points to a woman wrangling two more children on the other side of the carousel.

I glance at my tattoo, which is covered with a shiny ointment. It is one of those surprising days I will look back on when things are hard and I want to remember all the beautiful moments between us.

Finally, the carousel shudders to a stop, and after Ben makes sure the boy reunites with his mother, we hop off and step toward the park, where families run wild across the expansive lawn.

"Hungry?" I ask. "We could grab an early dinner somewhere. Or get takeout and eat in the park?"

"Sure."

Ben is agreeable as we find a spot on the hill and sit. There are several groups out throwing a football, playing soccer, or fishing at the water's edge. I'm sure it's odd for Ben to sit here instead of tossing a ball around with his buddies. Before he got sick, I rarely saw him sit down.

"What are you thinking?" I finally ask.

His thin arms are looped around his knees as he stares into the distance. "Just remembering."

It's something we say a lot in the quiet moments. "Just remembering," we'll say as we catalog all that's good. I just thought the same thing on the carousel, and here he is doing it too.

"It's a good day for that," I offer, letting my own mind wander. Back to the past. Back to even a few moments ago.

"So that journalist called again. From the *Times*," Ben finally says.

"And?" For some inexplicable reason, my heart begins to race.

His face darkens momentarily. "Listen, Harper. This whole 'find you someone to love' is a ridiculous idea. I know that. He and I talked about it a bit more, and I could see it playing out in real life like some terrible Hallmark movie." He looks at me. "I want you to know the idea came from a good place. If I'm being honest, I just feel so helpless. And responsible for all the pain you're going to go through." He sighs. "I was just trying to think of a way to make it better."

"So get me a puppy, not a fiancé." I bump his shoulder playfully. "But seriously, don't get me a puppy. I can't handle that right now."

"Noted."

I understand Ben's desperate need to cling to something that distracts him from reality. "Plus," I add, "how awkward for you to have to find me some new hottie."

Ben breaks into a grin. "Who said he would be hot?" His eyes are light, and he's smiling. "If you change your mind, though . . ."

"Zip it." I lay my hand in his and squeeze. He squeezes back. I rest my head on his shoulder and sigh.

I'm relieved he's choosing to drop this whole interview thing. I can't imagine some journalist taking a deep dive into our love story and Ben's big, beautiful, messy life. I don't want to share my time with him, not like that, not with a stranger.

Now that Ben's idea and this article are off the table, I snuggle in closer, wanting to relax, wanting to let it all go, wanting to stay present, but I'm still so anxious about what awaits us.

I'm still scared.

6

"The feature has been booked," Ben confirms the next day. "For the *Times*."

I'm sketching at the dining room table when he delivers this news. I stop what I'm doing and stare at him. "What?" After our brief chat yesterday, I assumed he would drop the whole thing.

"This could be huge for both of us," he hurries to add. "I know the article is about me, but once he finds out you're an artist, it could maybe help jump-start your career before . . ."

The unspoken *before I go* hangs between us, ominous. I don't want an easy win with art. If I go all in, I'm going to earn my place in the art world and not have it handed to me because the worst thing that's ever happened to me has now been made available for public consumption.

"I don't want to talk about my art," I say, a charcoal pencil clenched tightly in my fist. I knock away some of the shavings from the pad. "Isn't that beside the point? This is about you."

He sits at the table and folds his hands in front of him, his knuckles dry and cracked. "No, it's about us." His eyes burn into mine a beat too long, and I swallow.

"This is all so hard, Ben."

"Would this be a terrible time to make a sex joke?" He covers my hand with his and gives me a playful squeeze. "Look, if you don't want to do it, I'll tell him not to come."

I balk. "He's coming here? To the condo? I thought you'd be doing this over the phone."

He shakes his head, a small gleam in his eye. "It's going to be a really big feature. They want photos, backstories, in-depth interviews with colleagues and friends. He's going to be in town for a while."

My body involuntarily stiffens. "How long is a while?"

He scratches the back of his neck and glances toward our balcony. "Like a week?"

"A *week*? No." I don't tell him that a week could be all that we have left, and I most certainly don't want to share that time with a stranger. A week used to fly by in the blink of an eye. Time was often slippery, just out of reach. One day often bled into the next so that years passed without really understanding how. Now time has become our most precious commodity, and I don't want to waste it answering stupid questions about our lives. I want to live our lives, revel in the moment, make new memories. Instead of arguing, I close my sketch pad, ditch the pencil, and stalk to the kitchen to scrub the dark stain from my fingers.

"You don't want to do this."

It's a statement, and I don't argue as I vigorously scrub.

"I'm sorry, Harper. I guess I should have asked you first."

I stop and laugh. "You think? It's the *New York Times*, Ben! How did we get here?"

He stands across the room, searching my eyes for answers I do not want to give. There is so much in that single question: How did we get here? How did we find each other? How did we fall in love? How did we create a home together? How did we already reach the finish line when it feels like the race has just begun?

"He'll be here tomorrow," he finally says. "If you want me to cancel, I will."

"Tomorrow?" Suddenly my lofty dreams about lazy afternoons and quality time together vanish. It's all I can think to say as I shake off the excess water and smear my fingers across my jeans. "What do you want from all of this?"

He shrugs. "I'm not sure, really." He walks over and lightly strokes my arms. "If it's too much, let's just forget it."

I look up at him, my eyes trailing toward his mouth. I try to conjure the way we used to be. Were we ever really in the moment, or were we too busy planning for our next adventure? The future we assumed we'd have?

It seems we were always in a stage of figuring it out, moving faster and forward, when really, in these final hours, all I want to do is stand still with the man I love. I can't tell him this, can't tell him I want him all to myself. He has other people in his life: friends, colleagues, family. He needs to close doors too, to say his goodbyes. Maybe this is a way of doing that.

And who do I have? Over the past year, I've abandoned so many friendships during his cancer battle, pulling away from my girlfriends' invitations for drinks or trips in order to stay with Ben. Luckily, Wren and Jenna have always been firm fixtures in our lives, and for the past several months, they have felt like enough. I don't regret being picky with my time, not for a single second. But it's becoming clearer that in Ben's absence, I am going to have to rebuild more than just my heart. I'm going to have to build an entirely new life.

I have nothing to say, as I'm not going to tell him to drop this whole thing for me, so I kiss him instead. His lips are dry. A small sigh crests between us as I push my tongue into his mouth and wrap my arms firmly around his neck. I kiss him as though it's for the very last time, or the first, searching for something between us, some assurance that inviting a stranger into our lives won't backfire, that I am safe here, that we are still us.

He tugs me toward the bedroom and then breaks away, breathing heavily.

"Take these off." He motions to my clothes, and a shiver of delight passes between us. It has been so long. Too long. I undress slowly, and he teases my bare skin with kisses along the way. I remove his T-shirt, still not used to how thin he has become, and then I lower his pants and we both stand there, naked, observing, wanting. I lay him gently on the bed, as if he's made of paper and will blow away. I climb on top of him, and he smiles up at me, a passionate reminder of the way things used to be.

"Be gentle," he jokes.

"Not a chance." I lower myself over him deliberately and deeply, and my whole world ignites. Sensation spills through my stomach; heat surges between my thighs. I lose myself to the rhythm of him, of us, our breath merging and darting between us like a snake's tongue. I close my eyes, tip my head back, but Ben traces a hand up to cup my cheek and tugs me toward him.

"Look at me," he says.

I open my eyes and slam back to the moment, back to him. My eyes find his, and there are tears there. "I love you, Harper. I always have and I always will."

I kiss him, as if to devour his words, to wedge them inside me so I won't forget. We climax nearly at the same time, and then I collapse and roll off of him, more embodied than I've felt in months.

"Wow," he says, transitioning onto his side with a little groan to stare at me. "Why haven't we been doing that?"

There are so many reasons, but none of them matter now. He traces small circles on my arms, and my stomach clenches. In our earliest days, we would spend hours reveling in each other. I assumed we'd have all the time in the world. Now it seems the joke's on us.

I gather my hair on top of my head and sit up. "What time does the journalist get here?" I ask, realizing I am severing the moment, pulling this stranger into our afterglow.

"Nine, I think." He sits up too, yanks his T-shirt from the floor, then shuffles off to the bathroom.

Before I can get dressed, my phone buzzes. Thankful for the distraction, I glance at it. The local police department comes up on the caller ID. Panicked, I answer.

"Ms. Swanson?"

It takes me a moment to place the voice.

"Alejandro?" Alejandro is one of my favorite seniors. Though extremely talented, he has a knack for showing up in the wrong place at the wrong time. A foster kid, he doesn't have a stable home life, and I have opened my door to him on more than one occasion. "What's wrong?"

He fills me in. He was tagging the side of a train and got caught. Though normally the crime would just be a misdemeanor, Alejandro is already on probation and doesn't have the money to pay the fine. "How much?" I ask.

42

"Five hundred. I swear I'll pay you back, Ms. Swanson. You know I'm good for it."

"I'll be there in five." Luckily, the precinct is around the corner.

I tell Ben where I'm going, then rush out the door, knowing that yes, Alejandro is good for it, but only if he does bad things to get the money. He's a great kid, but despite all my best efforts, he keeps running in the wrong circles. Thankfully he's not been arrested, only fined, and I quickly settle up and usher him out the door with as little public scolding as I can muster.

Once outside, I grip his shoulders. "What were you thinking? Vandalism can be a serious charge. It's not worth it, Alejandro."

"I know." He stares at his sneakers. "But I like painting murals."

"And we've discussed this. There are plenty of places where you can spread your artistic wings. Just not on the sides of trains, okay?"

"Do you have a minute?" he asks. "I want to show you something."

"Sure." As we walk, I realize just how much I'm going to miss this pack of seniors. Though I helped foster their creativity, they really helped foster mine too. My kids' art serves as inspiration for my own work, even when I'm not actively creating.

"How's Mr. Ben?"

"He's doing okay. Thank you for asking."

We weave through a couple of sketchy alleys. "Just a little farther," he says.

I trail a bit behind, holding my breath as we pass rancid, over-flowing dumpsters. We approach a row of warehouses, all of which seem abandoned, until he gets to one at the end. He knocks three times, and then a giant metal door slides open and another one of my seniors, Kayla, smiles and fist-bumps Alejandro. Her nose ring glints in the light as she turns.

"Ms. Swanson! Dope!"

Even though I have no idea why Alejandro brought me here, I break into a grin and step inside. I am hit instantly with the smell of spray paint. My eyes have to adjust to the dark. It's clear I'm standing on a paint-splattered tarp, and when I shuffle farther into the room, I see why. Every square inch of this place is covered in art. Graffiti, murals, sculptures, and paintings in vibrant colors. Papier-mâché creations dangle from the ceiling. A few other former students stand among the sculptures and statues, and I'm instantly reminded of an underground gallery I went to in Brooklyn years ago.

"What is this place?" I ask in wonder.

"This is our gallery," Alejandro says. He stuffs his hands deep in his pockets. "But we're running out of room."

"I can see that." I take my time to absorb every piece. There is such pain here. Teenage angst and suffering. Pining. Raw, primal talent that so many of us lose as adults. I love each piece more than the last and finally turn to the group, bodies knotted around a giant wooden table on casters. They are all working on a collective piece.

"How long have you been working here?" I ask. I don't want to know how they found this place. That's an entirely different can of worms.

"A while," Kayla says. "We love your class, but there's nowhere that's just *ours*. So we found this." She smiles. "Do you like it?"

"Like it? It's better than most galleries I've seen." Immediately I know I'm going to text Wren about this place, see if she can do a

44

youth show. They shouldn't have to wait years for someone to deem their work good enough. If I can help give them an audience, I will. "Could you have a show here?"

What I'm really asking is whether it's legal.

One of my students, Leilani, speaks up, her dark hair twisted into ropy braids. "Yeah. It's my dad's. He's cool."

I sigh in relief. "Well, I know just the person to help you out. Have you all heard of Wren Terrington?"

An excited murmur crescendos around the room.

"Know her?" Alejandro says. "She's the shit."

"She is." I laugh. "She also happens to be one of my best friends."

"And you kept this from us *why*?" Kayla props a hand on her bony hip.

Why did I? Why didn't I ever invite Wren to class? Why didn't I work with my kids outside of school? Why didn't I talk to them about how to become a professional artist? Perhaps because *I* don't even know what it takes to be a professional artist.

"I have no idea," I say. "Give me a sec." I step outside to get reception and text Wren the address. I breathe in the fresh air, a little lightheaded from the lack of ventilation inside.

I hear the kids laughing as I wait for Wren. I text Ben to let him know I'll be home soon. I think about the interloper who will invade our lives for a week, starting tomorrow. I'm not ready for any of it, but it feels like I don't have much choice.

"Hey!" Wren shouts a few minutes later from the edge of the alley. "You dumpster diving now?"

I roll my eyes. "Inside." I pull open the door and watch her eyes light up as she drinks it all in.

She's quiet as she studies what's here and finally claps her hands. Excitement transforms her face as she casts them all a wicked glance. "Oh, children. Where have you been hiding?"

I leave them to it, saying goodbye to the kids and giving Alejandro a long hug and a stern warning to be good.

Now I'm back to reality and instantly reminded that tomorrow someone new will be in our home, watching us, becoming a part of us. Tomorrow I will have to share personal details with a stranger about my life with Ben. Smearing away the thoughts, I pick up my pace as I head home. I want to enjoy the rest of today.

Tomorrow can wait.

7

Early the next morning, I go for a run and make us coffee and breakfast.

We sit on our small balcony and watch the tourists below. Ben's eyes are pensive as he surrenders to being a witness up here while others live their lives down there. At first, it's what gutted him the most about treatment. He couldn't go for hikes or even long walks. He could barely get out of bed. He wanted to be out in nature, and instead he was confined to either the hospital or home.

But today he looks good, present, and I tell him so.

He sips his coffee and smiles. "I feel good."

Ben is freshly showered, in a black T-shirt and jeans. It's the first time I've seen him in jeans in months, and something stirs—a longing for the simple, normal things that used to define us. An outfit for going out, not staying in.

"Know anything about this journalist?" I ask, blowing on my coffee.

Ben tears a piece of toast with his hands and chews thoughtfully. "Just that he's won all sorts of awards, apparently."

I nod. My eyes scan the streets below and then up and beyond to the mountains. What I wouldn't give to go for a Saturday hike or do a yoga class, maybe take a nap later. Instead, we are going to open our doors to a stranger and rehash the last year of our lives. I want to remind Ben that instead of talking to a journalist, we could just be together today.

Before I can decide what to say, the doorbell rings, and anxiety flutters through my chest. "I'll get it," I say. "You stay."

Ben nods, and I smooth down my shirt and suck my teeth, rubbing the coffee from my enamel with my tongue. I unlock the door and pull it open to find a tall, lean man with wild, dark hair pushed back off his forehead in an impossibly perfect mess, standing comfortably in jeans and a fitted T-shirt with a blazer on top. He looks up from something he's scribbling on a notepad, and I almost faint.

"Liam?"

"Harper?"

We say each other's names at the same time. *Liam, Harper. Harper, Liam.* The ground shifts. My world upends. I search for what to say. "What are you doing here?"

He lifts the lanyard around his neck, jokingly checking his name and the *New York Times* badge, which is embossed and shiny. "I'm the journalist."

"I . . . How?"

He smiles that devastating smile, which manages to be both seductive and shy. Our one sacred week comes rushing back after a wicked ten-year gap. Liam is my secret. Liam is my only what-if. Liam *cannot* be standing at my door right now.

"You look well, Harper."

It's a lie. I look tired. I feel exhausted down to my bones. But Liam? Liam looks sensational. The glasses are gone, and it's clear he's not a young twentysomething anymore, but it's still him. *Liam.* "The last time I saw you . . ."

"Ten years ago, give or take," he says, glancing down at his vintage Rolex. He swallows, those eyes roaming over my face, drinking me in. I forgot how intense his gaze could be, that when he focuses on you, everything else dissolves.

I have a million questions, all of them slamming around in my brain like bumper cars. There's no way that Liam didn't know who he was interviewing ahead of time, right? Yes, technically I am now Harper Foster, but I still use my maiden name for teaching. "Did you take this job because of me?" It is audacious to even think it, let alone ask it, but to my surprise, he shakes his head.

"I don't do research ahead of time for my features," he explains. "I like to go in cold so I can be completely unbiased. Which means," he says, shifting in the doorway, "I don't read any previous interviews or dig into my subjects beyond the basics. I didn't even know Ben's wife's name." He swallows again. "I know that seems counterproductive for a journalist, but it produces the most unbiased work for me." He shoves a hand in his pocket and offers a tentative smile.

If he had known it was me, would he have come?

All my brain cells seem to have liquified, but I manage to swing the door fully open and usher him inside. "Well, Ben is on the balcony. Come in."

Now that he knows it's me, is he thinking about Ben's crazy idea and how ironic this all is? Oh God. I stop for a second. Does this also mean I have to tell Ben who Liam was to me?

"Ben doesn't know about you," I add, whipping around so fast I nearly crash into his chest. "Can we not, you know, bring up our past today?" *Or ever?*

Something like hurt registers in his eyes, but he swallows and nods. "Sure."

Liam steps gingerly inside, assessing the contents of my personal life. It's like having my diary on display for an ex-boyfriend, a whole life lived in the decade since we've seen each other. There is not a trace of him in my furniture or possessions, but when he locks eyes with mine, our story swirls around my organs like blood.

"Lovely home."

I shrug. "It's small, but we love it." My face flushes, and I dig my fingernails into my palms. Not knowing what else to say, I slide open the balcony door and Ben stands, extending a hand.

"Hey, nice to meet you. Ben Foster."

"Liam Hale."

Hale. His last name means "hero." On our first date, we walked across the Manhattan Bridge, and he'd taken my hand and told me stories of how his great-grandfather used to stand on that very bridge and recite poems about heroes to random passersby.

The two size each other up in a friendly way, and Liam whistles as he stares over the balcony. "This is quite the view."

Immediately I think about the first time I saw the view from his loft in Brooklyn, how I wanted a place just like his someday.

Ben grasps the rail and stares out over the city. "It is. We're lucky."

I banish the memories that are cutting into me like blades. "Coffee?" I ask Liam.

He turns, his back against the rail. He looks so at ease, so comfortable here. *How is this even happening?* "Sure, that would be great."

"Cream, right?" The words escape my lips before I can retract them. Liam started drinking coffee at sixteen. When his mom got sick, he'd made her a pot every morning at her insistence, but she could manage only a sip or two. He'd always drink the rest so it wouldn't go to waste.

Ben looks quizzically between us. "Wait, do you two know each other?" A flash of curiosity passes behind his eyes, and I consider lying but then concede.

"We do," I say. "Barely." That word is an affront to what we were, and we both know it. I avoid Liam's gaze and shrug. "What are the odds, right?"

I know how Ben's mind works, so he's probably ready to resurrect his Master Plan right now. I rush inside before that can happen, Liam and Ben close behind. I busy myself with the coffee as Liam stands by the island, gripping his crossbody satchel with one hand. I glance at his fingers, remembering the very first time he touched me, and how I'd never wanted him to stop.

Get it together, Harper.

Ben climbs on a barstool. "And *how* do you two know each other?"

The wheels are turning fast, his big idea sinking in like a fish-hook. I need to shut this down immediately, before he knows who Liam was to me and starts sending out wedding invitations to all our friends. Luckily, Liam motions for me to explain. I appreciate the opportunity, but I can't tell Ben the truth. At least not yet. I haven't spoken about our week with anyone except my friend Kendall, and I haven't talked to her in years. I hoarded Liam, kept our time together a secret, mainly because it hurt too much after it ended . . . which was really before anything began. It was easier just to pretend it never happened.

"We met in New York." That part is true at least.

"Oh yeah?" Ben smiles. "When was that?"

Liam offers an easy smile. "A decade back. Thought this one was going to blow up the art scene." He removes his satchel and takes a seat beside Ben. As I pull down a mug and pour him a cup, I stare at the only two men I have ever had deep feelings for: one is my husband, and the other is the one who got away. Or the one I let walk away. Though that sort of feels like a lie. I was the one who left.

Ben steeples his hands together. "I always encouraged Harper to go back to New York. Maybe she can soon."

I suck in a sharp breath at the casual toss of such impactful words. "Ben." I say it once, a warning.

"I just mean that I know how much New York means to you." He directs his attention to Liam. "She talks about it with reverence, like it's a person almost."

Because it is! And he's sitting right here! My mouth drops open as I toggle between Liam and Ben with what to do, what to say.

Liam smiles and looks Ben directly in the eye, always one of his best qualities. "Well, New York has that effect on people. It's a special place. Have you been?"

Ben launches into a diatribe about New York. It's where so many people in his profession live, but he finds it crowded and too emotionally charged. It kills his creativity. He needs mountains, fresh air, people who are friendly but will also just let him be.

Silence stretches between the three of us, sticky and warm. "So did you two know each other long then?" Ben slurps a bit of his coffee, and I look at Liam, almost warning him to stay quiet.

"Nope," he says, taking a silent sip of his own. "Just a week."

"A week?" Ben stares between us, and I can tell a little of his hopefulness slips. "Why so short?"

Yes, Liam. Why so short? It's something I've always wondered, because Liam wanted it to be more, and so did I. More than anything. But then things didn't go as planned, and I flew back home, back to my life. And that was that.

I shrug and swipe an invisible crumb from the island. "I went back to Chicago." Suddenly I feel desperate to extricate myself from this situation. "Look, why don't I let you two get started? I need to run a few errands."

I slip on my shoes and am out the door before Ben can protest or even say goodbye. My chest aches, and I rub vigorously on my sternum, willing myself to breathe. I take the stairs down to the main floor and burst outside, not knowing what to do or where to go. I turn and look back up at our building, where Ben and Liam are inside, in *my* condo, becoming friendly, talking about our lives.

Our private lives.

Liam Hale is in my home.

A million memories of that week flood my brain as I take a left at the corner and keep walking. I have no destination in mind. I just want to walk until I stop remembering.

I haven't thought of Liam in so long . . . Except that's not really true, is it? When you fall madly in love with someone after a single week and then you never see them again . . . Well, that kind of aching can drive someone insane. That is, until I met Ben, and he softened the edges, made me forget how much Liam once meant to me. Because Ben is a grown-up love. We know each other beyond the initial consumption of falling, the way it swallows you so completely.

I squeeze my eyes shut as I wait for the crosswalk light to turn green. I tell myself it's just a week, though the irony almost makes me laugh out loud. I, more than anyone, know how much life can change in a single week. I tell myself I'll just keep my distance, answer the bare minimum of questions, and distract myself with friends and painting.

My brain betrays me and circles back to the moment of opening the door and seeing Liam again after all this time. Much like the first time I saw him in Rita Clementine's gallery, my heart nearly stopped. It isn't because he is the handsomest person in the room (though he inevitably is), but because back then I recognized something in him. I just *knew*, like some sort of premonition, that we were going to be together.

While I thought it would last forever, I'm learning that nothing good ever does.

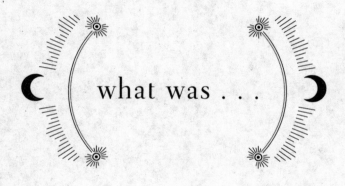

what was . . .

8

Kendall is late.

I attempt not to check my watch for the millionth time. My old college roommate is the entire reason I'm here. I tap my boot on the floor of this up-and-coming Brooklyn art gallery and turn nervously in a circle. This is perhaps the single biggest meeting of my professional life, and without Kendall I will turn into a tongue-tied mess. I just know it.

As one of the few people who refuses to buy a cell phone, unless I find a pay phone or borrow someone else's, I'm just going to have to trust she'll be here. "It's fine," I say to myself. "You're fine."

"Usually when people tell themselves they're fine, they're anything but."

I glance behind me to find the source of the voice and lock eyes with a tall, casually dressed man, whose eyes I could fall into, with wild hair like Robert Pattinson from *Twilight*. I swallow, trying to remember how to speak.

I'm not good with dating and have chosen my relationships with the same pickiness of a six-year-old sorting through wilted vegetables on their plate. I'd rather be alone than with the wrong person, which makes me somewhat aloof with men.

"I *am* fine," I insist. *I'm so not fine.*

He's leaning against the wall, legal pad in hand. "Clearly."

This strikes me as hilarious, and I burst into nervous laughter. "Point taken."

"Do you have a meeting?"

I nod and dig my fingers into my hefty portfolio. "I do. You?"

He hoists his notepad into the air. "Journalist. Doing an article on the latest Rita Clementine opening." He extends his hand. "Liam Hale."

"Harper Swanson."

He cocks his head. "Local?"

"Chicago," I clarify.

"Ah, the Windy City. I've only been there once."

"You're not missing much," I say. "Unless you like frostbite. Or midwestern accents."

"Two of my favorite dings," he says in a thick Chicago accent.

Again, I laugh, a sharp bark in the silent gallery. I look around as if I'm going to get into trouble, but no one is paying any attention. Luckily, small talk with this handsome stranger helps ease some of my nerves. My eyes keep tracking back to him. There's something oddly familiar about Liam, something warm, like a homecoming rather than a random introduction. In my whole history with the opposite sex, this has never happened to me, and it momentarily shocks me into forgetting the fact that my friend is late and that I might have to pitch myself alone to this infamous gallery owner I've only read about in art magazines. It's been my lifelong dream to be an artist, and this meeting feels like it's a make-or-break moment. I'm either in or out. I'm either catapulting myself onto the art scene or heading back to my cramped Chicago apartment to settle into the next phase of life.

"Ms. Swanson?"

I tear my eyes away from Liam to find Rita, smartly dressed in slacks and a cream blouse, staring down at a clipboard and back up to me with cold, intense eyes.

"That's me."

"Good luck." Liam pushes away from the wall, and I approach the world-renowned artist-turned-art-curator and newish gallery owner. She's made at least five solo art careers in the last twelve months, building up nobodies just like me into overnight sensations.

It's not that I care about becoming an overnight sensation, but I *do* want people to see my work on a larger scale. Kendall, who nabbed her position as the gallery manager, moved here a couple of years back and recently convinced me to fly to New York and show Rita my work. So here I am, though Kendall is still nowhere to be found.

I adjust my portfolio under my arm and am ushered into Rita's office at the rear of the gallery, which is larger than my entire apartment. This whole place, this whole city, has me sparking in ways I've only dreamed of. I want to live here, to be among people just like this, and I try to remind myself that I can do this. I can step into my future as an artist, starting now. Never mind that I've been trying for years and nothing has happened yet. Never mind that I barely make more than minimum wage working for a so-so gallery in Chicago. Never mind that I finally decided to go back to school to get a teaching degree in case this whole "being an artist" thing doesn't pan out. While I have options, this has always really been plan A. It's my dream, and Rita is in the business of making dreams come true.

She impatiently opens and closes her fist once she settles at her desk, her fingers flapping energetically against her palm. At first I wonder if she has a hand cramp. Then I realize she's signaling for me to hand over my portfolio.

"Oh!" I eagerly offer it to her, and her arm sags beneath the weight of it. I've been working since college to build the right portfolio—a mix of portraits and ceramics that showcases my versatility but doesn't make me appear sloppy or unfocused.

She yanks her glasses up from the gold chain encircling her neck and flips stonily through the book. I focus on remembering how to breathe as I fidget with my hands in my lap, my eyes sweeping over the classic but unusual art hanging on her walls. Rita consistently chooses what's unexpected, and that extends to the talent she's plucked from seemingly thin air. I hope she will feel this way about me.

There's a sharp knock on the door, and Kendall races inside, her cheeks flushed. She is so New York, from her black leather jacket to her vintage motorcycle boots to the giant coffee clenched in her hand, her nails painted black. She unwinds her red scarf and deposits it on the chair beside me. "Sorry. Subway issues." She pats me on the knee, takes a giant slurp of coffee, and sits. "I see you two have met."

Rita does not even look up to acknowledge her, but Kendall doesn't seem bothered. I smile at Kendall, not knowing if I should talk or stay silent. I just want to know what Rita thinks of my work, as this is all a Very Big Moment, but I try to tell myself that she's just one person and that art is highly subjective.

Finally, Rita slams the book closed and folds her hands on top of it. She looks from me to Kendall and back to me again. "You have some exceptional pieces in here, Harper."

My face flushes and my heart warms. *This is it. This is finally happening.*

"But I'm not sure any of them are quite the right fit for my gallery at this time."

Before I can respond to this inevitable rejection, Kendall crosses her long legs and butts in. "Oh, please. You say that to everyone. Then you push them to create something new, and you show them, and the rest is history. Blah, blah, blah. So let's skip the preamble and tell Harper what you want to see. She's here, she's game. She's ready to play ball. Right?" Kendall adjusts the gold bangles on her wrist that have gotten tangled in the hem of her sleeve. I cannot believe she just spoke to *Rita Clementine* this way.

To my surprise, Rita laughs. "Okay, then. Harper, *are* you game?"

This conversation is swinging so fast, I can barely keep up. I only nod because it seems like the right thing to do.

Rita stands and moves to the front of her desk. She steeples her fingers just below her chin and stares at me. "What scares you the most?"

Her question takes me by surprise. When I was younger, it was spiders, then an unusual phobia of holes, called trypophobia, then more normal things, like premature death. Now? Now the only thing that scares me is walking out of this gallery without representation. "Not living up to my potential," I say. "Not making it as an artist. Settling for a life that's . . . smaller than I want it to be. Ordinary. Having any what-ifs."

Rita's lips curl into some semblance of a smile. "There." She stabs the empty space around my chest. "That's the place I want you to create from." She reaches behind her and scribbles something on a piece of paper. "This is my personal address. I want you to create one piece and deliver it to my door a week from today. Make it a piece that represents all those fears and pain wrapped into one." She wiggles her fingers in the air. "It can be the start of a new collection. If I like it, you're in for the March show. Sound good?"

She folds the piece of paper with a sharp crease and extends it toward me. March? It's October. I work backward, wondering logistically if I could have an entire show ready in just five months. Kendall looks at me expectantly.

"How many pieces would you like in total?"

Rita looks toward the ceiling and calculates something under her breath. "Eleven?"

Eleven? I nod. "No problem."

She smiles again and glances at Kendall. "I like this one. Promising, I think. And I'm rarely wrong." She stands, and I follow suit, realizing the meeting is over. I scoop my portfolio from her desk and walk back into the gallery in a daze. Kendall clutches my arm and mouths, *Oh my God*, before tugging me out of earshot.

"This is it," she hisses, rattling my elbow. "You're in! I told you!"

Not to be a pessimist, but I'm not in, not even close. "Kendall, I appreciate your confidence, but she wants a piece in a week." I gesture to my clothes and extend my arms wide. "I didn't bring my art supplies on a plane from Chicago. Plus, I have to get back to work. I only planned to be here for the weekend."

"Babe, listen to yourself! This is Rita Clementine, not some no-name art dealer in Chicago. No, no. You're staying." She waves her hand in the air, and her bracelets get clogged in the butter-soft leather of her jacket again. "Change your flight and take care of work. I'll handle everything else. I know people."

I stare at Kendall, remembering a thousand nothing moments with the two of us at the Art Institute of Chicago. She has always been effortlessly chic, but New York has changed her these last few years. She is all business, and I want that confidence too. But I'm an artist. We make entire careers rooted in our insecurities, laying them bare for the world to see. I chew on my lower lip, hitching my portfolio higher under my arm.

"Even if I can get work covered, where am I going to find a place to work?" Already I know Kendall's studio apartment is out, as it's no bigger than a postage stamp and is all the way in Queens.

"Liam!"

Kendall startles me as she calls to Liam in the quiet of the gallery. I realize it's not yet open to the public, so she's not disturbing anyone, but still. Liam saunters over from the other end and smiles down at me.

"How'd it go?"

Kendall loops an arm around my shoulders. "Rita loves her. But she wants a piece in a week. I need to find her a place to work."

I extricate myself from Kendall's long arm. "Kendall, I don't have any of my supplies. I also can't afford to rent a studio space, so . . ." I don't mention that I could barely afford the flight out here and it's probably going to cost even more to change it. My job pays horribly, I'm in student debt up to my eyeballs, and even though I have roommates, Chicago rent is sky high.

"Harper, stop. This is *it*. This is your big shot, and you're not going to blow it because of logistics. I can take you to the art store, get you set up. Liam knows everyone. Right? Where could she go to work?" She takes out her phone and begins to scroll through her contacts.

"You can use mine," Liam offers.

My head snaps up to look at him. Why does a journalist have a studio space? Before I can ask him, Kendall laughs.

"Oh my God, I forgot you have a studio. Are you using it this week?"

"Nope." Liam offers me a smile. "Totally free."

I shake my head. This is all moving too fast, and I can't keep up. But for some reason, the idea of spending more time with Liam Hale does not entirely suck.

"Are you sure?"

He adjusts his glasses and smiles again in that easy way of his. I have already memorized that smile; I have memorized him. Am I a stalker and don't actually know it? I expect him to suddenly snap his fingers and remember that he can't lend me his studio after all, or that he has to work, or that he's changed his mind and doesn't want a stranger in his space, but instead he says, "I'd love to have you."

My heart pounds as if I'm staring over the edge of a cliff, about to jump. *I'd love to have you.* That could mean so many things.

Kendall pokes me between the shoulder blades, easing me forward toward Liam. "Great, then it's settled." Her phone chirps and she stalks off, answering the call. "Let me know how it goes! Harp, babe, we'll have lunch." She waves and disappears around a sharp, white corner.

I assess Liam once Kendall is out of earshot. "Are you sure you don't mind? I know this is a crazy request."

"It's not crazy," he says, offering his arm. "It's New York."

9

L iam's apartment is a masterpiece.

He has somehow snagged the most incredible corner loft overlooking the Manhattan Bridge in Dumbo. If his windows opened, I wonder if he could reach out his arms and touch it. At once, I am envious that someone my age has all this. In Brooklyn. And I'm also really hoping he's not a psychopath, luring young artists to his impressive home in order to chop them up into teeny-tiny pieces.

I set down my supplies, the cheap plastic having bitten angry pink tracks into my arms. "Liam," I say, as if we're old friends, "are you a drug lord?"

He laughs, and I realize that it might be my new favorite sound. It makes me momentarily forget about this amazing loft and his gigantic studio and the fact that he could be a serial killer and I could die tonight.

"Well," he says, dropping his satchel and two more bags of art supplies, "I found it right out of grad school. I dabble in art and photography on the side and sold some pretty big pieces a couple of years back, which helped me secure this place. Because it's so big, I decided to turn half of it into a studio so I can rent it out. I find that someone always needs it. And I like to be helpful." He shrugs sheepishly and stabs his glasses higher onto his nose.

"You *dabble* in art and photography? On the side?" I am suddenly achingly hot. I strip off my jacket and settle my nervous hands on my hips. "Will you show me some of your stuff?"

He gives me that sheepish look again and shrugs. "Sure." He leads me over to a few easels. I don't know what I'm expecting— something abstract, bowls of lopsided fruit, or bad portraits of all of his victims—but then he shows me a series of New York architecture and people that appear as black and white photographs. Except, as I lean in, I discover they are all charcoal sketches.

"Liam." I'm careful not to touch anything, but I dance from piece to piece, buzzing with the excitement I get when I clamp onto something really good. And this work—Liam's work—is really good. "If you write as good as you sketch, I'm going to gouge my eyes out with a paintbrush. These are phenomenal."

When I raise my gaze, he is looking at me as though he can see something deep inside me, something I don't even know how to name. My face flushes, and I avert my eyes. I don't know Liam Hale, but I do know I have never been looked at that way in my entire life.

"Thank you, Harper," he says. "That means a lot."

I glance around at the rest of the space: a king-size bed takes up the center of the room, flanked by a worn-in leather couch, a large TV, a guitar, and mounds of books stacked along a bank of windows with that breathtaking view. Art hangs on every square inch of free wall space. I am hungry to memorize every detail.

"So where are you staying?" he asks.

I wave my hand. "Some hostel." I don't tell him that it's awful and smells like cigarette smoke and sweat, and that I am dreading going back tonight.

He laughs. "Why?"

I also don't know how to tell him that I am the basic stereotype of a broke artist. The reality is, I barely have enough to make it month to month, much less book the Four Seasons.

"All I could afford," I find myself saying. It's the truth, after all. I don't mention that Kendall offered to let me stay at her place for the week but that made me claustrophobic just thinking about it.

"So stay here."

His words make me whip around from the gorgeous view. "What?"

He smiles while he makes a pot of coffee. He's so easy in the kitchen, so easy to watch. He's removed his jacket, revealing a Ramones T-shirt, and my heart gives a little kick. I love the Ramones. His dark forearms flex as he pulls down two mugs. "I have all this space, and if you're going to be working on your pieces, it might be nice to stay up late or get up early with no distractions. Right?"

I shake my head at this angelic man who might not be a serial killer after all and motion to the giant bed. "Won't that be putting you out?"

"Not at all." He presses Start on the coffee maker. "I've got a few stories I'm chasing, so I won't be here much. And I can crash on the couch."

The disappointment curls like a fist that I might not see him much, but at the same time, having the freedom to create at all hours of the day or night not in a gross hostel sounds like an absolute dream. I live with two roommates in Chicago, and I can never get any privacy. I often create in fits and starts. I don't think I've ever had one straight week to work on a piece outside of finals, and I become irrationally excited as I think about it. "Only if you're sure," I say. "I can cook, do laundry, whatever you need."

He smiles. "Just make something beautiful." He thrusts his hands into his pockets and looks at me again, practically *eye-fucking my soul*. I can't handle it. I can't handle this nice, studious, brilliant man who lives in my dream apartment in my dream city who just offered it all up to me on a silver platter. I want to ask him everything I can think of: Does he have a girlfriend? How long has he lived in the city? Who does he write for? But I'm already realizing that when Liam looks at me like that, I go completely brain-dead.

Finally, I find my voice. "Do you have to work the rest of the day?"

He pours us each a cup of coffee and holds up the cream. I nod and he pours in a generous splash. When he hands me a mug, our fingers touch, and my skin tingles with possibility.

"I don't actually," he says. "You?" He motions to my supplies. I know I need to get started, but I want to shake out this excess energy first. I want to explore Brooklyn. I want to have some fun. I want to be with Liam.

"Today I'd love to see the city through your eyes." *Oh my God, who am I and what am I even saying?* "That is, if you have time," I backtrack. "If not, I can totally entertain myself."

"Harper." Liam's gaze slices into mine before his eyes trail down to my mouth and back up again.

Eye. Fucked. Population: me.

"I would love to show you around."

I nod my assent, because now all the blood has rushed between my legs. I take a sip of coffee to distract myself and . . . *Oh my God, this is the best coffee I have ever had.* I decide then and there that I have to know everything I can about Liam Hale because I have never met anyone like him . . . and probably won't ever again.

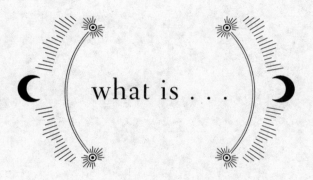

what is . . .

10

I'm so flustered by seeing Liam that I make a beeline for Wren and Jenna's without even calling first.

"Well, come on in," Jenna says when I blow past her entryway, scoop up one of their two hairless cats, Pickles, and cling to her like a lifeline. "Wine?" she asks.

"Advice first. Then wine."

She closes the door. "Is Ben okay?"

"Oh, he's just dandy," I say, burying my face in Pickles's soft, pink skin. "As you know, he had his grand idea for me to find someone else to love before he . . . you know . . . and just now my *ex-boyfriend* showed up on our doorstep to write a story about it."

I expect her to ask more questions or read my mind, like she sometimes does. Because didn't I *literally* just tell Ben that if I was meant to meet someone else, then a man would simply appear out of thin air?

Instead of probing further, Jenna gives me a curious smirk. "Maybe it's finally time for the cards." The excitement on her face tells me she has a lot to say but wants to do it through tarot. "You, go sit. Wren!" she calls behind her. "Cards!"

I'm not really that woo-woo, but Wren has given Ben some tarot readings that have blown both our minds. Predictions that have come true. Readings that have pinpointed, with frightening accuracy, what is going to happen. Though I've never asked for a reading before, getting guidance outside of my own muddled brain isn't the worst idea I can think of.

I enter their sacred meditation space. My anxiety settles as I breathe in the remnants of palo santo and sage. It's a small room, once an office, outfitted with white bookshelves that house all sorts of statues, metaphysical books, and hunks of crystal that, all together, probably cost more than most of the furniture in my condo. There are oracle decks and imported incense organized in happy little heaps.

I collapse on a meditation cushion, finally release their cat, and clutch a chunk of amethyst to give my hands something to do. A few moments later, Jenna enters, eyeing me with interest. "Wren is coming" is all she says.

A moment later, Wren enters with a lit sage bundle. She smudges herself at the entrance to the room, then motions for me to stand. I extend my arms as she waves the sage smoke over them, then down my legs, between them, and underneath the pads of my feet as I balance on one foot at a time. I turn and inhale the strong scent, hoping it can clear this strange sense of unease coursing through my veins.

I've been here for Ben's readings, so I know it's best if Wren doesn't know too much about the situation. She doesn't want to influence any outcomes. However, we both know that if I'm asking for a reading, this must be serious.

We sit. She grabs a deck from her shelf, takes a clearing breath, and hands me the cards.

"Shuffle, cut the deck three times, and then take three cards of your choice."

I follow her instructions. She fans them out face down and tells me these three cards signal the past, present, and future. Though I don't know what cards are coming, I'm waiting for them to explain what I'm supposed to do about Liam showing up on my doorstep *out of the blue* after a decade.

Wren turns over the cards and mumbles to herself before giving me the gist of what they mean. She doesn't always use a regular tarot deck, instead choosing individual decks for individual people. This is a deck I've never seen before, one called the Sacred Rebels Oracle, and the illustrations are stunning. She hands me the little guidebook to flip through while she talks.

"So, it seems you are facing the end of something, but out of this ending, you are also being given a gift." She taps the first card three times, then nods. "You're uncertain if you want this gift, but it's going to be up to you if you accept it. Whatever you decide, if you accept it or if you don't, it's going to change the course of your own fate or destiny. Interesting." She moves on to the second card. "This card is all about coincidences showing up in your life. Things that seem like a coincidence but aren't. These are signs. Signs you must pay very careful attention to because they could send you in a new direction entirely." Chills stud my arms as she moves onto the third card, which is the future. "Hmm, this is interesting." She holds up a black card with nothing but curly tendrils of smoke. "Your future is unwritten, a blank canvas almost. You hold the cards in your hands, Harper. It's up to you to make the next move."

I let out a sarcastic groan and smash my face into another pillow just as Jenna walks back into the room. I am buzzing with disbelief at what she just said. My insides feel like they have been shaken up like a carbonated beverage and are about to spew everywhere if I don't verbally unleash everything that has just transpired in the last few minutes.

I turn to them both, wide-eyed. I fill them in. I give them just enough info about my week with Liam all those years ago to understand this insane predicament. They cast each other a quick glance, and then Wren darts over to her bookshelf and pulls down a book.

"You can't make this shit up," she murmurs as she flicks to the right page. "Harper, this *means* something. You realize that, right?" She cocks her head as she assesses me, because they both know I lean more logical than woo.

"If you're referring to the man I fell madly in love with a decade ago and then never saw again showing up on my doorstep just now to write a feature on my dying husband, then yes, I'm getting the message loud and clear."

Wren studies me and encourages me to take a deep breath, but I feel like my lungs have collapsed. I root around on my meditation pillow and pull Pickles back into my lap. Her purrs vibrate my legs and help me feel instantly calmer.

Wren scoops the cards back into the deck and begins reshuffling. "Let's look at the possible outcomes here, okay? Ben made a wish. The answer to that wish showed up on your doorstep. I kind of don't see the downside."

Jenna scoffs. "Of course there's a downside. She loves Ben. She wants Ben. Not some dude from the past."

"I didn't say she *wants* him. I just said the universe is giving her a gift. The cards said so. Even Harper said so. She told Ben that if the universe throws her a bone, *then* she'll pay attention."

"As a joke," I remind them both. "I said that as a *joke*."

Wren shrugs. "Well, joke or no joke, it's up to her what she does with it."

Jenna huffs. "The only thing that matters is what Harper wants. This is about her life."

"Hello!" I wave my hand back and forth. "I'm right here. You two are talking about me like I can't hear you."

Wren cocks her head again and stares deeply into my eyes. "Fine. I'm talking to you now." She closes her eyes, opens them, then softens her gaze. "What do you want most, Harper?"

I almost laugh. What do I *want*? When, in the last year, have I even allowed myself to focus on what I want? I close my eyes and attempt to take her question seriously. After a moment, the fog clears, and I suck in a slow, gentle breath. With my eyes still closed, I answer.

"I want Ben to be cancer-free."

"What else?" Wren probes. "That one's a given, but what do you want for you?"

My eyes flick open. "What do you mean, what do I want for me? That is what I want for me!"

"No." Wren places her hands on my shoulders. "Think deeper. What do *you* want?"

I resist the urge to wriggle out of her grasp. I'm embarrassed to admit that I haven't thought about what I want since this whole cancer journey started. Ben's wishes have become my wishes. His battle has become my battle. I'm not sure where he ends and I begin . . . and I realize with a sudden jolt that that's what he's trying to prepare me for. He's trying to detach because it's clear I'm not going to be the one to make the first move.

Wren is waiting. I close my eyes again and really ponder. What do I want? How hard can it be to figure out something just for me? Small things like a hot bath or a spa vacation roll through my head, but those things aren't what I really want. Those are ways to escape. I replay the conversation Ben and I just had in the bathroom about taking my art more seriously and how defensive I'd become. Was he right? Am I playing small?

"Today, Harper," Wren finally says.

"Wren, give her a minute," Jenna snaps.

"Fine. Here goes," I say. I keep my eyes firmly shut so I can get this out without losing my nerve. "I guess, if I'm being really honest with myself, part of me would like to know what life would have been like if I'd pursued art instead of teaching." The words aren't even out of my mouth before I feel foolish for saying them.

"Good." Wren releases me, giving my shoulders a small squeeze. "Now you write it."

Jenna searches for a journal, rips out a page, then hands me the sheet of paper and a pen.

Begrudgingly, I scribble what I just said onto the paper.

"Now—and this is important, Harper, so really listen. Are you listening?"

I tamp down my annoyance but nod.

"On the next full moon, which is in just a few days, right before midnight, you are going to read this out loud three times, then burn it. Okay?"

Now it's my turn to roll my eyes. They're always trying to get me to do stuff on the full moon: manifest what I want, create my best life, cleanse the crystals they gift me but that I inevitably lose five minutes later. I stuff the paper in my pocket and lie back on the pillows, suddenly exhausted. Pickles climbs onto my chest and flattens against me, darting her little nose against my chin.

"How does that ritual help me with Liam? That's what I need to figure out, not calling in some fantasy world." I lift my head and smile at both of them. "How about I just live here for the next week? I can cat-sit and you two can take a vacation to some New Age conference. Boom. Problem solved."

"You can't run from this, Harper," Wren says, standing to replace the book on the shelf. "It's time to face your past. And your present. Literally and figuratively."

My phone dings. It's Ben, wondering when I'll be back. "Sorry, I've got to go." I slide Pickles onto the floor, pull myself up, give them each a hug, and walk to the door. Wren stops me before I jog down their steps.

"Harper, you owe it to yourself to explore this."

I balk at her words. "Explore what, Wren? Liam? Because that is one thousand percent never happening."

I can see that she wants to say more but doesn't. "Just promise me you'll do the ritual."

I don't want to make promises I can't keep, but I nod. "Sure." I wave and walk the short distance back to our condo.

I pause outside the door, a thousand memories from my past roiling to the surface. I've suppressed so much of that time, but seeing Liam again, here, so unexpected, feels like a small window has cracked open inside me, but the house belongs to Ben. *I* belong to Ben.

On the other side of the door, I hear laughing. I groan internally as I enter the condo. Though I didn't know Liam long, one of his superpowers is making fast friends wherever he goes. He practically let me live with him after knowing me for just five minutes, so I can't imagine what wonders he's working on Ben.

"She returns." Ben tosses up his hands as I enter. I stare at the two open beer bottles between them and rush forward.

"What are you doing?" I grab the neck of the bottle, but he reaches for it before I can snatch it away.

"I'm enjoying a beer with my new pal, Liam," he says, squeezing the top of Liam's shoulder. "I'm thinking we might need to revisit my crazy idea, but for me instead. He's a total catch."

I study Ben: his loose, sloppy movements; his red, ruddy cheeks. "Are you drunk?"

"A smidge." He squishes his fingers together, and I see the afternoon unfold after Liam leaves: nausea. More damage to Ben's liver. The relentless headaches. Getting sick.

Sensing my concern, Liam butts in. "He's only had half a beer."

"It's true," Ben says, his eyes a little glassy. "It's been a really, *really* long time. Too long."

I don't know what to say, and I hate feeling like a mother instead of his wife. Ben is a grown man. He can do whatever he wants. In fact, he should *only* be doing what he wants at this point. "I'm sorry," I rush to say. "I just haven't seen you drink in a long time."

"I think this could have been the key to everything all along." He hoists the beer bottle and drains the other half as Liam watches. Liam glances between me and Ben, the tension thick.

"Why don't I get out of your hair?" Liam picks up his bag and slings it across his chest.

"Where are you staying?" I ask. *Please say somewhere across town.*

"Across the street at the Edwin. I wanted to be able to walk. New Yorker and all." He shrugs, and a thousand memories slam back into focus: our perfect week in Brooklyn. The day he took me to all his favorite haunts. Our first kiss. Our last. That horrific, torturous goodbye. The dark void it created in the aftermath. The void it took me a long time to fill.

I swallow the rising lump and offer a smile. "Great."

"Why don't you two grab dinner tonight?" Ben asks. "I have a feeling I'm not going to be much in the way of company. But you two should totes catch up." He rests his chin in his hands, a crooked smile plastered on his face.

"Did you just say 'totes'?" I narrow my eyes at him, because I know what he's doing. He is thinking of his Master Plan, and I am not falling for it. I turn back to Liam, whose eyes are earnest, almost hopeful. I hesitate and tell myself it's just dinner, but it feels like more. It's facing a time in my life riddled with so much uncertainty and insecurity. So much possibility and disappointment. So much promise and heartbreak. Looking back, I didn't even know who I was or what I really wanted. And I'm not sure I want to spend time with someone who reminds me of that version of myself.

"I don't think tonight's the best night," I say.

Ben groans. "Liam, *please* take my wife to dinner. She never goes out. *Nev-er.*" He enunciates the word in two distinct syllables.

"I go out," I say defensively.

"Wren and Jenna don't count." He turns to Liam and tents his hands in a mock prayer. "Oh, please, sir, my wife needs to eat," he whines in a terrible British accent. "We eat mostly soft foods now. It's like we're senior citizens and—"

"Oh my God, Ben!" I laugh despite the situation. "I'll go to dinner if you promise to stop talking like that."

He mimes locking up his lips and throwing away the key. "I'll be quiet now."

For some reason, I can't look directly at Liam. "I'll make reservations somewhere."

"They have a nice restaurant at the hotel. Why don't we meet there around six?" He adjusts his satchel on his shoulder. "We can even sit outside so you can make a quick escape." He winks at Ben, who laughs.

What is actually happening?

"Okay." I walk him to the door and open it.

Liam turns, his dark eyes flashing. He opens his mouth, closes it. "It's really good to see you again, Harper," he finally says.

I want to tell him I don't feel the same way, that it's *not* great to see him; instead, it's like someone has sliced open a vein and I can't get the bleeding to stop. Because the truth is, Liam is the only man I have never gotten over. The only man I have wondered about. The only man, in my darkest moments, who, just by thinking about him, could make me pine for a different life. But not since Ben. Since Ben, life has shifted and bloomed . . . and yet now it's wilting like a rotting flower and there's nothing I can do to stop it.

I assumed the residue of my past with Liam had lifted long ago, but apparently it hasn't. It's still here, all those feelings and unmet possibilities so unfiltered and raw. "You too." The admission is a whisper, as if I'm betraying Ben just by saying those two tiny words. But it's not a betrayal. Because even though there's no one I'd rather travel this bumpy, messy, beautiful road with—not even healthy, very much alive Liam—seeing him again does feel like some sort of strange gift.

"See you tonight." He waves and takes off toward the elevator. I close the door and turn, marching over to Ben.

"You need water."

He grins wider, teetering on his barstool. "Do you think the *New York Times* planned this? That they looked into you, dug into Liam's past, and that's why he's here?"

"What? Of course not. We knew each other for, like, five minutes," I say. "It's just a coincidence." Even as I say it, I think of the cards Wren just pulled. This is *so* not a coincidence, and I know it. A headache hits me right between the eyes. I slide a glass of water over to him and wait until he takes a healthy slug.

"I'm going to sit out on the balcony and enjoy this buzz. Care to join?"

"Sure." We plop into our chairs and gaze at the cloudless sky. Ben is grinning and relaxed, while I feel tense, moody almost. Ben can't possibly know how much it has impacted me to see Liam again after all these years, and it hurts even more to keep the truth from him.

When we started dating, Ben and I promised to start fresh. We didn't bring up our ex-lovers, other than to share some of the bigger relationships we had and why we broke up. I never brought up Liam, however, because that week was just for me. Besides Kendall, no one knows about our time together. After a few years, it almost felt like I'd imagined it.

You're not imagining it, a voice reminds me. *Liam is back*. And that means I need to tell Ben the truth. I don't want any secrets between us, even if it's about the past.

Ben turns his head toward me. "He seems great. Quite a looker, that one. Like Ryan Reynolds, but, you know, less goofy."

I roll my eyes and push his water, which sits on the glass table between us, toward him. "And what about you? What movie star would you be?"

He squints his eyes and stares at the sky. "I've never thought about it before. Maybe someone like Henry Cavill?"

I whistle. "Wow, Foster. Aiming high, are we?"

He cranks his gaze toward me. "And you. You're *totes* like a Rachel McAdams. She could play you in a movie."

"I'll be sure to remember that when they make a movie of my life."

"Why did you guys only know each other for a week? Just fell out of touch?"

I open my mouth to spin some version of the truth, but I don't know where to begin. I don't know how to explain that for one amazing week, I had the whole world in the palm of my hand before I threw it all away. Before I messed it all up. "Yeah," I say instead. "He let me use his studio while I was working on a project." I think about how to explain beyond that, how to dip my toe into the whole sordid story without killing his buzz. Also, going down memory lane seems so futile.

Enjoying my husband before I lose him is the only thing that matters now. I make a promise to tell him the truth another time, perhaps after Liam is gone and everything settles back to normal.

"Huh," Ben says, staring down at his glass of water. "Do you ever wonder what could have been?"

I don't know if he's talking about Liam or New York, but it feels like a boot is trampling my heart. I reach for his hand. The pressure releases. I catch my breath.

"No," I say. "I don't."

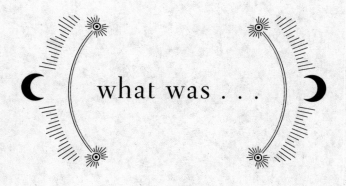

what was . . .

11

It is one of those perfect fall days I'm always dreaming about.

    I'm infused with the type of energy that usually comes only from a new idea. Except, I realize, as Liam chats happily while we walk down the street, I don't have an idea yet, and that's a problem. I have zero clue what I'm going to create for Rita Clementine.

I grip Liam's elbow, and he stops.

"What am I going to make?"

He smirks. "You'll figure it out. I know when I'm trying to start something new, I head outside, away from it all. That's actually when I get my best work done."

I agree. A lot of the magic happens in thinking about the project, not in the doing. I pepper him with questions about Rita: what she likes, what she expects to see, what would make her gasp in surprise. Liam is annoyingly tight-lipped and tells me not to create from a place of expectation but a place of inspiration. I sigh because I know he's right.

He takes me to a corner deli, and we eat the best roast beef on rye I've ever had. He shows me his favorite local museums, his go-to theater that plays late-night classic '80s and '90s movies, and the corner where he interviews the homeless population for an on-going photography series. This side of the river is bright, colorful, dirty, and real. It's everything and nothing like Chicago, and I love seeing it all through Liam's eyes.

When the sun starts to descend and my feet are tired, we stop under a tree by a park to rest. "So, is there anyone special in your life?" My words are light, but inside I'm desperate for him to say no.

He shrugs. "There was someone, yeah, but not anymore. You?"

I almost laugh. If he only knew. "I've never been in love." The words are out of my mouth before I can stuff them back in, but instead of feeling embarrassed, I feel relieved. "I don't think I've ever said that out loud before."

"I won't tell anyone." His voice is soft, his lips are full, and I suddenly want to kiss him. "Though I do find that hard to believe," he adds.

"Why?"

"Because I'm pretty sure plenty of people have been in love with you." His eyes are focused on my lips again.

My chest flutters at the word *love* on Liam Hale's lips, but I just smile and tuck an errant strand of hair behind my ear. "You must have me confused with someone else."

"I don't know, Harper. I think you could be a heartbreaker."

My throat immediately goes dry. Liam Hale doesn't know me. How can he see me as anything other than a loft crasher, a pest, an interruption to his schedule? "Let's hope so," I joke.

He taps the back of his head gently against the tree trunk as he stares at me, and there is something pensive in his eyes, a secret I want to extract.

"Do you believe everything happens for a reason?" I ask. I'm not sure I believe in fate or destiny, but it seems possible now. Everything seems possible today, as if I've stepped into another dimension where time and limitations no longer exist.

"Well, I try not to buy into clichés whenever humanly possible, but yeah, I guess I do believe everything happens for a reason." He smiles. "What about you?"

I move in closer, my knee brushing against his. "I'm beginning to think maybe yes." When my knee touches his, I feel a jolt in my stomach. I feel *everything*.

He rolls his head to gaze at me again, and my breath stops. Time stops. I want Liam to keep staring at me. Instead, he turns away, then stands. "Are you up for a little more walking?"

I nod, too afraid I'll blurt out something embarrassing. That my life in Chicago is so small: two roommates I don't really like, a job I'm not crazy about, no family close by, no real tethers or roots. Half the time I feel like I'm floating, like I'm circling around what I want to become without any sort of plan or anchor in place. And now, in the span of a single day, I have reunited with Kendall, I have an opportunity to change my career, and I have a connection to Liam that I've never felt with anyone, male or female. Is it because I'm outside my comfort zone? Or is this where I truly belong? Do I want to keep walking and figure out what all this means? Yes, I do. *Yes.*

Liam offers his arm, and I take it. We talk the whole way, until we cross over into Manhattan and grab falafel from his favorite street vendor. He buys a bottle of wine for later and we make our way back to Brooklyn on the Manhattan Bridge. He brings out his camera and snaps a photo of me. I don't like having my picture taken, but with Liam, I find that I don't really mind. I love the way he looks at me, studies me. I ask to take one of him, and then he expertly positions the camera to snap one of the two of us. My cheeks are flushed and cramped from so much smiling and talking.

We sit on a bench, and he asks for my hand. I give it to him willingly, as I'm coming to understand will be the way I am with Liam: giving, open, trusting. So opposite of how I've been in the years since college.

"Close your eyes," he says.

I do as I'm told, and he begins tracing words in the palm of my hand. I'm so caught off guard by the sensual zings ricocheting off every nerve ending of my body that I miss the first three letters and ask him to begin again.

I concentrate and make out each letter, one by one. M-A-Y-I-K-I-S-S-Y-O-U? My eyes snap open and I nod, because it's what I've wanted him to do all day. I don't understand why this is so easy or why we've been brought together, but when he cups his hand behind my neck and pulls me closer, I melt.

His lips touch mine, and there is an entire other world there, one where I am not Harper in Chicago or Harper the artist but Harper the woman, being kissed by someone I've only just met. But we kiss as if we've been kissing our whole lives. Liam's hands roam the length of my body, snaking under my jacket and sweater onto my bare, hot skin. I pull him into me, my fingers tugging on the hem of his shirt, and I am hungry for him in a way I've never been hungry for any-thing in my entire life.

Finally, I break free. My lips are swollen, my body hot. "Take me home," I say, realizing that for the next week, his home is my home too.

"As you wish." He quotes my favorite movie, *The Princess Bride*, though he cannot possibly know how much I love that line. He extends his hand and I take it, the two of us walking back to his loft, hand in hand.

12

I wake to a cheap wine headache and an overly dry mouth.

Apparently I fell asleep on the couch after staying up talking to Liam most of the night. Our conversation floats through my head now: stories of his family, my family, favorite trips, biggest dreams, least favorite foods, best places to shop, biggest indulgences. I run through his answers, committing them to memory: his mother, who died of cancer, and a father who was never there, Guatemala, write a novel one day, onions, Muji, two-dollar movie marathons at the old theater in his neighborhood. On and on the list went, until I was hoarding the details of Liam's life as if studying for a final. I search for him now and find a note on the coffee table. I rub the sleep out of my eyes and quickly scan it:

> *Didn't want to wake you. I have a story this morning, so I will probably be out most of the day. Please make yourself at home. Last night meant the world to me, Harper. Can we do it again tonight? I'll bring the pickles. Happy creating.*

Pickles. I told him that was one of my favorite indulgences: a crisp dill pickle on a hot summer day, because it reminds me of my childhood. I clutch the note to my chest. Last night was one of the happiest nights of my life. We stayed up talking until nearly four in the morning. I have never felt this connected to someone so quickly, and frankly, it's unsettling. The last thing I thought would happen in coming here would be to fall for someone, and never so quickly. Though we did not kiss or touch outside of that magical moment on the bridge, there is the promise of it, and for me, that is enough.

I gather my hair into a ponytail, brush my teeth, make a strong pot of coffee, and panic when I realize it's almost eleven. I don't ever sleep this late, and I've lost valuable time that I need. Suddenly Rita's expectations feel far too demanding. Besides college, I've never created from such an immense sense of pressure, and I'm not sure if I can rise to the occasion.

I take a breath and remind myself that I can do this. That's why I'm here, and that's why she's giving me this shot. My eyes scan Liam's loft, a loft I would kill for, a life I would kill for. If he can do it, then maybe I can too.

After coffee, a hot shower, and some toast slathered with honey and peanut butter, I get ready to shake out the contents of all four bags of my supplies but find that Liam has already done that for me. He has arranged all of my brushes, paints, and canvases on one of his long worktables. Another invisible check goes into the *I'm falling for this man* category. I decided last night that I would do a painting instead of a ceramic. Partly because of time, and partly because I don't want to turn Liam's studio into a dusty, dirty mess.

One of my favorite ways to work with paint is to add in other elements. I play with dimensions and sometimes bring in items from nature or fabric swatches to make the canvas a living, breathing thing.

Before I begin, I flip through my existing portfolio and wonder what is missing that Rita needs to see.

I try to assess my own work through Rita Clementine's eyes, a woman who has seen every type of talent and medium, and I quickly find that scanning now with a critical eye, she's right: There's no *pain* here, no suffering. No real inspiration. It's good, but it's a young artist's work. A student's, even. I close the book and stare at the blank canvas. What do I want to convey? What do I feel the most passionate about? Uncapping all the paints, I try to answer the question she asked: What am I most afraid of? My eyes drift toward Liam's window, where the Manhattan Bridge looms outside.

That's it.

In my bare feet, I rush to the window, studying the bridge: its angles, its weight, the water beneath it. Suddenly an image surfaces of me standing on the bridge, alone, then wrapped in the arms of someone I love, then climbing up the wires, then plunging into the still, black water. A woman in all of her possibility. A woman straddling an island. A woman whose life is fully realized, in all its agony and glory.

This could be my love letter to this city I barely know, a love letter to myself—my whole self. I chew over the idea, making sure it's not ridiculous or juvenile. How could I bring in different elements for the woman and the bridge? If I want to make the bridge feel real, I need to collect some items to capture the actual grit of the city. Glancing at the canvas now, I realize it's much too small. This piece needs to be large—not so massive that I can't get it out of Liam's door, but something that will stand out on Rita's gallery wall. It will be an homage to this city, maybe something like . . .

Just a Visitor Here.

The inspiration gathers in my bones as I rush to sketch my ideas. When I look up again, it's three in the afternoon, and I have a list of supplies and know just where I want to start.

As if I've conjured him, Liam comes through the door softly, like he doesn't want to disturb me, though this is his loft. "Harper?"

I love the way my name sounds on his lips.

"Over here." I finish up my list and smile at him as he emerges around the corner. His black glasses enhance his beautiful eyes, and he thrusts a hand through his hair. Now I know his scent, like fresh laundry and pine trees. My stomach clenches as I see him, and one word plays over and over in my mind: *mine, mine, mine.*

He glances at my notes once I tell him my idea. "This is brilliant."

"It is?"

"Yes." He leans in toward me, both hands braced on his work-table, and I fold into him like the sun. I feel it in my toes, this magnetism. I want to taste him. I want to know everything about Liam Carter Hale. My nerves spark like fireflies, and my stomach flips again.

"How was your day?"

"Good." He claps his hands together and rubs them vigorously. "Are we ready to start tackling this list or what?"

The thought of going on a scavenger hunt beneath the bridge for what I need excites me almost more than creating the piece itself. "Aren't you tired?"

"Nope." He swipes his keys. "Let's go treasure hunting."

I slip on my shoes, grab my coat and an empty bag, and we are out the door. I don't know how to tell him that I've already found my treasure: that in twenty-four hours I've gained more than I have in the last twenty-four years. Being here feels like a portal or a parallel life. I can't even think about the end of this week or what it means. I don't want to go back to Chicago, back to my life.

I want more.

I want Liam and this view and Rita Clementine and Kendall. I want to start over, here. I want to build a *real* life.

He takes my hand as we circle to the right outside of his building and toward the bridge that hulks above us, braced, waiting. I've never allowed myself to want more than what I have, but here I am, making wishes like a child.

Please let this all work out, I say to myself as we near the bridge.

Please let this be my new life.

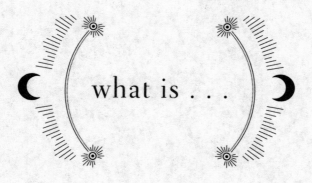

what is . . .

13

I arrive at Whitebird right at six.

   I don't want to be here. Though Ben passed out thirty minutes ago, exhausted from his afternoon, I still thought about canceling. I don't need a walk down memory lane. I don't need to catch up with Liam. But for some reason, here I am.

Liam has changed into a graphic T-shirt and black pants. It reminds me of his Ramones T-shirt on the first day we met. Even in Chattanooga, he looks fashionable and cool, so completely New York. I glance down at my own summer dress and sandals, suddenly feeling self-conscious. He smiles when he sees me, that dimple a pronounced comma in his cheek.

My stomach flips, and I feel momentarily caught. I haven't been looked at this way by another man in years. Ben flashes through my head like a neon sign, and I almost turn around on the spot, crawl into bed, and beg Ben to let me skip this entire week.

"Hi." He stands respectfully at a distance, and so do I.

"Hi." I feel foolish being here, and my entire body wants to bolt. Instead, I motion to the hostess stand. "Shall we?" After I give Liam's name, we are led to a lovely table outside. The sounds of the city swell around us, and I realize how much I miss going out to dinner with Ben, not a care in the world except what's on the menu.

"I can't believe you're here," I say when we're settled. It seems like a safe enough place to start.

He unfolds his napkin and drapes it across his lap. "I can't believe I'm here either." He steeples his hands together and looks at me intently. "I'm really sorry for what you're going through. I can only imagine how hard this is."

I have no words for that. A giant knot lodges itself in my throat. "It's the most heartbreaking thing I've ever been through," I say. The emotion fills my voice, and I'm desperate to change the subject. I wonder if Liam has suffered any great losses other than the death of his mother. I glance at his ring finger, which is bare. I realize I know absolutely nothing about his life. "But Ben has been so strong through it all," I add. If the situation were reversed, I'd have probably given up.

"And you don't think there's any way he can still reach remission?"

The question takes me by surprise. "No." I shake my head. "The doctors all confirmed it's too late."

He fiddles with the corner of his menu. "Well, doctors can be wrong."

"I know, but it's already spread to his organs. Stage four."

"And yet he's still here."

"He is." *For the moment.*

"I'm excited to get to know him better and learn more about his journey," Liam says. "I think his story can inspire a lot of people."

Though Liam is here to write an article about Ben, there's no way he can capture the *greatness* of him. The truth of who he was before the cancer and who he is beyond it. Who we once were together.

Who we have become. I want to scream from the rooftops how exceptional he is, how he's a person this world *needs*, how I selfishly wish the universe would sacrifice someone else. But I don't say any of that and quickly push the thoughts away, because every time I think about losing Ben, it feels like pieces of me are literally dying too. "Tell me about your life," I say.

He sits back and taps his fingers against the chair arms, playing them like a piano's keys. "Well, there's not that much to tell. I got a job at the *New Yorker*, then moved over to the *Times*. I've really made a home there." He shrugs. "I've gotten to travel and meet some amazing people. I still love the city. It suits me. Though I can see the appeal in a place like this."

"Are you still in the same loft?"

He grins. "Believe it or not, I am. I finally bought it about five years ago."

This gives me some strange bit of satisfaction, to know that I didn't imagine that loft or that week. I take a sip of water and wait to ask more questions until after we order wine and dinner. Once the server is gone, I motion to his bare left hand. "Married? Divorced?"

Something like regret passes over his face and is gone just as quickly. "Neither," he says.

"I find that hard to believe," I respond honestly.

"Why is that?" He cocks his head, and I remember that gesture well.

"I don't know. Because you're one of the good ones." This I am sure of, even if our time together was brief.

He laughs. "I appreciate that. But if I'm being honest, I haven't been lucky in love. Career, yes. The rest? Eh." It seems there's more he wants to say, but I don't press.

The server brings us our wine, and we clink our glasses and take a long sip. The alcohol loosens my nerves as we move on to other topics: my art, teaching, our life in Chattanooga. He listens intently, asking the right questions, but the whole time, I can't stop thinking about Ben.

"So this crazy idea Ben had," Liam says, as if reading my mind. "What do you think of it?"

"I think it's insane," I say. "Obviously."

"But completely romantic," Liam adds. "It takes a very selfless, secure man to want to do something like that for his wife. He seems like a very stand-up guy."

"He is. He's the best." I swirl my wine. "But he knows there's no way I could fall in love with anyone else." I know that's the truth, even though someone I used to love is sitting right across from me.

He folds and unfolds his napkin. "Earlier you said not to say anything about us. I'm curious. Does Ben not know about New York?"

The question, while innocent, makes me feel like we're doing something wrong. Suddenly it hits me: Ben unknowingly sent me to dinner with someone I used to have feelings for. Would he still do that if he knew what Liam once meant to me?

"No, he doesn't," I say simply. "Look, I know Ben says he wants me to find someone else," I continue, circling back to his initial question, "but he doesn't mean it. Not really. And my whole heart is with him." I'm not sure why I feel the need to tell Liam this, maybe to prove that I really have moved on and I'm okay.

I wait for Liam to say more or ask another question. Does he think fate has brought us together again, or that this is all just some wild coincidence? Or maybe he wants to talk about our breakup all those years ago so that we can finally get into all of the hard things that were never said. All the blame and hurt. Have some closure.

Sensing my discomfort, Liam changes the subject, and before I know it, I'm laughing as he recalls hilarious stories from his travels. Then we're ordering another bottle of wine. Everything leaves my brain: the stress, the sadness, my unending grief.

"I forgot what it's like," I finally say, dabbing at my eyes with a napkin.

He looks at me quizzically. "Forgot what it's like to what?"

"To laugh." My words are loose and free. "To just relax for a little while."

He sighs, swirls his wine glass, then lifts his gaze, taking a bated breath. "I'm so sorry you're both going through this, Harper. I can relate. Not completely," he rushes to add. "But I remember how hard it was."

I nod. "I know you can." Losing a parent isn't the same as losing a spouse, but loss is never easy, no matter who it is. The air charges between us in the silence, and for one fleeting moment, I remember how Liam could make me feel better. It still lives somewhere deep inside me, bubbling to the surface as though it never left.

Once the check comes, Liam insists on paying. "Can I walk you back?"

The question takes me right back to that first day we met, when he took me into his home, no questions asked. "Sure."

We cross the street, and he leans against the front of my building, closing his eyes for a moment before settling his gaze on me. "I know this is all so strange, Harper. Me being here. Doing this interview. I don't take any of it lightly. But for what it's worth . . ." His voice trails off before continuing. "It really is good to see you again." I can tell there's more he wants to say, but thankfully he doesn't.

We've both had wine. I know that's why he's being so honest, and it feels like we are walking a tightrope. I have to be careful of what I say, how I respond. I think of Ben, upstairs, the love of my life, the man who trusts me enough to go out to dinner with another man while he's sleeping.

"You too, Liam." His name should feel dirty on my tongue, like a secret. I haven't said his name in so long, but I find that it's a relief to say it again, to validate his existence in my world, however short.

"Well, get some rest." He pushes off the wall and walks toward me. For one excruciating moment, I think he's going to lean down and kiss my cheek, but he merely pulls me into a hug. I fold into him, breathing in his clean, sharp scent. Time slows. I rest my head on his shoulder and grip him uncertainly, our history pressed between us, everything that was once a memory now alive again. He is taller than Ben, built so differently, but still, I fit.

I pull away and take a few steps back. "Sleep well," I say.

I move inside and wait for the elevator. It was just a dinner, just a hug, but I still feel like I've done something wrong. I try to center myself as I walk down the hall toward our condo. When I open the door, the living room is dark. I peek inside our bedroom to find Ben still asleep. My heart aches as I see him tucked in our bed. I should have been here tonight. I shouldn't have gone to dinner without him.

I don't feel tired yet, and the last thing I want to do is disturb Ben if he's already asleep. I walk out onto our balcony, which overlooks the Edwin. I scan the many hotel windows and, shockingly, find Liam on his balcony too, arms draped loosely over the railing, staring right at me. My breath catches as I lift my hand in a small wave.

He waves back, his eyes piercing mine even from across the street. I don't know how long we stand like that, but eventually I go back inside. Confusion and guilt consume me as I get ready for bed and crawl in beside Ben. He stirs as I lie there and offers me a sleepy smile.

"Hey, you," he says. "Have fun?"

I smirk, outlining his jaw in the dark. "Define fun."

He reaches for my hand and kisses the back of it. "It's okay to have fun without me." He closes his eyes again. "You deserve to have fun," he murmurs.

Do I? Tears fill my eyes and trickle down my cheeks, as if by having a good time with a man I once loved, I have betrayed the man I love now.

I watch his breath deepen as he falls back to sleep, twitching every so often. I trace the outline of his eyebrow and lean in to kiss him softly on the forehead.

Here is my present. Not my future, as I would have thought or as I planned. But now, with Liam suddenly back in my life, everything feels muddled. I close my eyes and will my brain to stop turning. Liam will only be here a short time and then return to New York and his big, successful life there.

I am no longer a twentysomething, and we are no longer in each other's lives.

I am a married woman, to the love of my life, who is sleeping beside me. I grip his hand and snuggle in closer as our body heat mingles and rises.

Liam flashes through my mind again, but I ignore it and think only of Ben.

After a while, I drift to sleep.

14

The next day, Ben wants to take Liam on a crash course of his life: all the local race spots he's won, the music studio he still rents (but rarely uses), and the special places that comprise our life together.

I decide I don't want to be a third wheel, mainly because in the clear, sober light of day, the guilt of spending time with Liam last night lingers. While I had a good time and Ben was on board, if I search deeply, I don't trust myself around Liam. I'm afraid he will see right through me and understand that I am barely hanging on. I cannot afford to fall apart, not while Ben is still alive and breathing.

I tell the boys to have a great day, avoiding all eye contact with Liam, and decide to get organized in my studio. I call Jenna on the way. There's an audible struggle, and then Wren comes onto the phone, her voice smooth, like honey, which is probably why she can get any artist to do pretty much anything. That, and she's brilliant.

"Harper, honey. Number one: Don't forget about the full moon ritual. Number two: What are you doing August twentieth?"

"August twentieth?" I tip my face to the sun and try to suss out a smile. Normally, Ben and I would have made plans during the summer: little forty-eight-hour trips used to be our jam, followed by one big road trip, where we'd pick an ending location and spend about two adventurous weeks getting there before school started back up. There were the obstacle course races too, of which we'd usually do a few. But now there are no plans, no weekend trips or spontaneous adventures. There is our condo, a million takeout menus, and painful reminders of what we once were. And not enough time.

"I'm not sure," I say in response. "Why?"

"Oh, because I booked your solo show. Can you be ready?"

I stop on the sidewalk, stunned into silence.

"Harper, did I lose you?"

"Wren, in what universe do you think I would even want to do a solo show? Especially with everything that's going on?" I attempt to keep my voice steady.

She exhales, no doubt having taken a long pull from a joint. I can imagine her piling her dreads on top of her head and scrunching her beautiful dark forehead. "Because I think you're ready. And so does Ben."

All attempts at staying calm fly out the window. "Excuse me, what?" I turn in a semicircle on the street, as if Ben and Wren are going to jump out and tell me this is all some big joke. Is this what they were cooking up all along? "Did Ben put you up to this?" I think about his insistence that I give art a real shot. If this is his way of pushing me into taking my art more seriously, he has grossly miscalculated what might motivate me. As I wait for Wren to answer, her silence tells me everything.

"Harper, you've pushed your art to the back burner for too long," she finally says. "You're a great teacher. No one argues that. But just like you said, is that what you really want? To teach forever? Yesterday you told me you wished you could know what life might have been like if you'd pursued art. So I'm giving you that chance."

I think about the stupid wish I said out loud. Did Wren then go to Ben so they could scheme behind my back? I massage my temples, suddenly feeling exhausted.

"Okay, Wren, let me indulge your little fantasy for a second. Let's say I was up for a solo show. In case you aren't aware, I need pieces."

"You need at least a dozen for a solo show. Preferably more."

I begin walking again, but my legs feel rubbery. A dozen? The only thing I currently have is my half-baked series of Ben. Wren knows perfectly well how long it takes to do mixed media, or even portraits. And the more time I spend on portraits, the more I realize that's not how I want to memorialize Ben. I want a different medium; I just haven't figured it out yet. And I certainly can't figure it out with a deadline looming.

"There are going to be some big names there," she continues. "Collectors. Dealers. Other gallery owners. Give it some thought and let me know as soon as you can." She hangs up, and I cry out, staring at my cell phone in my palm.

"This is not happening," I say to no one. I walk the rest of the way over the pedestrian bridge, my mind in overdrive. While having a solo show is something most artists dream of, typically they would create their pieces first, *then* get the show. Now it's being handed to me on a silver platter, but the timing couldn't be worse.

I'm shuttled back to the opportunity I botched with Rita Clementine. If I'm being honest, I've always hated how that one opportunity killed my artistic spirit. I retreated to teaching because it felt like the safer option. I've been hiding ever since, never really giving myself a chance to shine. I stop again and someone nearly rams into the back of me. I apologize and wonder about Wren's real sense of urgency: What if this isn't really about me? Maybe it's about Ben seeing me doing something I love, and she wants him to know I can make this a true career before he's gone. Tears flood my eyes as I frantically text her.

Are you doing this for me or for Ben?

Is there a difference? she types back.

I'll think about it, I reply.

I know you will, she responds.

I take a shaky breath and unlock my studio, which is much too warm. I flip on the air-conditioning unit, crank on some '80s music, and assess all the pieces I have so far with a fresh perspective. Some of them are good; some aren't. I open a sketch pad to a new page and decide to brainstorm—just for fun—what a solo show could actually be. Maybe instead of just a tribute to Ben, it can be a tribute to us, to the life he will leave behind.

The ideas start to flow as I write down a list of what I might need. When I strip away the nerves, I find a bit of excitement lurking beneath the surface.

When I look up again, it's four in the afternoon. I've come up with a loose idea for the show and tried out a few new ideas. My body is stiff, my neck aches, and I'm starving.

I check my phone and am disappointed to find I have no missed texts from Ben. Hopefully he is having fun, but I also hope Liam knows not to push it too much. I chew the side of my fingernail as I think of them together, becoming friendly, swapping stories. Have they talked about me yet?

I pack up and text Ben on my way back. *How are you and your boyfriend doing?*

He types back almost immediately. *Like I said yesterday, I don't know why I came up with this idea for you instead of me.*

Great. I'll get you a wedding gift, I fire back. *Towels or china?*

Condoms, he replies. *Just lots and lots of condoms.*

Wow, I type back. *Where are you?*

Just about to get a bite. Want to join?

I hesitate. I'm covered in paint, in my stained overalls, and would love a beer and a bath, but instead, I tell him yes. They're getting burritos at one of our favorite dives, and as I walk back across the bridge, something like peace settles over me for the first time in a while. I'm painting again. I *could* have my first solo show. Liam is going to write an amazing article about Ben.

Ben is having a good day; therefore I am having a good day.

For now, it's a win-win.

15

I see them outside, drinking beers and talking like old friends.

I pause at the crosswalk, admiring the two of them while trying not to realize how odd it is that they are together, that Ben is drinking again, and that I am about to join them for a meal. I plaster on a smile and approach their table.

"I hear condoms are in order," I deadpan as I take a seat next to Ben.

Liam doesn't skip a beat. "We're actually headed to City Hall right after this." He takes Ben's hand. "We're not going to hide our love."

He pats Ben's hand affectionately, then wraps his long fingers around the neck of a beer bottle. "So, now that you're here, Harper, we were just talking about the way you two met at an obstacle race. But I'd love to know how Ben popped the big question."

His eyes probe mine and then swing over to Ben. Ben and I look at each other and burst out laughing. "Who wants to tell it?" I ask.

"By all means." Ben sits back and motions to me.

I extend my arms and roll my neck around as if I'm gearing up for a fight. This is one of my favorite stories, and it takes me a moment to remember who I'm telling it to.

"Well, this must be good," Liam says good-naturedly.

"Oh, it is." We wait until I've ordered some food of my own, and then I launch right in. "So, Ben had to attend the Oscars about six months after we met."

"Such an underachiever," Liam teases.

"I aim low," Ben says as he takes a sip of water.

"I was so excited," I continue. "I'd grown up watching the Oscars like everyone else, but I never thought I'd actually get to attend." I glance at him. "Naturally, he won, so we were forced to go to the after-party."

"Naturally." Liam sits forward. "You didn't want to go, man?"

Ben shrugs. "Not my scene. But I made an exception."

"He means once he found out his crush, Natalie Portman, was going to be there, he was all in."

"And once you found out Ryan Gosling was going to be there?"

"I almost changed my mind," I say. "About what I had planned next."

Liam looks between us, confused. "What do you mean?"

"So we're sitting there, schmoozing with Hollywood elite, and we move onto the dance floor when 'Hallelujah' by Jeff Buckley comes on, which I had requested the DJ play," I explain. "Everyone was confused why a slow song was playing at an upbeat party." I smile, remembering. "Right there, in front of all these A-list celebs, I dropped down to one knee, which was not easy in my gown, by the way, and asked Ben to marry me."

"Wait, *you* asked *him*?" Liam slaps the table. "Please tell me someone recorded it."

I roll my eyes. "It made the news, in fact." I look at Liam. "If you'd done any digging, you would have found it."

He laughs. "Oh, well, I'm totally going to now." His eyes linger on mine before floating back to Ben.

If the situation were reversed, would I want to watch Liam propose to someone else?

"I was blown away by the gesture," Ben says, bringing me back to the moment. "I had no idea she was going to do that, but then I figured she was just trying to beat me to the punch."

I laugh. "In fact, he had planned on proposing to me a week later, but I did beat him to it. Just like I beat him during that race the first day we met."

Ben lightly pokes my shoulder. "Not everything is a competition." His eyes twinkle.

"Oh, yes, it is." I tap my beer to his and sit back, enjoying this easy banter and the sun on my face. I haven't thought of that day in so long, or what it meant to both of us.

"We've come a long way since the days of our Hollywood lives," I say. I reach over and grip Ben's hand. He threads his fingers through mine.

"We have."

I lose myself to the moment but am acutely aware of Liam taking it all in. He clears his throat and mimes writing something down on a notepad. "And the cutest couple award goes to . . ."

"You two?" I quip.

Liam laughs and then glances at Ben, the easy smile slipping from his face. "Hey, man. You okay?"

Ben places his hands on the table and breathes deeply.

I gently touch his back. "Are you going to be sick?"

He shakes his head, and I rub soothing circles over his shirt, then dip my napkin in ice water and drape it over the back of his neck. I fish peppermint oil from my bag and dab a drop into his water, which he greedily sips. The whole ordeal lasts a minute or two before Ben opens his eyes and sucks deep, slow breaths.

"Sorry about that."

Liam looks worriedly between us but tries to lighten the mood. "Does the idea of our love make you sick?"

Ben offers a weak laugh but doesn't respond.

"Nausea comes and goes," I explain to Liam. "Sometimes it's tied to food, sometimes not. At this stage, anything can cause abdominal bloating, backaches, and even swelling in the arms and legs." I want to ask Ben how much they did today, if he needs to go home and rest. But as the days pass, I know he wants to spend less and less time in our condo and more time out in the world, which I can't argue with.

Liam searches for what to say, but I fill the gaps instead by asking how the day went. Ben excuses himself to the bathroom, and Liam senses the shift in mood.

"It's just like that sometimes," I offer by way of explanation. "One minute he feels great, and the next he doesn't."

Liam shakes his head and takes a sip of his beer. "It's strange. All day I kept thinking, 'This guy is going to make it. The doctors got it wrong.'"

I nod. "Trust me, I know. I think that all the time, actually. Like it's not real, or a miracle can happen. But he's really sick, Liam. He's just great at hiding it."

He stares into the distance thoughtfully. "I'm sure not doing chemo or taking all those drugs at this point probably makes him feel slightly better, though, yeah?"

I nod. "Much better. We know from endless research that infection from treatment is often what kills people, not necessarily the cancer."

"You're right." He swallows painfully, and I lean in.

"Your mom."

He smiles and leans back. "Yep." Ben has shared that Liam has covered a lot of stories about alternative therapies for people who are terminal, just like his mom. Suddenly it dawns on me why he might have wanted to take this job.

"You're not trying to convince Ben to seek alternative treatment, are you? Because at this stage, it's really too late."

I can tell Liam is contemplating what to say. "It's never too late," he says. "And yes, I did float an idea by him, but it's obviously up to Ben. I wrote a big story a while back about this advanced neuroscience workshop. I literally saw miracles happen with people who were terminal, Harper." He snaps his fingers. "Suddenly, just like that, they were completely healed by harnessing their own minds in meditation to create a new sense of reality, a new environment of internal health."

My mind spins rapidly. What, so Ben is just going to "think" his cancer away? I want to scream that it doesn't work like that. I know Liam means well, but he doesn't understand that any sort of false hope is a lifeline I'm not sure we have the energy to cling to. I can't get my hopes up. Ben can't get his hopes up. "Liam, I know you have good intentions, but we're both finally coming to terms with the inevitable. I'm not sure now is the time to shake things up."

"Now is all there is," he says quietly.

We sit in silence for a few moments until he changes tactics. "Look, I've obviously gotten to know Ben a bit, but I'd love to hear more about him from your perspective. What makes Ben, Ben."

I search for what to say because I can say so much. Glad for the change in subject, I think about all the little details that compose Ben. For instance, even at his sickest, he never gets out of bed without spooning me first and planting kisses on my cheeks, eyelids, and neck. I decide to keep that little nugget for myself and instead share how he used to go on a run every morning and take at least ten dollars with him to give to the unhoused man on the corner. Often, he'd take that same man for coffee and breakfast and ask him questions about his life because no one else did. I share how much he loves his work, that music has been the guiding compass of his life, just as art was once mine.

I tell Liam how Ben never complains when his work is interrupted but instead calmly stops and pivots to the new task at hand. I share how his biggest fear is being attacked by bats and one of his deepest regrets is not going on a camping trip with his dad when he turned thirteen because he felt too "cool" for camping, and then his father died in a terrible car accident a week later. I share how he always leaves the last of the coffee for me, how he opens doors for the elderly and engages animatedly with children, even if he will never become a dad himself.

I tell Liam how his positive attitude through cancer has never wavered beyond the initial shock and inevitable disbelief; it's why all the nurses and doctors loved him so much, and why, when he told them he was finally done with treatment, they respected his wishes and let him go.

I know Liam will paint the picture of Ben well. Before I can say more, Ben returns and offers a pained smile.

"Are you okay?" I attempt to clear the emotion from my voice.

"I am, but I think I might have had enough for today."

Liam gestures the server over. "Let's get the check. In fact, why don't you two go on ahead and I'll pay?"

"Are you sure?"

"It's on the *Times*. Trust me, it's fine."

"Well, in that case, another round," Ben says weakly.

We tell Liam goodbye, and I loop my arm through Ben's. "How was the day other than that?"

He sighs as we stop on the corner. He turns to me, tears in his eyes. "Harp, I'm so tired of these ups and downs. I get to a point where I feel so good that I forget I'm dying, and then other moments my body takes over, and I just . . . I just want the pain to stop." A few tears slip down his cheeks, and I smear them away as emotion racks my chest.

"I know." Even as I try to reassure him, I know that I *don't* know. Not really. I can't tell him that it will all be better, because the only way the pain will stop is if he stops breathing.

He sighs and looks at me. "I have to tell you something."

My heart skips a beat as I look at him. "Anything."

We cross the street as the light turns green. "I just signed up for a Dr. Joe Dispenza workshop."

I don't ask him to elaborate, as I know who Dr. Joe Dispenza is. Wren loves him. But then something dawns on me. "Is this Liam's idea or yours?"

He looks at me sheepishly. "Both, actually." When Ben first looked into alternative treatments, he read most of Dr. Dispenza's books and contemplated signing up for one of the workshops, but his doctors convinced him it was much too late for that.

"When is it?"

"The day after tomorrow. In Georgia. Less than an hour by car."

"Georgia?" I think of the road trip, the germs, the exhaustion, the travel. "What about the article?" Liam is supposed to be here for an entire week.

"Liam's already got a lot of what he needs from me, and your interviews are next anyway. I thought he could finish up with you while I'm gone." He takes my hand and stops on the sidewalk. "I need to do this, Harp. Please."

He doesn't know how dangerous the words he's just uttered are. He can't leave me here with Liam. He can't leave, *period*. I calculate how to talk him out of this. "How did you even get in at the last minute?"

"Liam knows Joe. He made a call."

I sigh, annoyed. Of course he did. In his line of work, Liam probably knows everyone. After what he told me about his alternative therapy research, this makes sense. We both know what Ben's not saying: it's his last chance. These workshops are famous for curing the incurable. When an opportunity like this comes around, you jump. You take it. You go all in. I'm not sure my heart can take this sudden swerve back toward hope, however. And yet Liam's words burrow back into my heart: *"Now is all there is."*

"How long is it?"

"Just seven days."

I sigh. "Can I drive you there at least?"

He scans my face and rubs his thumb gently over my cheek. "Like I said, Harp, I need to do this alone. I need to focus on healing my body without any distractions. Plus, you know, the article."

I don't care about the article, and he knows it. The sounds of the city balloon around us as I try to wrap my head around what he's telling me. All of my fears run in rampant circles on a relentless loop. *What if something happens and I'm not there? What if he gets an infection? What if he needs me?*

As if reading my thoughts, he sighs. "You've got to stop worrying about me, Harper. Worrying does nothing, as we both know. It doesn't make me better, and it doesn't keep me safe."

"Worrying has become my full-time job, though," I retort. "I've become abnormally good at it."

We continue walking, and I notice his shortness of breath, the way his stomach protrudes just slightly, bloated and tight.

"You've already made up your mind about this, then?"

"I have." He stops again, cups my face in his hands, and kisses me deeply. My insides stir, mourning a life we haven't yet lived. "Do you trust me?"

I don't even have to think about the answer. "I do." I tap him playfully on the butt, but inside, my nerves are frayed. "Let's get you healed."

what was . . .

16

On the way to the bridge, Liam explains why Dumbo is called Dumbo.

"So it's not named after the love of an elephant?" I tease.

"Down Under Manhattan Bridge Overpass," he clarifies. "This was once a robust waterfront district selling tobacco, sugar, coffee, and other products. And there used to be lots of fishing too." He points to all of the warehouses and factory buildings. "These are all original, but they've been converted."

"For the elephants, clearly." As we step outside, the subway rattles the bridge overhead. "So why did you choose Dumbo?" I ask, realizing we never discussed why he chose this side of the river last night. "Cheaper than Manhattan?"

He pauses on the street as a knot of people balloon impatiently around us. "I love Manhattan, but I also love rooting for the underdog." He spreads his arms wide. "I like being on the outskirts, connected to the action but not in it all the time."

"I always feel like I'm on the outskirts," I admit. "Like I'm on the outside looking in."

I expect him to wave me off or tell me that's not true, but his eyes lock onto mine, intense and probing. "You're not an outsider here."

My heart thuds in my chest as we start walking again. I want to call his bluff. Aren't I, though? I don't really belong here, don't really belong anywhere. But when I stop to search my heart, I realize I *don't* feel like an outsider here . . . at least not today.

Liam points to the Waterfront, a large, converted structure that houses a museum and restaurants in one of the old warehouses. I struggle to absorb the details when really I just want to know more about him. He leads me to the underbelly of the bridge. There's a small, squat brick building to the right and an open fence to the left. Liam easily steps through and motions to the concrete around him.

"Let the foraging begin."

We work silently. He gives me room to wander and explore. I don't know exactly what I'm looking for, but that's what I love about pulling other mediums into my art. Sometimes I surprise myself. As I push deeper beneath the bridge, Liam startles me as he appears beside me.

"So why Chicago?"

It's the same question I asked him just moments ago. Last night we discussed my path from college to landing my job at the gallery, but not why I've stayed there, since it's clear I don't really love it.

I toss a rock up and down in my palm, weighing it, before launching it back into a patch of dirt. "Well, for starters, I went to college there, so it made sense to stay for a job. The gallery is a decent gig, but I'm just not lit up by Chicago the way I am here."

"Well, nothing beats New York."

"I agree." I dig in the dirt for another rock or pebble. "It's not that I'm not grateful, because I am, but it almost feels like a place-holder, like I'm waiting for my real life to begin."

"Would you move if you got another opportunity? Let's say with a very prominent gallery owner who loves your art?"

"Without question," I respond.

"Then what's the problem?" he asks. "Chicago is just temporary."

I shrug. Do I really want to get into all of this? "I really thought I wanted to work in a gallery," I explain. "But galleries don't pay the bills. It's also hard to find time to focus on my art. And yet I can't afford to go all in on my art without another job. So last year, as a backup, I decided to go back to school and get my teaching certificate, so now I have options. I can do, I can sell, or I can teach."

He smiles. "Well, that sounds like a smart plan to me." He stoops down and offers me a perfect leaf. I clutch it as if he's handed me a flower. I resist the urge to smell it. "But for this week, you're an artist."

"I'm an artist," I say. *And I want this more than anything*, I think. Suddenly I don't know if I'm talking about him or the opportunity. Before I can say anything else, he leans in, and I almost close my eyes in anticipation of another kiss. I've been thinking about it since last night. Instead, he flicks something from my shoulder and I step back, embarrassed.

"This is the big dream. New York. Art. You're here for a reason," he says.

Am I? The subway rumbles past, and I wait until the shaking has stopped before I respond. I hate that my knee-jerk response is always "Well, yeah, I'd love to be an artist, but there's so much of the art world that's out of my control." I always have an excuse as to why I haven't made it yet. I know I'm not too old—I'm still in my twenties—but I look at all these people who are younger and more talented, and the panic seizes me. Instead of feeling inspired, I feel paralyzed. I tell him as much.

"So what *is* in your control?"

I ponder the question as I gather more supplies: rocks, a few pieces of sea glass, a button, scraps of fabric, a pair of reading glasses, a few objects that will make a wonderful miniature ladder. "I've never thought about it before," I say. "Beyond what I create, I mean. That's always in my control, I guess."

"It's like writing," he says, pushing off a column to keep up with me. "As a journalist, I have to stick to the facts. And how a reader interprets what I write isn't up to me. But the way I tell the story? That's all mine."

I want to tell him that if a reader doesn't like his work, he can always find another job. But if no one buys my work, I'm not really an artist, am I?

"What's holding you back?"

It's similar to the question Rita asked. I toss a few more objects into my bag and then turn to look at him, unpacking the question. I'm afraid of getting so close but never making it the way I want to. I'm afraid of never living the life I really want, or finally getting what I want but still dreaming of something else. I don't usually verbalize these things. Instead, I paint them. Or journal about them. "Me, I guess."

"Oh, well, that's an easy fix," he says. "Just become someone else."

I laugh as we begin walking back to his loft. "Great! Problem solved. Can I be you for a day?"

"Harper." He stops me with my name on his lips and turns to me. He's so close I can smell the mint on his breath. "No one has it all figured out, especially me." He searches above him, as if waiting for the right words. "We show the world what we want to, right? For the most part, I'm content, because I've realized the only thing I can really control is how I feel. So most days I choose to feel good."

"Well, that's stupid," I deadpan. "Feeling miserable is *way* easier."

Now it's his turn to laugh. He cocks his head at me. "I used to think so too. But stick with me, kid, and we'll have you painting unicorns and rainbows in no time."

"I'll just ignore the fact that you called me 'kid,' even though we're around the same age," I say. I don't let myself worry that he might have also just friend-zoned me. People don't usually call you "kid" if they want to see you naked.

Back inside, I shake all of the contents out of my bag and sort through all the goodies on Liam's worktable. He says he has to run a few errands but will be back in a bit. The moment he's gone, I study all the objects. I weed out some of the junk I know I won't use and sift through the sea glass, buttons, and reading glasses. I know this is an opportunity to go deeper. To believe in myself in a way I never have before. To create something new.

Hours later, I have transferred several of the scenes onto the canvas, and though it is still unfinished, that tingle tells me I'm onto something good. The sun is beginning to set, the sky achingly clear as I wrap up for the day. Liam's not home yet, and I have no way to call Kendall without a cell phone.

I realize I don't have anyone else to share my excitement with—that I am here creating, that I am finally in New York. Somewhere between college graduation and entering the real world these last few years, I've forgotten to make friends. I have my parents, but my mom and dad live in Ohio, and we aren't especially close, even though I'm an only child.

This hard truth makes me sad. Maybe that's why I'm so eager to start my life over again somewhere new. I can leave the old disappointments behind. I can have a clean slate.

Luckily, Liam walks through the door to distract me from myself. He drops his bag from his shoulder, his T-shirt sliding up to reveal a smooth patch of olive skin. My eyes drink him in. He grins as he approaches and braces his hands on his hips.

"How's it coming?" He studies what I've put together on the massive canvas: bits and pieces of Brooklyn, bits and pieces of me. I've sketched all the different versions of the girl, but I haven't put paint to canvas yet. That will be last, because that part always goes quickly for me. Liam swipes a hand over his mouth, then drops it. "Harper, this is really good."

His praise warms me to the bone. "Thank you. I'm excited."

"Are you done for the day?"

"I am."

"Good. Come. We're going on an adventure."

I don't even ask where he's taking me. I simply grab my bag, slip on my shoes, and we are out the door again. The evening is crisp, and I zip up my jacket and arrange my scarf in a single knot. He points out his favorite park and his local coffee shop, where they know him by name. As he rattles off all the ways he's made a life here, I tamp down the jealousy. I, too, have creature haunts, but it feels like I'm always hiding or observing or simply in a rush. I never try to put myself out there, to linger and make small talk with people in my community.

We walk and walk, and finally, winded, I stop him in the street. "Are we walking to New Jersey?"

"You'll see."

126

A small thrill works its way over my body as he extends his hand, and I take it. His fingers thread through mine as if they've belonged there my whole life. I know people talk about love at first sight, but I never believed until now. And I'm not sure what I believe in terms of a higher power, but I have never felt stronger that Liam Hale was somehow put on this earth just for me.

After an hour of walking and sightseeing, he stops in front of a nondescript building. "Okay. You ready?"

I search for signage, but there is none. "You're not selling me into a sex-slavery ring, are you?"

He throws his head back and laughs. "Not even close." He holds the door open for me, and I move inside to a dimly lit hallway. There's the buzz of animated voices in the very back, but I stop as my eyes adjust, and then gasp. There's art everywhere: hanging from the ceiling, on every inch of the walls; even the floors have been painted in graffiti. I take a moment to absorb it, to feel the inspiration that went into this unique space, and finally, I find my voice.

"What is this place?"

"It's an underground gallery, put together by kids from all over New York. I volunteer here. They're getting ready for a show in a couple of weeks."

"This is incredible." I almost ask him when he has time to volunteer on top of everything else, but I'm not surprised. He leads me deeper into the belly of the gallery, and I see all sorts of portraits, paintings, and sculptures. And they are stunning. And painful. And raw. And real. Liam lets me wander and absorb. I don't know why he brought me here, if it's for inspiration or validation, but there's nothing I love more than witnessing art: how it can light you up, how it can talk to you, how it can change your mind just from the simple act of looking.

I lose all sense of time and space as I drift from room to room. When I'm done, Liam introduces me to a small group of kids who are at the kiln. He's so comfortable here. I lift my hand as he introduces me and tells them I'm working on a piece for Rita Clementine.

I don't expect these kids to know who she is, except apparently they do.

"That's my dream," a young girl named Keisha says. "To be shown in that gallery. To show her what I can do."

Her confidence floors me. Here I am, given the biggest opportunity of my career, and I'm still doubting myself. And here's Keisha, ready to snap it up, to believe in herself, to *take the spot*. I make eye contact with Liam, understanding in an instant why he brought me here. He brought me here to understand that if I don't want it badly enough, there's always someone else who does.

We make conversation and even dabble with clay before we leave. The sun is just now descending, and he tugs me toward the fire escape ladder, where we climb to the top and step out onto an expansive roof. I stop as I see a picnic basket and bottle of wine near the ledge.

"Is this for us?"

He smiles sheepishly. "Yeah. Too cheesy?"

"Cheesy?" I fear I might faint from the sheer romanticism of it all. Is this the errand he was running while I was working? "Try perfect."

We slide onto a fluffy blanket and watch the sun descend as we tuck into our falafel sandwiches. He pours us each a glass of wine, and when we are full and warm under the blankets, I turn to look at him.

"Why did you do all this for me? You don't even know me."

He looks at me so intensely, tears spring to my eyes. "But I do, Harper. Already, I do." He swipes a napkin across his mouth and crumples it in his fist. "You are so wildly talented. I want you to really let yourself believe it this week. See what you can do."

It's unnerving for someone to see me so clearly after just a few days. Are my insecurities that visible? Instead of closing up, however, I nod. "You're right. I know this is my chance. And I want it." I look at him, something unsaid passing between us: *I want you*.

"Then mission accomplished." He lies back, propping his head in his hands.

I take a mental picture, wanting to memorize absolutely everything about this week. I tuck in beside him and rest my head on his chest. It fits. He fits. We fit.

"Are you sure you have to go back?" He traces small circles on my arm.

The moment is broken as I think about what happens after this week. My boss didn't seem to care that I asked for extra time off, and my roommates haven't even checked in. Can I fathom boarding a plane and going back to my life and my job when I know I can feel like this in another city, in another life? I sit up and smile. "No," I say suddenly, angling back to look at him. "I don't have to go back."

Liam grins and sits up. "Is that a real possibility?"

I calculate the reasons why I wouldn't be able to uproot my life, and there's only a void where excuses should be. I'm an adult. I can do whatever I want, and that includes moving to the place I've always wanted to live. Even if it doesn't work out with Rita, I can find another job here. The answer is swift and simple, like most good things. "Yes."

He tugs on the hem of my T-shirt and pulls me closer, stopping right before his lips find mine. "I'll make it worth your while," he teases.

His lips are so close I can taste them. "You already have." I close my eyes and press my mouth to his.

In our kiss, there's an entirely new world I am eager to claim. Him. Me. This. Art. A life worth living. A life of no regrets.

When I'm breathless, I break away and roll to my back, searching for stars through the clouds and artificial lights of the city.

Can I really leave Chicago? Pack up my life and go? I think through the logistics and feel a wave of giddiness as I imagine boxing up my few belongings and telling my roommates I'm moving out. As I quit the gallery. As I buy my one-way plane ticket and set up shop in Brooklyn.

It is possible, I realize now.

I can have my dream life.

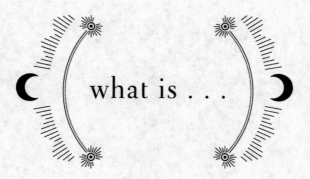

what is . . .

17

The day after tomorrow comes too quickly.

Ben has not been on a solo trip since his diagnosis. I have basically been by his side every waking minute. We know we've grown codependent, that we've been living from a place of survival, and that this separation, however painful, will be good for us both. Probably.

As Ben shrugs on his backpack and walks to the car, his eyes shine with something I haven't seen in a while: adventure, possibility, change.

A miracle.

"Call me the moment you get there," I say.

"I will. I promise." He kisses me again, and I try to soak in this moment, try to stop time. I don't want to lay all my worries at his feet. I know he needs to do this alone, to stay focused on healing, but everything in me wants to scream to stay here, with me, in our condo. But I know getting out of the place he's been so sick in will most likely make him feel better.

I wave until he is out of sight and then slump against the brick wall outside our building. I want to believe in miracles, but I also believe in reality. Though I remind myself, if anyone can beat this, it's Ben. Maybe a miracle really could happen. Maybe it's not too late.

My phone chirps with an incoming text from an unknown number. My heart flutters as I read the text. It's from Liam.

How are you holding up? I thought we could go down by the river, maybe have a picnic, and I can interview you there since it's so nice out?

Seeing his message on my phone floors me. Did Ben give him my number? After I left New York, I'd wanted to reach out a million times. I didn't have Liam's phone number or his email, but I could have found him. I could have looked him up at the paper and gotten in touch that way. But as weeks turned into months and then years, I figured he didn't want me to find him. He wasn't on social media, so I couldn't even low-key stalk him when I finally got a cell phone, and I never allowed myself to look up his work because it was just too painful.

Tiny, beautiful moments of our time together in Brooklyn throttle back to the forefront of my mind. I have never felt so special, so alive, so *on purpose* as I did that week, and if I'm being radically honest with myself, I'm nervous to be in Liam's presence again. He has an effect on me that no one else does, not even Ben. It's the closest thing to magic I've ever felt, and the fact that Ben has brought up this crazy notion that he wants me to fall in love before he goes, and now has left me with the *only* other person I *was* madly in love with, is all too much to be a simple coincidence. It's a sign of some sort, just like the cards said, but of what, I'm not yet sure.

I think about how to respond. Should I suggest we just do the interview over the phone? No, I'm not some lovestruck twenty-something anymore. I'm a grown woman, married to the love of my life. I can handle one interview.

I'm sad, but I know he needs this, I reply. *Your plan sounds lovely. What can I bring?*

We decide to meet in a little over an hour. Here I am again, all these years later, needing to focus on my art but instead choosing to spend time with Liam. As I leave my apartment and make the brief journey toward the water, I realize meeting this time is under very different circumstances. This isn't all fun and games, and we aren't falling for each other. He is here for a story, and I am here to help honor Ben. That's where this story ends.

I remind myself of that as I catch a glimpse of Liam spreading out a blanket on the soft grass, arranging food on compostable plates before shoving a hand through hair I can almost still feel beneath my fingertips. My heart betrays me by beating much too fast, and I contemplate turning around, locking myself in my studio, and sending him a "sorry, can't" text.

Instead, I stalk down to the water's edge as he blinds me with that devastating smile. "Hey, you." He spreads his arms and motions for me to sit. "Good day for a picnic, right?"

It's like stepping back in time as I offer him a tight-lipped smile and sit on the very edge of the blanket. It's impossible not to remember the picnic he made for us on that rooftop all those years ago. My whole future was ahead of me then, and I foolishly thought it would all work out.

Liam lowers himself beside me, and I swear I feel the heat from his body even with five feet between us. He offers me a can of sparkling water. I take it and stare at the calm river, my thoughts dancing all over the place.

"He'll be fine," Liam says, popping the top of his water and taking a swig. "These workshops are wildly transformational. People who have been diagnosed with chronic lifelong illnesses leave completely in remission."

I feel a flush of guilt as I realize I wasn't even thinking of Ben just now and focus on the entire reason I'm here. I search for what to say. I can't think about Ben being fully healed. I've already been there in my mind, and with every doctor's appointment, reality caused me to come crashing back down. "I don't know how he can do this to himself," I finally say, plunging my fingers into the grass beside me. "Give himself this type of hope."

"What's the alternative?" Liam shakes his head. "The mind is a powerful thing, Harper. I watched my mom give up because the doctors told her there were no other options. She lived in fear, and then she died." He shakes his head. "Whatever we believe, that's what happens. I've studied this. I've covered stories on it for years. I've done the research. And I can tell you that it is one hundred percent possible that Ben can walk away totally healthy next week."

I want to believe that too, but I simply can't. Not with advanced pancreatic cancer. Not with how much it's already spread. And what if the impossible *does* happen? Would Ben and I still live the rest of our lives in fear of it coming back again? Would we think with every cough or bad day or stomach bug, *Well, here we go again*. It's not the actual diagnosis that's the cancer, I've realized; it's all the uncertainty that comes after. I know Liam already knows this; he went through it, and his mom did not make it to the other side.

"So what do you want to ask me?" It's a sharp swerve, but Liam acclimates and brings out his phone to record.

He swallows, and I try to drag my eyes away from his throat and lips, but it's harder than it should be. "Well, Ben has told me how you two met, and I know the infamous proposal story now, but I'd like for you to take me to that moment of his diagnosis. What happened. How you felt."

"Starting off easy, huh?" I joke, hitching my knees up to my chest. I drape my arms around them, the can dangling loosely from my cool fingertips. "He got really sick on our honeymoon. I knew something wasn't right. I could just feel it." I tell him that after Ben fainted on our honeymoon, he started complaining about stomach pain and darker urine. Then it was unexpected weight loss and nausea. He thought it was a bug. My mind went straight to cancer.

"I finally forced him to go in for bloodwork. They immediately called him in for more tests and to biopsy a spot they found on his pancreas. I should note here that Ben hates doctors, hates blood, hates all of it. He used to say that anyone who walks in for extensive testing doesn't leave without some sort of diagnosis. When the doctor came in to share his results, Ben joked and asked, 'Am I dying?' and instead of laughing, she simply offered a frown." I swallow, remembering. "At that moment, I literally thought, 'This is it. This is the moment everything changes.' She started explaining advanced pancreatic cancer, what it meant, how it was diagnosed. They practically forced him into treatment on the spot, and it's one of our biggest regrets. That we didn't take time to explore our options. They made it sound like if he wanted to live, he had to start treatment immediately. You don't know Ben, but this was not the way for him to enter a fight. I remember that all he asked was how long he had left, and she told him six months without treatment, maybe a year or two with."

Liam shakes his head and scribbles something on his pad.

"He worried that amount of time wasn't even worth it for what his body would have to go through. But I asked more questions—about treatment, side effects, the cost with health insurance—and I realized this wasn't just his diagnosis. It was mine too." I pause and take a shaky breath. "I remember being so angry. Ben was the healthiest person I knew. We were newlyweds. We had plans. I didn't understand why it was all happening. We left, and when we walked outside, he looked at me and said . . ." My voice trails off and I try to keep my emotions in check. "He said, 'I've only just found you.'" My eyes lock with Liam's and something familiar passes between us.

"Then he burst into tears, which was the only time I'd ever seen him cry." I sigh and look up at the cloudless sky. "That was one of the hardest days of my life. It all felt so unfair."

I know Liam wants to chime in, say something positive, but this is our story, not his. I take him through the subsequent treatment, how it made Ben so sick, how he experienced such negative side effects and developed several infections that nearly killed him. It didn't seem possible that there could still be an ounce of cancer in there with all the drugs and treatments, but the cancer somehow still grew and spread.

"Does Ben have any unprocessed trauma? A rough childhood, things like that?"

I'm surprised he's asking me instead of Ben, but I just shrug. "He definitely has some things he doesn't like to talk about, mainly with his dad's unexpected death. He often works it out in his music."

Liam nods. "That makes sense." He scribbles something else and then presses Stop on his phone. "Snack time?"

I nod and dip into the turkey sandwiches, salad, and fruit he's brought. We munch silently, staring at the water, a few paddleboarders and boaters soaking up the day.

"Harper?"

My heart thuds in my chest the moment I look at him. "Yeah?"

"Why did you leave?"

My mouth is dry, my head is swimming, and I don't want to answer. There are so many reasons I left New York, none of them good. I know what he's really asking: *Why did you leave me?*

"It's complicated," I say.

He nods, pensive. "Okay, but all this time, why didn't you reach out?"

"Why didn't you?" I toss the question back, and he actually laughs.

"You're kidding, right? I reached out constantly."

"No, you didn't." He *definitely* didn't.

"Yes, I did. You didn't have a cell phone, so I tried to track down where you work, but you'd already quit. I even tried to reach you through Kendall and Rita."

My head is spinning. He *what*? Not long after I came back to Chicago, I quit my job, got a new email address, and moved out of my apartment. When I finally got a flip phone and thought of reaching out, I didn't have Liam's cell phone number; all I had was his physical address. I even wrote him several letters but never sent them.

"I thought about reaching out a thousand times," I finally admit.

"Why didn't you?" He turns to face me fully. "Because I tried, Harper. I emailed you but it bounced back. I tried to look you up online. I even flew to Chicago once."

These admissions hit me one after the other, until I am unable to keep up. *He flew to Chicago? He tried to find me?*

"That wasn't just some random week to me," he finally says. "It was my whole life, my future. *You* were my future." His voice cracks, and so does my heart.

139

I know we shouldn't be having this conversation. Ben's earnest face rolls through my mind, front and center; I scurry to stand, taking a few steps back, as if Liam has physically threatened me. "I can't be here. I can't do this. I'm sorry."

I turn to go and break into a run. Maybe if I run far enough, fast enough, I will start to forget.

what was . . .

18

In the morning, I can hardly believe where I am.

I am in Liam Hale's bed, which sits like a monument in the middle of his loft. He is adorably tangled in the sheets next to me. I trail a hand over his bare back. Last night was incredible, for more reasons than one.

I close my eyes for a moment, remembering the tender but urgent way we connected. His lips on mine. The intensity of his breath and words. The way my body responded, as if it had been seeking his body my entire life. Making love with Liam was intense and passionate, and I will never forget it as long as I live. Then, to top it all off, he took me to a late showing of *The Princess Bride*, which officially made it the best night ever.

Now, I feel awakened to something I've been missing; strangely, it has less to do with Liam and everything to do with myself. I've been playing small. I've been in hiding, doing what I think I'm supposed to do instead of following my instincts.

Sitting up, I gather my hair into a ponytail and once again study the outline of Liam's body. My eyes trail from him to the piece I'm working on, then to the windows that frame my inspiration: the bridge. Already life is stirring down below, people hurrying to work, getting on with their day. I know I need every hour I can get today to sink into this piece, but I want to revel in this moment and what happened last night just a little longer.

Crawling out from beneath the sheets, I tiptoe to the kitchen and make us coffee. As I'm searching for cream, I give a little yelp of surprise. On his refrigerator, under a tiny magnet, hangs the photo he snapped of us. I trace the edges of it, the evidence of all that is possible here, with him. With a shiver, I make us two strong cups and then whip up some breakfast.

"What smells so good?"

I turn off the pan, the bacon still sizzling, as Liam walks over, his voice still heavy with sleep.

"Hungry?"

His eyes lock with mine as I ask it, and he offers a wicked smile. "Starving." Before I can think too deeply about last night, he envelops me again, his lips making contact with every inch of my body. I am coming to learn that Liam loves to touch, to kiss, to hold, to *claim*. He is physical, so different from what I'm used to.

After, we eat on his balcony, overlooking the gritty city below. Pungent smells waft up from the sewers, but I don't mind. Once we are full, he sighs. "So what's on the agenda today?"

I motion behind me to his studio. "Nothing but that. I've only got a few days left and a ton to do."

He nods. "Got it. I'll get out of your hair then."

Though I should feel guilty about kicking Liam out of his own loft, this arrangement already feels normal. Once he is showered and gone, I get to work. I forget about Rita Clementine and her gallery and what it would mean if she accepts me. Instead, I focus on this giant canvas and the way I am filling it.

A knock at the door shakes me from my flow. I stop where I am and rush over to answer it. It's Kendall.

"What a happy surprise," I say, opening the door wider. "Come in."

"Thanks." She glances behind me, probably expecting to see Liam. "Can I see?" Before I can answer, she makes a beeline for my work, and instantly I feel completely bare, exposed. She studies it thoughtfully, moving left to right. "This is good," she affirms. "Rita will love it."

"You think?" I swirl a few brushes into a cup of water and wipe them dry.

"I do. Are you at a stopping place? I thought we could catch up."

"Sure." I suggest we go for a walk since I haven't been getting enough fresh air. Outside, she steers us north, and I can tell she's distracted.

Though Kendall and I used to be roommates, we haven't kept in close touch until she reached out about this opportunity. I'm not sure what's happening in her daily life, though it's clear she takes her work very seriously. When we get to a park bench, she motions for me to sit.

"I just wanted to talk to you about a little something. It's no big deal *at all*," she emphasizes, "but I thought you should know."

"Okay." I sit and smile at a toddler who is playfully running from her mother. The mom scoops her up and kisses her belly until the little girl erupts into giggles.

"It's about Rita."

Now she has my full attention. "What about her?"

She fiddles with her bracelets, her hair, the lapel of her jacket. "I know I didn't say anything before, and like I said, this totally doesn't matter, but she's my aunt."

"Wait, what?" How did I not know that?

She gives me a tentative smile. "So I may have pulled some strings to get you in to see her. But I believe in you, Harper. I've always believed in you. We both have a lot riding on this, so I need you to really show up, okay?"

"What makes you think I wouldn't?"

"Because I know you," she says, tapping me playfully on the nose. "You get in your head."

She's not wrong. I search for what to say to assure her, but she continues before I can find the right words.

"Also, I know I'm the one who introduced you to Liam—and he's a total dreamboat, by the way—but an opportunity like this doesn't come along that often, and I want you to be one hundred percent focused on your job here. Rita Clementine doesn't make offers to just anyone."

I feel like she's slapped me. "I know that. I'm focused, Kendall. I swear."

We sit in awkward silence for a moment as I think of all the ways I'm *not* focused, all the ways that I'm more excited by what's happening with Liam than the piece and what it means for my career. Sensing I have nothing more to say, Kendall claps.

"Okay, I've said my piece," she says. "And not to put any more pressure on you, but think about how much fun we'll have if you move here. It would be like old times. But, you know, without boring classes."

I want to focus on what she's saying, but I also can't help thinking about Liam. *Is* he a distraction? Am I somehow sabotaging myself by paying more attention to him than why I'm here?

"Let's not get ahead of ourselves," I say. "I have to impress her first."

"You will. It's your time to shine, babe."

I relax against the bench and try to absorb what she's saying. It certainly feels like my time to shine, but it's also so much pressure. And I've always caved under pressure. Growing up doing team sports. Being put on the spot. Public speaking. I've always run away from what's hard, and I want this to be different. I *need* this to be different.

We chat about other things, and then she's walking me back to the loft. I say goodbye, and as I step inside, I feel a bit disgruntled and no longer in the mood to create. I walk over to the refrigerator and trace the photo of the two of us. Is Kendall right? Am I using Liam to sabotage something I really want? As I stare at our smiling faces, I realize I don't just want this opportunity with Rita. I also want Liam, and I want to be the kind of person who believes she can have both.

That wild possibility is what excites me the most . . . but if I'm being honest with myself, it's also what scares me.

19

After a few more days, the piece is ready.

As I assess the canvas, I feel strongly that it is one of the best things I've ever created. Part of me wants to hold on to it as a keepsake for how I've felt this week. But it's time to hand-deliver it to Rita Clementine's house, which, according to the address, is a brownstone in one of the wealthiest parts of Brooklyn.

Liam's friend who owns a pickup truck agrees to give us a lift. As I sit in the bed, guarding my precious cargo, I replay these last seven days and how they've brought me here, to this critical moment.

Once his friend parks, I take a deep breath as we carefully lower the canvas to the sidewalk. It's not yet noon. We are early. Because I don't have a cell phone, Rita emailed me instructions, which I have printed and memorized.

Let yourself in. Walk straight back to the in-home gallery, which is the last door on the right. Arrange the piece as you wish for it to be experienced. Call upstairs when you're ready.

I steady myself. This is it. The moment I've been waiting for. With a calming breath, I hoist my end of the canvas under my arm while Liam takes the other. At the door, I nudge it open and almost alert Rita that we're here. I don't want her to think an intruder is entering her home. But I remind myself that wasn't part of the instructions. I don't want to give her any excuse to kick me out.

We hobble toward the back, and I briefly take in the terra-cotta floors, the exquisite, powerful art, the sculptures and statues that clog every space. At the door to the gallery, I prop the edge of the painting on my hip and push it open. We waddle in, gently set the canvas on the rug, and I loosen my shoulders as I stare at the bare white walls. There are nail holes everywhere, evidence of other art that's been hung or shown, and for a moment, I wonder if there's a camera in here. If this is all part of some weird game to see how well I can follow directions.

"Where do you want it?" Liam is just as excited as I am, which helps.

I study the walls and the proximity to the door. I want Rita to stumble upon the piece. I want it to engulf her. I want her to be drawn to it, like fire. Finally, I decide on the west wall, which has the most beautiful light, thanks to the adjacent window. As we hang it and make sure it's level, the light plays on some of the sea glass we found. It offers an unexpected explosion of color, which adds to the overall effect. When we have it centered, I stand back. "Well?"

"It's your time to shine, kid."

He squeezes my shoulder and tells me he will be right outside. Before I call up to Rita, I take a moment to give myself a pep talk. Normally I'd keep a running tab on all the little things I would tweak or fix. I would prepare myself to lose out on this opportunity before I'd even given myself a chance. But this isn't the Harper Swanson from Chicago. This is the Harper Swanson who is on the precipice of something great.

149

My fingers tremble as I shove them into my pockets and walk out of the door and to the foot of the stairs. With as much confidence as I can muster, I call, "I'm ready!" and then scurry back into the room, perching in a chair in the corner to wait. Finally, she enters, and I stiffen, as if I've been caught doing something wrong.

But I do not take my eyes off of her; instead, I stalk her every movement as she moves fully into the room. I watch the way her eyes sweep over to me first, almost bored, and then snag on the piece. She takes a tiny, audible breath, which in my book is a victory, before creeping forward, folding her arms, and standing in silence for what feels like an hour.

She's so still for so long, I wonder if she's lapsed into a trance, but then she's touching, moving, mumbling under her breath. Finally, she looks at me, and I don't know what I'm expecting—maybe a smile or nod, some sort of acknowledgment that I've done a good job.

Instead, she simply sniffs and says, "I'll be in touch," before turning in her flats and heading for the door.

All the pent-up excitement, hours of work, lack of sleep, and physical and mental effort are about to walk out that door with her.

I stand and can't silence myself before I blurt out, "That's it?"

She stops as if I've yelled at her, her shoulders hunched by her ears. She rotates slowly and narrows her eyes at me. "Excuse me?"

I know I should stop talking, but I can't. This means too much to me: this moment, this opportunity, my art on her wall. "I'm sorry, I just . . . I'd really love to know what you think. If this is what you had in mind."

"And I said I'd be in touch. Good day, Ms. Swanson."

She leaves, and I fear I've blown it. I snap a quick photo of the piece and walk out of the room, visibly deflated. Liam doesn't hear me coming because he's on the phone with someone. I sit on the stoop as I watch his back. He laughs, and despite how down I am, my face cracks into a smile.

When he turns and sees me, he says he has to go and shoves the phone in his back pocket. "So? Did she love it?"

I shrug. "She said she'd be in touch." Inside, I'm panicking. I know what "be in touch" usually means; it means, "Sorry, not interested." I replay the moment she walked into the room, though, the genuine surprise on her face.

"Maybe she's playing it cool while secretly plotting your rise to the top." He lightly touches my neck. "Let's do something to take your mind off it."

Suddenly I'm exhausted. The whole buildup and adrenaline dump have left me feeling drained. "Is it okay if we head back to your place?"

"Of course."

It's not a long walk, and Liam chats most of the way. I try to pay attention, but I'm too in my head, dismantling my dream before it's even fully built. Just when I am thinking of a hot bath and a glass of wine, we pause at Liam's door.

There, with a bag slung over her shoulder, looking like she stepped off a Milan runway, stands a stunning woman.

"LaTasha?" Liam's voice registers actual shock.

My gaze bounces between the two of them, and all thoughts of Rita and my art fly out the window.

The woman tosses her arms wide. "Surprise!" Her teeth are blindingly white against her smooth, dark skin. Liam steps into a hug, and I watch the two of them embrace. It is evident, from the look on her face and the way her fingers comb through his hair, that they have history. A pit forms in my stomach as I step out of the way. Her hands linger on his elbow, his shoulder, and then lightly caress his face.

I feel like I've been punched. Finally, as if remembering I'm there, Liam turns. "Harper, this is LaTasha. LaTasha, Harper."

She extends one gorgeous hand my way, fingernails perfectly manicured. I am paint-splattered and scrubbed free of makeup, but I shake her hand and mumble hello. I can see the question in her eyes, the same one I'm practically screaming internally: *Who is she?*

Liam unlocks the door and motions us both in. I hesitate for only a moment, contemplating if I can run away. I don't want to know who this woman is, not really. I don't want to step inside.

I'm afraid of what it might cost me to learn the truth.

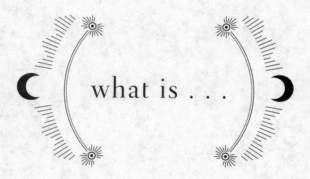

what is . . .

20

I end up at Wren and Jenna's after walking most of the day.

Though I've tried to untangle the truth of what happened that day in front of Liam's apartment, I'm still reeling over the fact that Liam tried to find me.

None of it adds up. I try to focus on what Jenna is saying about some drama that happened at summer school today, but my brain is still back at the water, back with Liam. *Liam tried to find me. Liam flew to Chicago. Liam said I was his whole future.*

Sensing my disinterest, Wren kisses the back of Jenna's neck and scoops up Gremlin, hooking his spindly body in the crook of her arm. "Let's talk about your show, Harper."

I roll my eyes and sip my glass of wine. "We'll see."

"No, don't do that. You're doing this show. There's no 'we'll see' about it. Ben believes in you. We believe in you. Your kids believe in you. Think how proud they would be to see their teacher doing what they want to do someday. It's time to believe in yourself too."

At the mere mention of my kids, I close my eyes and sigh. I think of the talent in that art room, how so many of my kids wouldn't think

155

REA FREY

twice about the opportunity for a solo show. That makes me remember when I met Keisha in Brooklyn, how openly hungry she was to state her goals and rise to the top. What's stopping me now? I'm off for the summer. Technically, I could pursue art, but with Ben's diagnosis, I am deflecting, stalling, second-guessing, just like always.

"And," she adds before I can interject, "there's never a perfect time to follow your dreams. It's like having a kid. Sometimes you just have to run into the fire and see what shakes out." Wren folds in beside Jenna, all sharp angles to Jenna's soft curves.

"Okay, Wren. I think she's got it. Next subject." Jenna grabs Gremlin from Wren and possessively cuddles him. "How's Liam?"

I stare into my wine, not knowing how much to say. Explaining anything beyond the basics about Liam is complicated, but these are two of my closest friends, and I know I can trust them. Loosely I explain what just transpired between us and that, per usual, I ran away.

Jenna bites her lip, glances at Wren, then back to me. "You realize tonight is the full moon, right? You have to do the ritual, Harper."

"You do," Wren confirms. "We can even do it here, if you want."

"Enough with the ritual!" I yell. "That's not going to fix any of my problems. Figuring out what to do now, in my *real* life, is."

"Okay," Jenna says, scooting forward to pat my knee. "What does Ben say about all this?"

I hesitate. There's no easy way to say I've basically lied to Ben, that I brushed off my relationship with Liam because I don't want to dredge up the past when he needs to stay focused. I'm realizing, however, that it's more for my sake, not Ben's. "He doesn't know."

"Harper, you have to tell him."

"Definitely don't tell him."

156

They both speak at the same time, and my brain scrambles even more to decipher their advice. Now it's Wren's turn to place a hand on Jenna's knee. "Harper, do not tell him. That will just give him more to worry about."

Jenna moves Wren's hand. "You have to tell him." She blinks widely at me. "This was his plan in the first place, Harper! He basically manifested this into existence by delivering Liam to your door, and you're not going to tell him that the universe answered him back? How is that fair?"

"I have a headache." I rub my temples. Pickles hops onto my legs before Gremlin knocks her away and plops into my lap instead.

"Look, do what you want to do," Jenna says. "But just remember whose journey this is."

"Hers!" Wren shouts. "It's hers."

"And Ben's," Jenna adds. "He deserves to know what's happening."

"Why give him more anxiety when he's got enough to worry about?"

"Who says it will give him anxiety? It might give him hope!"

The two of them bicker while I listen to Gremlin's soft purrs. I came here to get clarity, and now I'm more confused than before.

Wren's phone dings and she reaches for it, still disgruntled. Then she breaks into a satisfied grin. "Well, well, well. Look who it is." She flashes me the text. It's from Liam.

"How does he have your number?"

"Ben gave it to him," she says dismissively. "He needs to interview us. Tonight." She stabs a finger my way, then taps out a furious text. "Oh my God, you're coming. We're having a cookout. We want to see you two together, and then we can decide what to tell Ben. Deal?"

Jenna rolls her eyes. I shift in my chair. "I'm not sure that's the best idea. Considering I literally ran away from him at the first sign of talking about the past."

"All the more reason you should let us assess. I want to get a sense of his aura," Wren says, wiggling her fingers in the air. "See if he's right for you."

"Ben is who's right for her!" Jenna sighs and hoists herself from the couch. "Ben is the only man in her life. Ben is who matters right now, not some dude from the past."

"Well, obviously I don't mean right for her right now," Wren clarifies. "I'm talking about the future."

"I need a nap." I lower Gremlin to the ground and stand. "Just let me know what time tonight." I give each of them a hug, and Wren walks me to the door.

"Look," she says, steering me outside so Jenna can't hear. "You know I love Ben. Everybody loves Ben. He's one of my dearest friends. But like I said the other day, Liam being here isn't a coincidence, Harper, and we both know it. Ben knows it, and he doesn't even understand the full extent of your connection with Liam. But you owe it to yourself to figure out why he's here and what this means."

"I know." I actually *don't* know, but I understand it's the only thing I can say right now to get her to drop it.

"Okay, see you tonight." She kisses my cheek and leaves me standing on the stoop more confused than before.

21

"It was one of the coolest days I've ever had," Ben says over the phone.

It's near dinnertime, and he fills me in on the first day of the intensive. I struggle to listen and absorb every word, but my brain is all over the place. Wren's words hammer a soft spot in my heart, but so do Jenna's. Of course I want to tell Ben who Liam is to me, what he meant. But as I hear the uptick in his voice, infused with an energy I've never heard—not even when he was healthy—I know I need to wait until he returns.

It's just a week, I tell myself. But I know, more than anyone, what can happen in a week. How much can change. How much can begin or end.

"This sounds so incredible already, Ben," I say instead. "I'm so happy for you."

He explains that there have been studies of people entering these intensives with life-threatening illnesses and by the time they leave, they are completely cured. It's not anything that Joe is doing or not doing; it's simply showing people how to enter a new state of consciousness that creates infinite possibilities. It's a lot to wrap my head around, but Ben sounds clear and focused. I want to ask him if he's eaten and hydrated today, if he will get to rest much tonight, but I bite my tongue. I want him to ride this high as much as he can. If he needs me, I'm only a short drive away.

"How's it going with Liam?"

"It's fine," I say, though my body tenses as I say it.

There's an awkward silence between us, and then Ben laughs. "Oh-kay. You sure everything's good?"

I can feel the words bubbling up my throat, but now is not the time. This week is about Ben, not me. "Yeah."

"Harper. You know I can tell when you're not okay. I promise I'm going to be fine. Better than fine, actually. I haven't felt this physically good in a long time."

"No, that's not it."

"Then what is it?"

I squeeze my temples as I stare at my phone on speaker. Should I FaceTime him? Would it be better if I could see him? "I need to ask you something," I finally blurt, deciding to change the subject. "Did you suggest to Wren that I should do a solo show?"

"Oh," he says gently. "That."

"Yeah, that," I say. "Ben, I appreciate the thought—really, I do—but now could not be a worse time for me to create a show. I don't think I've ever felt less creative in my life."

"I understand that," he says. "It was just an idea. I thought . . ."

He trails off, but I want to hear him say it. "Say what you want to say, Ben."

"I just thought it would be amazing to see one of your shows before . . ."

Again he trails off, and we both know what he's not saying. I take a deep breath, and in one messy gush, I explain why I'm not ready. I tell him about my big shot in New York a decade ago and how I blew it. While I've alluded to that time in my life, I've never really taken ownership of the fact that I just couldn't cut it, that my work wasn't good enough, that *I* wasn't good enough. And now Wren is giving me a second chance. "Even if I could get it all together by August, what if I blow it again?"

"First of all, you didn't blow it. It just wasn't the right time." I hear another audible squeak that must be him shifting on the bed. "But now it is. It's time to manifest what you want, but you have to get honest about what that even is."

Ben has never used the word *manifest* in his life.

"Get honest about what I want?"

"Yes. What do you want? What's your biggest, wildest dream?"

I open my mouth to respond, but then stop. Hadn't Wren asked me the same thing? I recall what I told her: that I want Ben to be cancer-free. That I would like to know what life would be like as a working artist, even though I also enjoy being a teacher. "I do think it would be amazing to reach as many people as I can with my art," I finally say.

"Oh, come on, Swanson," he encourages. "You can do better than that."

"Fine." I search my heart—not my ego—and share what comes up. "I would love to earn my place in the art world . . . to sell pieces, get written up in articles, to make a solid living doing what I love." It's the first time I've said any of these things out loud to Ben. I haven't really thought much about what I want out of an art career since that fateful night when my dreams crumbled around me like dust.

161

"There it is," he says. "So go get it."

"Ben."

"Harp."

"It's not that easy."

"Why not?" His voice is hyper, energized. It's been so long since he's been able to offer *me* advice, and I realize how much I've missed it. "Why can't it be that easy? Why can't I walk out of here without cancer? Why not us?"

I'm speechless. He's right, but it seems like it should all be so much more complicated. "I've never been able to pluck out what I want from the universe and actually have it." Even as I say it, I know that's not true. It did happen, once. If only for a week. But I know it's more than possible.

"So start now." His voice is kind but determined. "Talk to Wren about it. She can help."

"I'm not sure what I think about this law of attraction version of you," I joke.

"It's not the law of attraction." He laughs. "It's science."

"Look, I'm sorry I brought all this up," I say. "Especially with how important this week is for you. I hope you can do what you need to do there."

"Harper, stop. I'm happy to talk about what's on your mind. You've sacrificed this last year of your life for me. You've been there as my caretaker, my wife, and my best friend. I want you to focus on *you* this week. Focus on your art. I'll be fine. I need this, but I also need to know you're doing what's best for you too."

"Well, I appreciate it," I finally say. "Let me know how day two goes, okay? Don't, like, scale a mountain or something without telling me first."

"Do you remember when we hiked Mount Whitney? Man, that was a great trip." Our conversation swings into safer territory: reminiscing about the past, which sometimes feels fruitless, but right now it's a welcome distraction. We used to only think about the future and what we would do once Ben got a clean bill of health. In these last few months, however, it's been all about the past, about honoring the time we had together and what time we have left.

"I love you, Ben." My eyes fill with tears, and I miss him so much, I can hardly breathe. The way he smells. His smile. His hands. The way he makes me feel. Ben is my home.

"I love you too." He clears his throat. "More than you possibly know. I'll call you tomorrow, okay? Sleep well, my love."

We end the call, and I gnaw on a cuticle, ignoring the five text messages Liam has sent. My stomach is in knots, and I feel reckless, unhinged. The sun has long since set, but I step outside, the night inky and humid. I tip my head up toward the moon and see the stars, reminding myself how infinite it all is. My eyes lower and pass across the street to the Edwin. Part of me expects Liam to be standing on his balcony again, staring at me, like he was the first night, but his room is dark.

I sigh and head back inside, feeling Ben's absence. Before I can wallow in it, there's a sharp knock on the door.

"Harper, it's Liam. We need to talk."

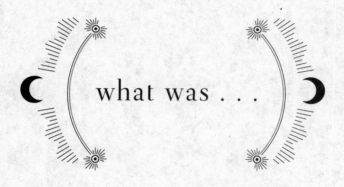

what was . . .

22

"M an, I've missed New York," LaTasha says as she drops her bag by the door.

Liam catches my eye and gives me a pained, mildly panicked smile as LaTasha excuses herself to the bathroom after her long flight. He grips the back of his neck and sighs. "Sorry about this. I wasn't expecting her."

My heart is racing, but I attempt to stay calm and not jump to conclusions. "Who is she?" I shift from foot to foot in my beat-up combat boots. Inside, I feel as though my heart is closing and I am on the verge of losing both Liam and my career in a single night. But maybe she's just a friend. Maybe I can still have my happy ending.

"She's . . ." Before he can answer, LaTasha reappears and squeezes past Liam into the kitchen, making herself at home. She uncorks a bottle of wine and flips a braid over her shoulder.

"So how do you two know each other?"

There's an awkward beat before Liam explains. "She's a friend of Kendall's. I lent her my studio so she could make something for Rita Clementine's gallery."

His explanation hurts more than I thought it would. A friend of Kendall's. Not a friend of his. Not a lover. Not anyone.

LaTasha rolls her eyes. "Always the martyr, my love. Did you finish?" Her eyes swing back to me, but I'm still hung up on the words *my love*. So not a roommate, then.

"I did," I barely choke out before staring at my shoes. "You know what, why don't I let you two catch up? I'm going to get out of your hair."

I grab my backpack and stuff random items inside. I practically sprint to the bathroom, scoop all my belongings into my shaking arms, and force them into my bag. I can hear them talking in hushed whispers but can't make out what they're saying. In the main room, my eyes linger on the refrigerator, where the photo of us hangs, a potent reminder of our time together this week. I can't very well take it when LaTasha is standing right next to it, so I zip my bag and contemplate my choices. I have nowhere else to go, but I know I can't stay here.

"You don't have to go," Liam rushes to add when he sees my full bag, sloppily packed, but I can tell LaTasha wants alone time with him, that she is eager for the "friend of Kendall's" to scram.

"No, it's fine," I say, my eyes lingering on the art supplies I will have to leave behind. "I appreciate you letting me stay here." My words are cold, and we both know it. I wave goodbye and practically sprint out the door before tears sting my eyes. I rush down the stairs and hit the street in a total panic. I have no idea where to go.

I need to find a pay phone to call Kendall. Is this what she was really trying to warn me about, because she knew I'd end up hurt? Before I can decide what to do or which way to walk, Liam bursts from the main door and sighs.

"Hey, Harper. Don't go. Please."

Something is happening between my brain and body, because I can't make myself register what he just said. I keep seeing LaTasha's beautiful eyes and her long, brown fingers touching every part of the man I am madly in love with. My mouth is dry, my muscles tight. I stab a shaky finger up toward the loft. "Who is she, Liam?"

Liam may be many things, but he's not stupid, and thankfully he doesn't say something like "no one." Instead, he sighs and leans against the blood-red brick. He kicks a shoe against it, jutting his heel roughly against the surface in a staccato motion. "I haven't been entirely honest with you."

My heart ratchets up to my throat, and I think I might be sick. Deep down, I knew all of this was too good to be true: Rita. Brooklyn. Liam. I know I'm doing what I always do and I'm closing up before I have all the facts, but I can already tell how much this is going to hurt either way. "Just tell me." My voice sounds odd to me, flat and hard.

"LaTasha is my ex. She's been in Bali for a year working with a nonprofit to protect sea life. We broke up because of the distance, but she's back. We're not together," he adds, "but we are friends. She just needs a place to crash for a few days until she finds a new apartment."

I shake my head. Nothing about LaTasha's mannerisms screams *friends*. I smack away a few tears, humiliated. "She called you *my love*, Liam. How is that friendly?"

"Harper, look. We were together for five years. She's an important part of my life, but trust me when I say it's no longer romantic."

"Did you live together?"

His eyes catch mine, and there is a flash of guilt there. How had this not come up? I'd cracked myself open to him, told him everything, and he'd left out this vital part of his story? Why? When I'd asked him if there was anyone special in his life, he'd just said there was someone but not anymore. A one-sentence summation now standing in his kitchen while I'm down here on the street.

"When we were spilling our hearts out to each other, you didn't think to tell me about her?" To be fair, my side of the conversation had been short, mainly because I had nothing to share. But apparently he did. I know Liam has a past, and I'm okay with that. But not when that past shows up at his doorstep with me still inside.

"I didn't think it was relevant. This week was about us."

Until it wasn't. "I'm an idiot." I spin in a circle, gauging which way to walk. "You know, this whole week has been make-believe. All of it. It all felt too good to be true, and now I know why."

"Harper, don't." He pushes away from the wall, but I'm just out of reach. "This week has been real. I've never felt this way about anyone."

I lift a hand to stop him. "Please don't say something trite like that. It only makes it worse." I don't know which direction Kendall lives, but I begin to walk. Liam jogs easily to catch up.

"Harper, seriously. Stop. Let's talk about this. I don't want you to go."

"What is there left to talk about?" I whip around so fast, my overstuffed bag slams against his chest.

"Us," he says. "How you're feeling. Our future. All of it." He reaches for me, but I step back.

What future? The fact that he kept a secret from me hurts more than the fact his ex-girlfriend has returned. I thought I knew him, *really* knew him, but how can someone know anyone in just a week?

"I need to go home," I finally say. "Back to Chicago." My voice echoes on the nearly dead street. Suddenly I am embarrassed. I don't want to react this way. I don't want to feel this unglued or shut down, especially over a guy. But this, *all of this*, has opened my heart in a way I did not expect and am clearly not ready to handle.

He sighs and drags a hand down his face. "Harper, please don't go back to Chicago. Let's just take a breath and we'll figure all this out, okay?"

"And what? Be a third wheel with you and LaTasha? No thanks."

"Hey, come on. You're not a third wheel. I promise." He moves toward me. "Besides, you have to wait to hear back from Rita, right?"

I shake my head, and the slow, sad truth shifts into focus. "Come on, Liam. She said she'd be in touch. We both know what that means. It wasn't good enough. I'm not good enough. This week was a total waste of time."

The words land like a bomb. Liam's eyes dim, and he takes a shaky step back. "You don't mean that."

This is my moment to undo all of the damage I've just done, to tell Liam that he's right, I *don't* mean it, that I *do* understand, that I'm just being petty and jealous and am clearly self-sabotaging and that we can work it all out and begin again.

I realize, as I stare at him, that this isn't about LaTasha at all. Because deep down, I do believe Liam. I trust him, even if I don't know him as well as she does. What I don't trust is having what I really want: him, this city, my art. It feels like too much to lose.

I grapple with what to say, knowing how easily I could make this tension disappear. I simply take a step forward. I move closer. I show that I trust him, that I trust myself, and believe that it will all work out in the end.

But instead, I do what I've always done when I'm afraid of getting hurt. My self-preservation kicks in, and I shake my head as I stare into his eyes.

"I do mean it," I hear myself say. But I don't. Of course I don't. I waver for a moment, understanding that by leaving, I am tarnishing everything good between us. Maybe just for this moment. Maybe forever. Am I willing to take that risk?

"Harper, please."

His words burrow a hole in my chest as he reaches for me, his fingers brushing mine. My hand tingles as my eyes catch his. *Oh, how I love this man.* I hesitate again, my heart and mind ripping me into two distinct pieces: Go or stay. Hurt him now or hurt him later. Be hurt now or be hurt later. He waits, eyes pensive, before I shake my head.

"I'm so sorry, Liam. I can't." Better to cut it off now. Better to run.

I turn and walk away before I can see the devastation cross his face.

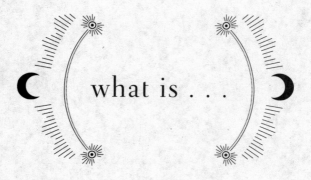

what is . . .

23

I open the door after composing myself.

Liam skips the niceties. "May I come in?" A bottle of wine and flowers are in hand, though I know they are for the cookout tonight, not me.

I nod and allow him to enter. The two of us here without Ben feels dangerous. He sets the flowers and wine on the island, bypasses the couch, and steps onto the balcony. I follow and wait for him to speak first. He palms the rail and stares out at the beautiful night, and then he turns, his eyes catching mine in the darkness. Despite who I am and where I am, my breath catches as it did that first night we spent together. I hate that my body is betraying me this way, especially after the conversation I just had with Ben.

"I'm sorry about today." He exhales and leans against the railing. "I know I'm here for a story, for Ben. But I also think it's important that Ben has all the facts." He crosses his arms. "That's how you felt, isn't it? With LaTasha?"

LaTasha. Hearing her name after all this time makes me feel trapped.

"I just want to give him the same courtesy. Even though," Liam rushes to add, "it's all in the past. But I just don't want to feel like I'm keeping anything from him. Especially since I'm writing this article."

I think about how blindsided I felt when I found out about LaTasha and how I wished Liam would have told me sooner. "You're right," I say. Though it's not exactly the same thing, it's still technically keeping something from the man I love. I sigh and sit on one of the chairs. "I'll tell him when he gets back. I promise."

His eyes sweep over my face just like they did that night on the street. The night I broke my own heart. Looking back, I realize that Liam was asking me to stay, to take a chance, to choose him. To trust him. And I didn't. I couldn't. And now, here he is again, at the worst possible time. "I just don't want him to get any ideas," I say. "About you showing up out of the blue. He won't think it's a coincidence."

"Do you think it's a coincidence?" He's looking at me again, and I can see he wants to say so much more.

"I don't know," I answer truthfully. I don't ask him the same thing in return because I don't want to know the answer. I scramble to hold on to any semblance of self-control, to remind myself of what's real and what should stay in the past. I think about the conversation I had with Ben, how right I feel when I'm with him, how I don't have any questions about who I am or where I'm supposed to be in life. "Ben just called," I blurt. "He had a great day."

"Oh yeah?" Liam's eyes brighten as he sits beside me. "What did he say?"

I fill him in on what Ben shared. "Thank you for encouraging him to go," I say. "I haven't heard him this positive in a really long time."

"I'm glad." He clears his throat, taps a shoe. "And what about you?"

"What about me?"

"Are you okay?"

I'm silent, but it's written all over my face. Of course I'm not okay. I'm not okay that Ben isn't here. I'm not okay that a man I was once crazy about is sitting on my balcony instead. I'm not okay that the safely stitched fabric of my past has come undone and that the stuffing is oozing everywhere. I'm not okay that I will soon become a widow. I'm not okay with anything.

I want to continue our conversation from earlier today, to really understand what happened in the aftermath of me leaving New York. Who is truly to blame for why we never got back in touch? I could have easily reached out to Kendall, or she could have told me that Liam was trying to find me. I never wanted to admit to her that I'd let my feelings for Liam cloud my potential with Rita. I'd let both of them down, and it was easier to walk away than explain I'd made a stupid mistake.

Now knowing that Liam tried, however, makes me rethink everything. He tried. I didn't. What does that mean? I want actual answers, but I'm so afraid of what I might find there, how I might want to rewrite history. "Look, I know there's a lot we both probably need or want to say. But you're here for one reason, Liam. Ben. This is about his story, like you said, not our past. I just want to keep it that way, okay?"

Liam waits a beat, then nods. "Understood. From now on, we'll stick to the story."

Relief washes through me. "Thank you."

He pats the tops of his thighs, as if deciding something. "I should get going."

"Well, I'm actually going too. Wren and Jenna invited me." Before I can gauge his reaction, I dash into my bedroom, take a moment to breathe and freshen up, then enter the foyer with a smile plastered on my face. "Ready?"

The night is warm, and we walk in silence. I fear I've shut Liam down completely, but I'm sure he's processing everything like I am. Luckily, Jenna and Wren live close. When we arrive, he stares up at their modern town house.

"Nice place."

"Wait until you see inside." I let myself in, and Wren hollers that they are out back.

Liam whistles as he walks in, because their town house truly is its own eclectic masterpiece. Impeccable art, mismatched furniture, imported rugs, crystals, statues . . . It is a mishmash of styles and cultures, but somehow it all works. Incense burns in almost every room, leaving the entire place hazy and fragrant, and when we step outside, the sizzle of burgers makes my stomach growl.

Jenna is lounging by the hot tub, among her potted plants. Wren stands at the grill, flipping real burgers and veggie burgers. She wears a bathing suit and a silk robe, her dark skin inked everywhere that's visible.

"Welcome to our humble abode, reporter man," Wren says.

I stare between the two of them as they giggle uncontrollably at that statement. "Um, how many edibles have you both had?"

Jenna stands to greet us. "Not nearly enough." Liam grips her hand, and she holds on a beat too long. "Good lord, you're attractive. Much too attractive to be a writer."

"Ignore them," I say as Liam offers Wren the wine and flowers.

Wren winks at me as we all settle in. We eat first, and then Liam launches into his easy line of questioning. He never makes the conversation feel stiff or uncomfortable. Before long, Wren and

Jenna are sharing all sorts of tales about Ben. The time they got high in a cemetery and got caught. A midnight hike where they were chased by a bear. A hot-air balloon ride where the fire sputtered and they almost plummeted to their death. The soundtrack he wrote for their wedding. As I listen to them now, it's hard to remember a time before we were all friends.

"We've always been protective over Ben," Wren says now, one arm draped across Jenna's shoulders. "Being in the public eye, even behind the scenes, can attract some trolls, for sure. But he's always been such a stand-up guy. He didn't date often, but when he did, sometimes he would pick the *worst* women. Ugh. Until Harper, that is."

"Oh," Liam says, looking between us. "So you two knew Ben before Harper did?"

I jump in to explain. "Ben met Wren years ago at some Hollywood shindig, and they hit it off. When she opened her gallery, he would come visit sometimes and fell in love with the city. After we met, he introduced me to both of them, and the rest is history. It's why I applied to teach here. The fact that Jenna also happened to be a teacher at the same school was an added bonus."

Jenna squeezes my knee, and I smile. Liam writes something down and then looks at me. I hold his gaze a beat too long, and they both notice.

"You guys up for the hot tub?" Wren asks. "You got what you came for, right, Liam?"

"Sure thing." He stops recording and flips his notepad closed.

I gesture to our clothes. "We don't have bathing suits."

"So? We're all adults."

"Wren." My voice is a bit sharp. I know she is a completely free spirit, but there is no way in hell I am going skinny-dipping with Liam Hale.

"Don't freak out, babe. We have spares in the back. I'll grab them."

"I'll help," Jenna trills, running off behind her.

I turn to Liam and offer a nervous smile. "I'm sorry about that. You don't have to get in the hot tub."

He shrugs and stuffs his hands into his pockets. "Sounds nice, actually. I haven't been in a hot tub since college. Sounds like a nice night for folliculitis."

I burst out laughing. Before I can respond, Wren tosses him a pair of trunks.

"Are those Ben's?" I ask.

"Who else's would they be?" She motions to where Liam can change. Thanking her, he disappears, and I squeeze my hands into fists at my sides as Wren and Jenna pounce on me.

"Oh my God, are you okay?"

"There seems to be a connection here, Harper."

"I really think you should talk to Ben about this."

"No, she most definitely does not need to talk to Ben."

"You guys, stop," I say, putting a hand on both of them. "I can't deal with this right now."

"Dude," Wren says, her eyes glassy. "I know we talked about this earlier, but seeing you two together?" She mimes an explosion. "There's something real here, Harper. And Ben came up with his idea for a reason. And now that reason is changing in the bathroom."

I snatch the bathing suit Wren is still holding and begrudgingly change in their bedroom. This feels like crossing yet another line, getting into hot water, half naked, with someone I once fell so hard for. I compose myself, walk back out, and swallow the lump in my throat when I glimpse Liam's fit body in Ben's old trunks.

I am instantly transported back to Ben standing here when he was healthy, flexing and preening until we would all laugh. He would often pretend to curl Gremlin and Pickles like they were dumbbells, and the cats loved him so much, they would flop in his fists, totally trusting. There were so many early days when we would come over for nights like this, followed by hours in the hot tub until we were all pruny and dehydrated.

We slip into the steamy bubbles now, and I force myself to relax. Wine is poured all around, and I drink greedily, trying to numb myself as quickly as possible.

Wren and Jenna pepper Liam with questions about his life, and then Wren and Liam venture off on a tangent about the art world, since he has roots there. Jenna floats over to me.

"How you doing, hot stuff?"

"Oh, just dandy. How are you?"

She looks at me. "This is a lot, Harper." She gestures to Liam. "Not just this, but everything." She drops her voice. "You know you can talk to me, right? You don't have to listen to Wren."

"I know." I bite my tongue as a flood of emotions threatens to erupt to the surface. Luckily, Jenna takes the cue and turns to lighter conversation.

Suddenly it's late, and Wren excuses herself to get Jenna, who has had way too much to drink, into bed. While she's gone, I am left with Liam, in the hot tub, alone.

"Hi," he says, at a safe distance.

"Hello."

We stare at each other, and again, all those questions I had from earlier threaten to tumble out.

"You've got great friends," he says. "You both do. You're very lucky."

"I am. We are," I say. "They're the best."

"Wren really believes in your art," he continues.

"I know." I sigh and rest my head against the back of the tub. "Now I think she's waiting on me to believe in myself."

This feels like the same conversation we had so many years ago, when Rita Clementine was the one who was giving me a chance and I was second-guessing everything.

"And do you?"

Do I? "Remains to be seen." I shift and glance at my watch. It's almost midnight. "I better get back," I say. "Get some rest."

"Yep."

We exit the tub and towel ourselves off. I avoid all eye contact, not daring to look at a dripping-wet Liam in my husband's bathing suit. We quietly slip back into our clothes in separate rooms and then tell Wren good night on the way out. She asks me to call her tomorrow as I hurry down her porch steps.

Now the night feels cool, and I shiver beneath my slightly damp clothes. Once again, we are quiet on the walk back, and I am thankful for not having to pretend.

At our block, he stops, something clearly on his mind, but then he shakes his head and keeps walking to the entrance of the hotel.

I stop him before he goes inside. "What are you thinking, Liam?" It is a loaded question, especially when I told him I need to keep our time together about Ben.

He hesitates. "You really want to know?"

No. "Yes."

"I'm thinking that now I know none of this is a coincidence." His eyes are intense as he looks at me. "I'm here for a reason, Harper. I found you again for a reason. I'm just not sure what it is yet."

I don't know what to say. I stand still for so long, he finally takes the cue, tells me good night, and enters his hotel. Part of me wants to run after him, to tell him to wait, to explain that even if this isn't a coincidence, the timing is all wrong. I spent the better part of ten years wondering what my life would have been like if I hadn't left New York or my one big opportunity or that loft or Liam, and then I forced myself to move on. But it wasn't easy. It was never easy. And now, when time is so precious, so finite, I don't want to waste time on what-ifs. But then I remind myself that almost everyone has that one big what-if, or a story about the one who got away. I'm no different, except my what-if is literally a few feet away.

The past and present mingle in my mind as I let myself into my building, rinse off in the shower, and climb into bed. It's been a long time since I thought about where my career went off the rails. So much of it feels like my fault because I wasn't brave enough to fight for what I wanted. Instead, I ran away from it all before I could inevitably fail. And yet here I am, in this life, with a man I love and a man I used to love. A man I have to learn to lose. And once again, I have an opportunity to be an artist.

But what if I try and fail again? I flip through a book, not really absorbing the words. Maybe that's what this is really about. I'm afraid that if I put myself out there again, I'll somehow mess it up. That in this life I'm destined to be a teacher in Chattanooga. Nothing more. Thinking about what could have been is just a waste of time.

I slam the book closed, plug in my phone, and text Ben good night. When we first met, Ben would always call me right before bed and stay on the line until I fell asleep. Hardly anyone I knew actually talked on the phone, instead communicating in poorly spelled text fragments. But not Ben. Now he gets tired if he talks too long, so we simply text. I know he needs to conserve his energy, that he is hopefully fast asleep, but a huge part of me wishes I could talk to him. I scroll through my texts and pause when I get to Liam's number. If I'd had his number ten years ago, would I be somewhere else? If I had a cell phone? If I hadn't run away?

Before I can think about it, I shoot him a quick text.

I really hope you understand, Liam. It's all just too much.

The message goes from delivered to read, and then he's typing back. *I do understand. I will always wonder what would have happened if things had turned out differently, but the past is the past, and I will always treasure our time together, Harper. Maybe in another life.*

Tears slip down my cheeks because this feels like an ending to something . . . closure, maybe, after all these years. *Maybe in another life*, I quickly type back.

I place my phone on my nightstand and stare at the empty spot on Ben's side. How will I sleep without him tonight? I've had to sleep plenty of nights alone when he had to stay at the hospital and insisted I come home to get rest, but I never really slept. I would worry about him in that stark room alone, with the whir of machines and the stench of sickness everywhere. I would feel so guilty for being able to take a hot shower and sleep in our own bed that I would stay up half the night, defeating the whole purpose of being home so I could rest.

I roll over to smell his pillow and pull out something crumpled behind it. I smooth the balled piece of paper flat and see it's Ben's Master Plan. My eyes fill with tears as I read it again:

Master Plan: Find Harper Someone to Love Before I Go

1. *Get Harper to agree to my crazy idea.*
2. *Once she is done telling me I'm an idiot, explain crazy idea.*
3. *Come up with a time line for crazy idea.*
4. *Find dates for Harper.*
5. *Find dates for Harper who don't make her want to gag.*
6. *Find dates for Harper who aren't sociopaths, psychopaths, or just lame.*
7. *Find the one for Harper who can make her laugh and take care of her the way she has taken care of me.*
8. *Remind her that I will be watching from beyond the grave . . . so she better not love him too much.*

Now this list has an entirely new meaning. Knowing what I know. Having Liam show up out of the blue after Ben wrote this . . . I smooth my fingers across the list again.

Tonight Ben is somewhere good, experiencing things with a group of people who all have something in common. A sole purpose. And I am here, trying not to think about a past that was left so unfinished, that steered my life to what it is today.

I sigh and close my eyes.

What would life have been like if I'd stayed in New York?

As the question tumbles through my head, my phone dings and my heart kicks. Maybe Ben sensed that I need to talk. I hungrily reach for my phone and realize it's just a text from Wren.

DON'T FORGET IT'S THE FULL MOON! You MUST do the ritual tonight, Harper. Don't forget. I mean it!!!!

I groan and replace my phone on my nightstand. I don't even know where that piece of paper is. Part of me wants to go to sleep, but I know if I try, I won't be able to. Not yet.

Before I can distract myself, my phone begins to buzz. Knowing it's Wren before I even look at it, I swipe open my FaceTime and see her face pop onto the screen. She's whispering, Jenna asleep beside her. "Did you do it yet?"

"You literally just texted me thirty seconds ago," I hiss.

She climbs out of bed and steps into her dark hallway. I can barely make out her features. "You have to do this, Harper. I have a feeling."

"A feeling that if I say some magic words and burn some paper that I'm going to get my happily ever after?"

She lights up a joint, takes a deep inhale, then exhales through her nose. The gray smoke curls around her, blocking the screen. "Something like that." She coughs.

"Ugh, hold please." Throwing the covers back, I rummage through my clothes, trying to remember what pair of pants I was wearing. Finally, I fish the piece of crumpled paper from the front pocket and wave it so she can see it. "Happy?"

"Not until you actually do it," she says.

I read what I wrote, wondering if anything could really be that easy. Just say some words, make a wish, and boom! Your life will be different in the morning.

"Are you going to stay on the phone while I do it?"

"Yep."

Understanding that I am not going to win this fight, I grab a lighter from the bookshelf, next to a manifestation candle that Wren gifted me. If I'm going to do this, I might as well set the mood. I prop the phone on my nightstand so she can see me, then light the candle and place it next to my phone.

"Now get comfortable," she instructs.

I climb onto my mattress and sit cross-legged, tugging a pillow into my lap.

"Close your eyes and take a few deep breaths."

I do as I'm told, taking a few stabilizing breaths, with the paper clutched in my hand.

"When you're ready, open your eyes and repeat the words three times. But do it slowly, with feeling."

Part of me wants to click the End Call button, but after a few beats, I open my eyes and stare at the words—my words—on the page. Slowly, I begin to repeat them.

"I want Ben to be cancer-free. I want to be known for my art." I take a shaky breath, slightly embarrassed, but continue with more conviction. "I want Ben to be cancer-free. I want to be known for my art." I pause for a moment and let those words sink in before repeating them a third and final time. "I want Ben to be cancer-free. I want to be known for my art." Even if I feel silly, by the third round, my body begins to tingle and my fingers heat up around the piece of paper.

"Good. Do you feel that?" Wren murmurs.

How can she know I feel anything? Too stunned to speak, I simply nod.

"Now, I want you to burn the paper, and after it's done, say, 'And so it is, and it is so,' to make it official."

Clutching the paper, now warmed by my touch, I dangle it over the candle's flame. I know that these are just words, and I'm only holding a simple piece of paper, but this whole thing suddenly feels significant. I let the edge of the paper catch fire and watch as it curls into a hot, black fragment, then bursts into ash.

"And so it is, and it is so," I say.

After a few beats of silence, Wren lets out a massive sigh. "See you on the other side, sister. Sleep well." She ends the call, and my heart begins to pound in my chest. What does she mean she'll see me on the other side? I sit there, unsteady in my own body, before I blow out the candle and am thrust into darkness.

After a few minutes, my body still tingling, I snuggle under the covers and will myself to calm down. Though logically I know nothing is going to happen, the idea of Ben being cancer-free is a gift I rarely allow myself to cling to anymore. Maybe that's why I feel so resistant: I don't want to feel hope, even a shred of it, in case it doesn't work out.

The words keep repeating in my head as I hover above sleep and then finally drift off, Ben and Liam clashing for space in my heart and head.

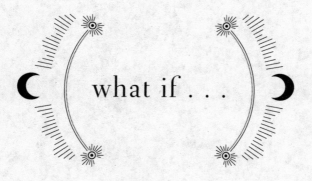

what if . . .

24

I open my eyes and blink into the early morning light.
My fingers graze the nightstand for my phone, except my wrist knocks into something long and flat, not my wobbly side table. I glance to the left and realize I am not in my bed. I roll my head to the right slowly, as if it might detach from my shoulders, to find Liam sleeping soundly. One of his bare legs is hitched over the blanket on his massive king-size bed. He is shirtless, in fitted black briefs, and I take a moment to admire his physique before shooting up in bed.

Holy hell, why am I in Liam's bed?

I close my eyes again and realize I must be dreaming. I literally pinch myself and wait to wake up. After counting to ten, I blink again and let my eyes trail to the window. The Manhattan Bridge hulks outside, just as I remember. Suddenly I am aware of two things: *I am in Liam's loft. And I am mostly naked.*

I must be having a stroke.

I scramble out of bed, but Liam doesn't budge. He is a hard sleeper, at least from what I remember during our week together. I stumble backward and stare down at myself. I am wearing only a white T-shirt—his, by the looks of it. My legs are bare and pale. I study my hands, as if I'm expecting to see someone else's. I glance at my wrist where my *I see you* tattoo is.

Instead of the tiny words, there's only a bare swatch of skin. I rub at it, as if my tattoo will suddenly reappear. I spin in a circle, hyperventilating. *Where is my tattoo? Where is Ben? Where is my condo? How did I get to New York?*

I run back to the bed and grip Liam's shoulders. I shake him roughly. "Liam, wake up. Wake *up*."

He opens his eyes and moans, hooking an arm around my waist and tugging me toward him. I wriggle out of his grasp, horrified, though his hands work their way over my thighs and send an electric jolt through every traitorous inch.

"Let me sleep, woman. You kept me up half the night." He taps me lightly on the bottom.

"Liam, what is happening?"

"What is happening with what?" He cocks himself onto one elbow, stomach flexing, eyes still closed. His hair is mussed, and I look anywhere but at his well-defined torso.

I spread my arms wide, then drop them. "How did I get here?"

He looks at me, eyes thick with sleep. "Is that a metaphorical question?"

I stab my finger toward his window. "Last night I was in Chattanooga. You were in a hotel. This morning I woke up here, in this loft. A loft I haven't seen in *ten* years, Liam. Am I dead?" I spin in a circle and pat the visible parts of my body. "Is this some sort of fever dream?"

"Did you hit your head, my love?" A smile plays at the corner of his lips, and I want to shake him. I glance at my hands again. My wedding ring is gone. Where is it?

"Liam, I'm serious. Where's Ben?"

He sits up fully and rakes a hand through his hair. "Who's Ben?" He slides on a pair of sweatpants and a pang literally hits my gut like a knife.

"*Ben* Ben! My husband. The man you are doing a story on for the *Times*."

Now Liam looks worried. He stands and presses a hand to my forehead. "Harper, I don't work for the *Times* anymore. Are you sleepwalking or something?" He waves a hand in front of my face. "You're scaring me."

"You're scaring *me*. I'm not supposed to be here. I'm . . ." I turn around, and that's when I see it: Liam's studio. Or should I say, *my* studio. My art is everywhere, big and small pieces, ceramics and mixed media. "Oh my God." I rush over to the workspace, poring over every piece. This is my art. My supplies. My clothes. My decorative touches. My eyes roam over the loft and soak it all in. So many things have been updated, but much of it is the same. I search for something with the date on it and see a copy of the newspaper crisply folded on the desk. I reach for it, hunting for the date at the top. This paper is from yesterday. I touch my body, making sure once again that I am real. Is this a dream? It doesn't feel like a dream.

What's the last thing I remember? The ritual before bed. "Oh my God," I say again. I lower the paper. *Am I time traveling?* Even as I think it, I know things like that aren't possible . . . are they? "Liam, how long have we been together?"

He's already making coffee and turns to me, eyebrows scrunched. "Is that a trick question?" Seeing the seriousness on my face, he continues. "Um, a decade. But you know that already."

I collapse in the chair behind me. This is real. This is happening. Somehow I'm in an alternate reality with Liam, which is playing out because of a full moon ritual I was basically *bullied* into doing last night. I squeeze my eyes shut and try to remember what I said. The words come to me in a sweet, ironic rush: *I want Ben to be cancer-free. I want to be known for my art.*

My eyes snap open again. Is this some cruel trick of the universe? Ben is cancer-free, but I'm not with him? A cold panic sweeps across my skin, and I fear I'm going to be sick. Things like this just don't happen, except in movies or books. I do not believe in time travel or portals or parallel time lines. I've never even thought about it. My eyes lift to Liam again. But I *have* thought about Liam. Hundreds of times. And now I'm here, with him.

"What day is it?"

"Wednesday." He places the coffee bag to the side, pads over in his bare feet, and squats down until his face is flush with mine. "Harp, what's going on?" *Harp.* Only Ben calls me Harp. I open my mouth again to try to explain, but I know my best bet is to play along until I can figure out what's going on. I place my trembling hands on Liam's face, because this is what Harper who has been with Liam for a decade would do, and summon up a smile.

"I think I had a very weird, very real dream, and I'm just super confused." My eyes flick to the studio and back again.

"And in it, you were married to some guy named Ben?" His fingers dance over mine. "If you won't marry me, you certainly aren't marrying Ben."

Won't marry Liam? What on earth is he talking about? There are so many questions, but I don't want to bombard him any more than I already have. "Just a dream," I say in an attempt to keep my voice calm. Before I can stop him, he leans in and slides his thumb against my cheek. My entire face ignites and my legs instinctively open to make space for him. He glances down, one eyebrow cocked, and leans in for a kiss.

Realizing where I am, who I am (Ben's wife!), and what is happening, I snap my legs closed and gently push him away. Inside, my brain screams to *get up now*. Though I would never cheat on Ben, my body seems to have other ideas.

Liam moves back without complaint and stares deeply into my eyes. "You still take my breath away," he says, "even after all this time. You know that?" One hand slides up my thigh, and I practically bolt from the chair.

"I need to pee," I blurt. I rush to the bathroom, close the door, and gaze at myself in the mirror. "Wake up, Harper. Please wake up." I stare into my own large brown eyes in the mirror and practically demand answers. My auburn hair is wild and loose around my shoulders. There's still the dark freckle above my lip, the slight bump in my nose where a rogue elbow in an obstacle course race broke it, the full lips, the strong chin. It's still me, but it doesn't *feel* like me. I look at myself until my eyes blur, practically willing something to happen. Maybe for the ground to shake. Or lightning to strike. Something to get me back to my life, back to Ben.

After it's clear I'm stuck in this psycho dream, I take a few breaths and open the door. I peer out carefully, as if monsters might jump out and attack. Instead, Liam is busy pulling down mugs as the last of the coffee bubbles into the pot. Ben flashes through my head again. Beyond anything that is happening, I know I must find him.

"Everything okay?" Liam asks.

"Yeah. I just really had to pee." I shift uncomfortably from foot to foot, tugging on the hem of my T-shirt. Don't I own *pants*?

"Hungry?"

I motion to the coffee. "Coffee's fine." He pours a healthy dash of cream into a mug, just like I prefer, then slides it over and stares at me pensively while I take a distracted sip.

"I'll be right back." He excuses himself to the bathroom. In his absence, I hunt for my phone. I find it underneath some sketch pads and try my same code. "Ha!" It works. The phone unlocks, and I pull up my contacts first, scrolling to find Ben. There is no Ben.

"Don't panic," I say. "You're most likely dead or in some kind of made-for-TV rom-com." I gnaw on a nail and dial his cell. He doesn't answer, and when the voicemail clicks on, I consider leaving a crazy, *Hi, it's your wife you might not have met yet!* message, but the recording says I've reached the cell phone of Lisa Howard.

I hang up and then stare at my phone as though it will give me answers. Where is Ben?

I move to my calendar, open it, and am shocked to see a bunch of color-coded meetings that take up the majority of every day for the foreseeable future. "What in the world?" I scroll through them, and my mouth literally drops open. Interviews, podcasts, gallery visits. Who am I, and what have I become?

I open my email and scan through the messages. I rack my brain for who to contact, who could give me some insight into my life here, and then snap my fingers. Kendall! I type her name in my phone and there she is. I read through our text chain, a text chain I never created, and am surprised to find that we are still in contact. Does she still work at the gallery?

Before I can dig anymore, Liam emerges in a T-shirt and sweat-pants, a lazy smile on his face. Though it still feels like a betrayal, my heart kicks. I know this is not my life. This is either a dream or a glimpse of some alternate future, and I will most likely wake up tomorrow and all will be as it should. But to be here, even for a moment, in this fantastical reality, with Liam, in this loft, as an artist—and a successful one, by the looks of it—fills me with a strange kind of joy I can't articulate.

And then I think of Ben, wherever he is, and a pit in my stomach grows to the size of Texas. If I'm in this life, does that mean I never met him?

Liam pours himself a cup of coffee, and I join him on the balcony. I think about sitting with Liam just last night, on a different balcony. But here, it's *our* balcony. I settle into a chair, glancing at all the herbs and plants spilling across the black wrought iron. My fingers fondle the petals. I wonder whose idea it was to bring in plants.

The city beckons below, and something sparks in my chest. A calling. A remembrance. After I left New York, I would think of this place, and this loft, figuring I was romanticizing the whole "grass is greener" life. Because in truth, I did only know Liam for a week. We didn't go through the daily grind of domestic life. We didn't really go through anything, beyond falling for each other and then letting it dissolve just as quickly. But at this moment, I feel weirdly validated. Being here feels exactly how I always thought it would feel. I glance at Liam, who props his feet on the rail. Even though it feels like a deep betrayal to even think about it, in this moment, this place feels like home.

"You going to the gallery today?" His eyes are warm. I cannot get over that we are still together, that he apparently still tells me I'm beautiful ten years in, that he makes me coffee and wants to kiss me good morning and lets me sleep in his T-shirt.

I freeze, because I don't know what gallery he is referring to. "Probably," I answer. "You?"

He smiles. "Oh, you know. The life of a writer never ceases. Just trying to prep before I hit the road. There's still a lot to do."

"Where are you going?"

He stares at me with his head cocked. "I told you all the cities they put on this book tour. We talked about it last week."

"You wrote a book?" The words are out of my mouth before I can stop them, but Liam laughs.

"Har har. I know. I thought I would never write books, but here we are." He reaches over to squeeze my knee. "It's basically your fault."

"My fault?"

He rolls his eyes. "Harper, come on. You used to constantly complain about all of my deadlines working for the paper."

What, so he just quit his successful career because I had a problem with it? "Did I?"

He looks at me. "What's with you today?"

I lift my coffee. "Give me one more cup of this and I'll be able to tell you."

We sip in silence, but my brain works overtime. I want to know everything about my life and who is in it, but first I have to figure out what is happening.

And more importantly, I have to find Ben.

25

After I'm showered, to-go coffee in hand, I tell Liam goodbye and settle onto the streets of Brooklyn.

While I was getting ready, I poked around enough to know that I now own Rita Clementine's gallery. *Rita Freaking Clementine*, the woman I ran away from all those years ago because I couldn't hack it. I've also learned a few more things.

1. *Apparently Rita helped make me into the art sensation I always wanted to be, which means I must have never left New York.*
2. *At some point, she handed over her gallery to me.*
3. *I'm kind of a big fucking deal.*

Because I have no idea if I've died and gone to some parallel semi-heaven, I'm indulging in this false reality for the sheer fact that my life turning out this way is something I once dreamed about, and now it's here, staring me in the face. But the more realistic part of me knows that Wren has somehow issued a strange spell and her words of "see you on the other side" have come true. Do I know her in this life too?

Quickly, I scroll through my phone, but I don't see her contact info. Luckily, I know her number by heart and will call her the moment I get settled at the gallery.

It is a cool morning, despite being the start of summer. Though I am confused and am wondering about Ben—*Where is he? What if I can't get back to him in time? What if I never see him again?*—I also can't help but revel in the fact that I'm in Brooklyn. That this is my home. My home with *Liam*. This Brooklyn looks a bit different from the one I visited a decade ago. For starters, it's packed. I dodge people on the street and feel a tiny thrill at what's ahead.

After a short walk, I approach the gallery from memory and almost faint. I assumed the gallery would have the same name, but instead it says "Swanson Gallery." I swallow, taking a mental picture for when I wake up from this crazy dream, then tug on the door. Locked. I rummage in my purse for a set of keys and try a few of them until the right one slides into place with a satisfying click.

Inside, I flip on the lights and take a sharp breath. The art is stunning. Every piece is exactly something I would have chosen. I'm reminded of working at the gallery in Chicago and how I used to fantasize about owning my own space someday.

I almost clap my hands in excitement as I see a series from local artists and squint as I spot one of the names: Keisha Hollis. Could this be the same Keisha I met at that underground gallery so long ago? The girl who was so hungry for my spot?

An immediate sense of satisfaction overtakes me as I assess the eclectic mix of mediums and talent here. Did I choose all these pieces? Did I get to deliver the news and change an artist's life as

Rita must have changed mine? I ransack my memory for something concrete and walk the halls like a stranger, taking my time to memorize everything I see.

Finally, I wander back to where Rita's office used to be, except my name is now etched on the door. My fingers trace the gold embossed letters before I spin in a circle, waiting for someone to jump out and tell me this is all some big joke. When no one comes, I carefully open the door. Inside there's sleek, modern furniture, a stack of art books on oak shelves, and photos of my life with Liam jamming up any free space. I study each one. There's one of us on a boat, one in the mountains, and one in the loft. In all of them we seem happy, the evidence of our life that I have somehow missed, displayed on a clear time line.

I drop my purse on the desk and pore over the contents of my life. Another photo of me and Liam, arms wrapped around each other, perches next to my desktop computer. My heart gives that achy kick again. *Is this really happening?*

Before I can answer that question, Kendall bounds in, and I smile when I see her. She looks virtually the same, except one side of her head is shaved. "Yo, what's up? You never texted me back."

I open my mouth to respond, but I don't know what to say. Instead, I motion to the chair across from my desk. "Sit."

She sighs, adjusts one of a million signature bracelets, and crosses her impossibly long legs. "What's going on?"

I fold my hands together and exhale. "I actually have no idea." I contemplate how to explain my situation in a way where she doesn't immediately assume I'm crazy. "This morning I woke up in Liam Hale's apartment."

She waits. "And?"

"And yesterday I was in Chattanooga with my dying husband."

She makes a face. "Chattanooga? Ew. Why would you be in Chattanooga? And what husband? What are you talking about, Harper?" She sighs again. "You know we have a big day today. So whatever this is"—she waves her hands in my direction—"needs to wait."

I stand, cross the tiny space to shut the door, and sit back down. "I know this sounds insane, but somehow I have time traveled from my life in Tennessee to Brooklyn."

She waits a beat, then bursts out laughing. "Harper, come on. What's this really about?"

I know how I sound, but I continue. "Ten years ago I walked out of this door and never came back. Rita didn't like my piece, and I never saw Liam again. Or you, for that matter. And now, suddenly, I'm here, in this version of a life I once wanted."

She blinks at me, her dark eyes even moodier than normal. "I'm not following."

In strange scenarios like these, there's always one supporting character who believes the time travel story could be true, right? I need this to be Kendall. I need it for my own sanity. "This is not my life," I say. "I have no idea what I'm doing or how I got here."

She stands, her impatience dissolving as she adjusts her Gucci belt. "Not this again, Harper. Look, everyone's getting really tired of this whole 'woe is me' act. Rita gave you this opportunity because you deserve it. You've earned your spot here. You belong, so do your job, okay? You've got this!" She moves to the door. "I've got a busy day, but when you're done having this whole midlife crisis thing, let's do lunch. Okay? Bye, babe!" She leaves me sitting there, even more confused than before.

I think back to ten years ago, when she gave me a gentle reminder to keep my eye on my career, not Liam, but had I listened? No. When

I walked away from art and Brooklyn, it seemed I'd lost her friendship too. But that wasn't her fault. It was mine.

But in this life, I stayed. In this life, she is here and so am I. In this life, I am with Liam, *and* I have a thriving career.

I ransack my office in an attempt to bring myself up to speed. It seems I have two assistants who run my entire life, and I ask both of them to clear my schedule for the next couple of days. The last thing I want to do is mess up something for this version of myself. Instead, I need to figure out why I'm here and how to get back.

On my computer, I google Ben's name and find a few old articles about some of his work as a composer. But there's nothing within the last couple of years. As I'm just about to pull up his Instagram, there's a succession of rapid knocks on my door. Rita Clementine sticks her head inside.

She looks the same too, just a little older and sharper. Her cheeks are hollowed and stained with rouge. "What's this about you canceling the next two days? Are you ill?" She stares me down over her bright-red reading glasses.

"No, I'm fine. I just—"

"You just *nothing*, Harper. Unless you're dying, you're working." She crosses her arms. "Do you remember when I had my heart attack?"

"You had a heart attack?"

Rita rolls her eyes. "You told me you could handle it. Is taking a few days off handling it? No, it's not."

I try to piece these stray bits of information together. So Rita had a heart attack. Is that why she gave me the gallery? "I can handle it," I say, even though I'm pretty sure that *no, I definitely cannot handle it*—whatever *it* even is.

203

"Well, good. We have artists to greet, so chop-chop." She claps twice and leaves me once again stunned by the hurried tone. Why is everyone in such a rush?

I think about my life back home, the kids I teach, the lazy mountain days, the slow pace. Is it just a New York thing, or an art thing?

The next few hours pass in a blur, though I find that my brain knows just what to do. Somehow I understand how to critique and what to say, as if this version of my brain is being channeled through the other Harper's body. Is this what an out-of-body experience feels like? By the end of the day, I am utterly drained. Liam texts that he wants to go out for dinner and tells me where to meet.

Though I am exhausted to my bones, I'm also starving, so I hightail it out of the gallery before Rita or Kendall chain me to my desk. The air is muggy, and I realize I didn't even step outside today. As I stare at my pale arms, even though it's summer, I wonder if this is why. Am I a workaholic in this life?

Liam is standing outside the main gallery door, looking as handsome as ever. I wave awkwardly and try to keep as much space between us as I can while we walk.

Sensing the tension, Liam maintains the distance and shoves his hands in his pockets. "How was your day?"

I think about trying to tell him the truth too, but refrain. "Busy. Yours?"

"Same."

We move silently down the street. I ask him questions about his work to keep him talking so I don't have to. He is about to launch his second book, after his first did surprisingly well. I study the way his face lights up as he talks about this new career path. What a departure from the journalist he has always been: the Liam who chases stories, who lives out of a suitcase, who is comfortable behind the scenes. I remember when he told me one of his greatest dreams was to write a novel. Now this Liam is front and center, owning his own work.

At the restaurant, we sit at a tiny table outside, which is across the street from a park. The table wobbles, and rather than complain, Liam wedges a coaster underneath the leg. As we sip our beers, we watch kids running wild in the park, overtired parents sitting on benches, chatting as the sun prepares to set. The thrum of this life fuels me, even after such a weird, crazy day. My mind still struggles to catch up, but there's something so right about being here that I don't want to miss a thing. Liam scans the menu and chats easily with the server.

After we've ordered, I close my menu and ask him something that's been on my mind all day. "Why aren't we married?"

He pauses with his beer at his lips. "Uh, because you don't want to get married?"

I open my mouth to protest but then close it. The real me chose to get married, but what if this city and my career have changed me? When I look at Liam, however, I can't imagine a world where I would choose not to *lock that shit down*. I was smitten after only a week with him. What changed? We're obviously committed to each other in every other way.

I shrug. "Well, people can change their minds." Even as the words leave my mouth, I have no clue what I'm saying. I'm not going to get married in this fake life when my real husband is in another universe.

"*Are* you changing your mind?" There's something uncertain in his gaze, and I wonder if I've hurt Liam by saying no.

Again, I shrug and try to keep it light. "Who knows?"

"No, really, Harper. Are you changing your mind?" He reaches across the table and takes my hand in his, rubbing his fingers over my bare ring finger. It feels strange not to wear my wedding band, to let another man hold my hand, to sit in Brooklyn, talking about marriage with someone else. How am I here? *How* is this even happening?

"I guess not." I stumble over my words, more confused than ever.

He gives a terse nod and sits back, a numb look on his face as he downs his beer and orders another. This is too much to absorb. I try to steer the conversation into different territory, mainly asking him questions so the conversation doesn't turn back to me.

Amazingly, we finish our dinner without revealing the fact that I am *time traveling* and make the long walk back to the loft. It feels good to walk, to soak in the city I haven't seen in years. I don't know how long I will have a glimpse into this reality, but it's been validating to know that I didn't imagine what I felt all those years ago, to see what life could be like . . . if only I had stayed. I glance at Liam, who has grown mute, and wonder what must have happened between us on that fateful day to make me stay. Why I didn't run away. Why Rita said yes. How I was so brave.

The sun has set, and the streetlights play tricks on my eyes, but still, I can see Liam's profile as he digs in his pocket to find the keys for the loft. A loft that has become our home. I instantly think of my condo with Ben. Ben pulling out his keys. Ben opening the door.

Liam holds the door open for me. "You coming?"

But this isn't my real world, and I'm not with Ben. Standing here, looking at my past, however, I suddenly waver between wanting to wake up and wanting to stay right here for just a little bit longer, in the place I feel I once belonged.

26

When Liam is asleep, I sneak out of bed and onto the balcony with my phone.

I look up Ben's Instagram page but am shocked to see it doesn't exist. *What does that mean?* Instant dread slinks through my body as I assume the worst. What if, in this life, the cancer won? Anxious, I try Wren's old number. She answers on the third ring.

"Hello?"

"Wren, thank God." I lower my voice in case Liam can hear me. "What have you done to me?"

I wait for her to make a joke, but she's silent. "I'm sorry, who is this?" she finally asks.

"It's Harper Swanson Foster, one of your best friends and also the woman you did an insane full moon ritual on last night so that today I have woken up on another planet, also known as Brooklyn."

She mumbles something and then a door closes. "Say that again?"

"Was that Jenna? Get her on the phone too. I'm serious. I need to know what is happening, and I need to know right now."

"You know Jenna?" Her voice trembles, but I can clock the excitement there. "Wait, you're that artist who owns Rita Clementine's gallery in Brooklyn, right? I've been trying to get a meeting with her forever."

"Wren, please. *Focus.* This is not about art."

"Okay then, what's it about?"

"It's about me being stuck in some weird parallel life because *you* put me here! You have to believe me." I think of ways I can prove it. "Look, I know you. You and Jenna are two of my closest friends. You have two hairless cats, Gremlin and Pickles." I recite the layout of their apartment, their most annoying habits, and some personal details. Then I dig a little deeper. "You didn't come out until you were thirteen, though you knew you were gay at five." I recite the story she's only told to a few close people in her life and then try to drum up as many other intimate details as I can remember. It's enough, I realize, as she sucks in a sharp breath. She believes me.

"Okay," she says after a few moments of contemplation. "Tell me exactly what happened to you last night."

I start before that, with going to her house, the card reading, and then the ritual. I tell her exactly which book she pulled from her shelf.

"Oh my God! I have that book. Let me grab it." I hear one of the cats meow as she passes it, her dreads rough against the phone. "Where are you, where are you . . . Ah, here you are." Pages rustle through the phone until she finds the right one.

Thoughts tumble through my mind while I wait. Images of worst-case scenarios flicker through my head. Being stuck here forever. Never finding Ben. I don't know much, but I know I have to get back.

"Got it. Okay." She recites the ritual and then whistles.

"What? What is it?"

"This says that in order to reverse the spell, if you do happen to time-hop, you do the inverse of the ritual."

For the first time since I woke up in this strange reality, I exhale. "Okay, great. What do I need?" Already I'm standing up, eager to grab supplies.

"There's, um, just a little hitch," she says.

"A hitch? What hitch?" My voice is the only thing hitching up as I worry about what she's going to say next.

"It's not a big deal. It's just that you can't do the ritual, er, until the next full moon."

Silence blooms between us as her words sink in. "You mean I'm going to be stuck here for an entire *month*?" My voice echoes across the dark void of my balcony, and I don't even care who I've disturbed. "Wren, I cannot be here for a month. Look in your book. There has to be another way. I have to get back. Like, *today*." There are so many things I don't say. Ben could die in a month, and I'd never get to say goodbye. I could get hit by a train. I could do something really stupid, like kiss Liam or accidentally fall onto his naked body. I could screw the entire future of mankind by being somewhere I am not supposed to be.

"This isn't really happening, right?" I say. "It's just some sort of blip, or glimpse of another life, or a weird hallucination. It must be."

Wren's voice shakes slightly. "I'd like to say no, but I've heard about things like this happening . . . just never this close to home." The phone is muffled as she whispers what's happening to Jenna. I miss my two closest friends. I miss Ben and our tiny apartment and our complicated, beautiful life. I need to get back to all of it. Right now. If something happens to Ben while I'm gone, I will never forgive myself.

"Do you both still know Ben?" This gives me a little jolt of promise. "Who?"

The disappointment is swift and cruel. That means Ben must not live in Chattanooga. Where is he? I ask Wren a few more questions about my time here. Do I have to do anything or complete some weird life lesson like in all the time traveling movies in order to get back? She thumbs through the book a bit more but says she can't find anything. I hang up after she promises to keep me updated on anything else she discovers.

I close my eyes and rest my head back on the hard outdoor chair. The city still hisses below me, always alive, even this late. Reality sets in. I cannot get back to my life for a month. A *month*! How am I possibly going to fake my way through this version of my life for thirty days?

Eager to escape my own thoughts, I reenter the loft and plug in my phone, staring down at Liam. I play a game with myself and wonder if I can focus on what I have in this life instead of thinking about ways to get back to my old one. Isn't that the point of a glimpse? To be here now, not thinking about my other world?

As I slip into bed, I'm racked with guilt. Liam moves in his sleep and rolls toward me. I study his features. Despite how much I love and miss Ben, being here with Liam isn't entirely awful. I miss my life, but here I'm a successful artist. Isn't that what I wrote down on that piece of paper? Suddenly I sit up.

Yes, I asked to be a successful artist, but I also asked for Ben to be cancer-free. Which means he really could be out there somewhere, healthy. A small spasm of hope rips through all this uncertainty. I steady my breathing, but it's all I can think about before another realization dawns on me. My wish to pursue art means I haven't met Ben. Maybe it means I never will?

The guilt consumes me once again as I close my eyes and demand my brain to settle, to stop pinging all over the place like a pinball machine.

None of this makes sense, but it will soon. It has to. One way or another, the thirty days will come and go. I will do the ritual, and then everything will go back to normal.

I will find my way back to my real life. Back to Ben.

27

The next few days are so busy that I barely have time to ponder this strange new existence or why I'm here.

Liam is usually gone by the time I wake up. I'm starting to understand that with my hectic schedule and his prep for the book tour, we are like two ships passing in the night. This isn't the life I imagined for the two of us in my former daydreams, but at the same time, I know that getting to the top of any career always comes at a cost.

At lunch, Rita takes me to a nearby restaurant, but she is all business. I find myself nervous around her, as if I'm still that young artist trying to prove herself. Once the server has taken our order, she folds her bony hands on top of each other and studies me over her cat-eye frames. I can't get over how much older she seems, how fatigued. None of the fire I once recognized in her from a decade ago is present. She seems wrung out from the inside. Maybe that heart attack she mentioned?

"Harper, we need to talk."

I pause with my water glass near my lips. The phrase "we need to talk" rarely leads to anything good, but I nod. "Okay."

She sighs and smooths her napkin in her lap. "We have to close."

I rack my brain for what she could be talking about, but I can't play along. "Close what?"

"The gallery, Harper. What else?" She rubs her napkin along the edge of her water glass, buffing out a stain.

I try to remember any emails concerning feedback around finances. I don't think I've seen anything, but I've been in this fake version of my life for exactly 2.5 seconds, so I know I don't have a grasp on the entire picture. "But why?"

She looks at me again, head cocked, as if I'm a stranger. "Harper, we are hemorrhaging money and have been for years. You *know* this. It's why I brought you in in the first place. To do whatever it is someone your age was supposed to do." Rita waves her hand in a dismissive motion and stares sharply to the left. "It's not all your fault, of course. No one is buying art like they used to. It's all about NFTs and TikTok and god-awful influencers and pay-to-play and blah, blah, blah." She rolls her eyes and visibly shudders. "True art is a dying breed."

Just ten years ago she created influencers before that was even a thing. She was ahead of her time, pushing boundaries, forging the way. When had that fire gone out? I try to make sense of all of this, but I can only offer a simple retort. "But we seem so busy. *I* seem so busy."

"Well, you are. And I have no doubt you'll be fine, no matter what happens with the gallery. But do you really think those of us on the board aren't paying attention to the numbers? Me, of all people? The books are the books, and we can all see that the gallery's days are numbered." She whips off her glasses, and they bounce against her concave bosom, dangling from her signature expensive gold chain. Pinching her nose between her two fingers, she begins to cry. Never, in my real life or any imagined scenario, has there ever been a reality where Rita Clementine cries.

I move from my chair to comfort her, but she shrugs me off. "These aren't sad tears, Harper, they're angry tears. I *never* should have handed my gallery over. My legacy is dying." She balls the napkin in her hand and tosses it on the table. Her fist quakes with rage, the blue veins swollen beneath her thin, milky skin.

I feel stung. I remember that night, ten years ago, when she told me she'd be in touch. I remember the way she'd dismissively flicked her eyes over me, as if I was beneath her. I'd worked hard on that piece, bent over backward to make something she wanted to see. Yes, I was creating from a sense of urgency, from needing to please someone else, but I'd also really loved what I created. I was proud of it and what I'd achieved.

I stand on shaky legs. I never said what I wanted to say then because I was intimidated by Rita Clementine, by her success, by what she could make me. But I am a grown woman now, and this is not then, or my real life. I clear my throat, and she looks up, startled.

"I've worked very hard to uphold your legacy," I say, even though I have no way of knowing that's true, other than what I intuitively feel. "I can't control what people are or are not buying, but I do know that the gallery needs an infusion, something ahead of its time, which you have always done so well. Perhaps it's time to bring some fresh ideas to the table."

She sniffs and stares at me warily. "Like what?"

"Honestly? I don't know yet. I need some time to think."

She nods, pushes her chair back, and stands. "You have until the end of the week." She walks away, leaving me with literal whiplash. There's no way I can handle being in an alternate reality *and* helping a practical stranger save her gallery. Or technically, my gallery. It's all too much. I close my eyes, thinking again about Ben. I miss him to the very depths of my being. Taking a breath, I send Wren a quick text.

Find any loopholes yet?

She replies almost immediately.

I haven't, Harper. I'm sorry. Still looking. Meanwhile, enjoy your hot man and life as an artist! Embrace it, sister. You deserve it.

The knot in my belly grows. I don't deserve anything. And there's nothing to embrace! This version of Wren doesn't know me, doesn't know Ben or what's at stake. As I toss money on the table and stand on shaky legs, I think of Ben again. I have to find him. Instead of going back to the gallery, I decide to take a walk to clear my mind. I'm shuttled back to that week with Liam, how he would get me out of my head and onto the street, pointing out some of his favorite places. Most of them have been replaced, though when I come up to the movie theater, I see it's still there. I smile, remembering the night we watched *The Princess Bride* together after we'd first made love. That was one of the happiest nights of my life.

Everything seemed so simple then. No dying husbands. No dashed dreams. No time-traveling portals. Just a girl falling in love with a boy and wanting her career to work out. Where did it all go so wrong? And why—and how—am I back here now?

I walk until my feet hurt, because apparently this Harper owns no sneakers, only heels. When I'm back in front of the gallery, I stare up at it again, wondering what idea I can possibly come up with to save this esteemed gallery.

I think of Wren and how many cool ideas she's come up with over the years. As I try to conjure something amazing, my brain vetoes everything. I feel like I'm wading through mud.

As I'm standing there, the gallery doors burst open and a few people trickle out, lost in animated conversation. One woman stops, then turns and trots up to me with enthusiasm.

"Hi! Are you Harper Swanson?" She is young, tattooed, and looks like an artist herself.

"I am," I say.

"Oh my God, I just have to say, you are my hero," she gushes, glancing at her friend. "Your collection last year on impoverished Jewish communities was one of the most touching tributes I've seen in a while." She goes on and on, talking about work I didn't create and can't possibly take credit for. I nod and thank her before dipping back inside.

The air is arctic, and a moment of dizziness consumes me so abruptly, I rush to the window and sit down on its ledge. This all feels like too much. Too much change. Too much that doesn't make sense. Too much at risk.

Too much to lose.

28

At the one-week mark, I owe Rita Clementine an idea.

I've been staying up late most nights, attempting to come up with something brilliant that will impress her, but most ideas have been juvenile or too far-fetched or completely out of line with what she'd want. Finally, after an all-night ideating session, I think I've got something.

During this week, I have also managed to avoid all physical contact with Liam, who unfortunately doesn't have a clue as to why his supposed girlfriend won't touch him. It has caused a serious rift between us, as I've been treating him like a chummy pal instead of a romantic partner of ten years. I know I can't get away with this behavior much longer unless I fake some sort of virus.

And even though I've been keeping my distance, I can tell there are deeper cracks between us, silent wounds that go way back. But I've been too absorbed with trying to save this gallery to give it much more thought, because after a month, it won't really matter, will it? *And neither will this gallery*, I suddenly realize.

Once inside, I knock lightly on Rita's office door and she barks to come in. When she sees me, she folds her arms and sits back. "What have you got?"

No hello or casual niceties. I don't even bother sitting down. "Well, good morning to you too."

"Good lord, Harper. Always so sensitive. Good morning! Did you sleep well? How's Liam? Yada, yada." She narrows her eyes. "Now, what have you got?"

Despite her rudeness, I laugh. Early this morning, a kernel of an idea began to pop. As I find a sketch pad and begin to draw my idea for her, my whole body ignites. This is what I have always imagined. This moment, right here. Not being told what to do. Not running around Brooklyn with my head craned over a phone, hopping from meeting to meeting. Not owning a gallery. Just the well of fresh ideas tumbling from an inspired place. This is what I have forgotten how to do in my life with Ben.

I feel a stirring in my belly I haven't felt in a long time, not even while contemplating a possible solo show. Up until this point in my real life, I've always created from a sense of needing to prove myself: I need to prove I can make it. I need to prove I belong in the art world. I need to impress Wren. But what if I allowed myself to create from a different place? A place where the wild lives? After all, in this life I'm not some novice artist who needs to prove her worth. I've done that already, and that's what I need to channel for Rita now.

I pause for a moment, pen in the air, suddenly struck by a sobering realization. Part of me has been blaming Ben's diagnosis for the reason why I haven't taken my art more seriously. Or that I have a day job. There's always an excuse as to why I don't have time to pursue my passion. Instead of using the pain, agony, fear, and grief, I've been hiding, insisting it's a terrible time. I flip to a fresh page on the notepad and begin to scribble down new notes.

Rita doesn't say a word, but when I finally look up, she has a twinkle in her eye that I remember from ten years ago.

"There she is," she finally says, clutching one of my hands in her own. "I've missed you."

I am so excited that she likes this idea, I forget this is not real. Instead, I lap up the praise I never received from her then and lean into it like an affection-starved dog. I know I'm not really a gallery owner and have no gallery to save. But I do have a good idea, and I can see that Rita thinks so too. This is a small victory I will take.

"You approve?" I place the cap on the pen and stare down at the loose structure of the show.

"I approve. Get everyone on board. We have about three weeks to get this off the ground." She flips through her digital calendar on her phone and spits out a date.

My body tingles as she says it, just as it did the night of the ritual. Three weeks from now, on the date she just chose, will be the next full moon. That can't be a coincidence. "On it," I manage to say before leaving her office, my body trembling from the obvious synchronicity.

I tuck away this tidbit of serendipity and breeze through the rest of the day, updating the staff on what we are going to attempt to do by the end of the month. When it's dark, I'm practically vibrating as I let myself into a loft I do not own, coming home to a man who is not really mine. But Liam's not here. I find a handwritten note taped to the fridge.

My editor wanted to meet. He's got news. Hope you had a great day. See you soon.

Though I have been keeping my distance, the intensity of my feelings for this man are not lost on me. All this time I have carried a flame for someone I spent just a week with. I told myself that I romanticized it. But I haven't. I *didn't*. I know, when I get back to my other life, that I have to tell Ben about who Liam really is to me. It's only fair.

My phone dings, and I check it, hoping it's Liam with an update on when he will be done. It's Wren.

Just wanted to make sure that I didn't have some sort of ethereal hallucination where someone named Harper jumped time lines and blamed it all on me.

I laugh.

Who is this? I respond back, then hurriedly type, *Just kidding.* Wren sends a sweating GIF and then, to my surprise, she calls me. I love that about Wren. She's never much liked texting, always preferring to hear someone's voice over digital communication. She's like Ben in that way.

"So I was thinking," she says, launching into the conversation. No hello. No small talk. "According to all of my research on the deep, dark web, you can't just complete the ritual. You actually do have to, you know, learn a lesson."

I groan and collapse onto the bed. "I was afraid of that." I twirl a piece of hair around my finger and roll onto my stomach, pressing the speaker and plopping the phone beside me. "Any chance you know what that lesson is?"

"Negative," she says.

I fill her in on the date of the gallery show, and she gives a little squeak. "That's it. That's the night of the next full moon. Something big is going to happen. We just don't know what yet."

"World peace?" All jokes aside, I'm too afraid to ask what I really want to know: What if I can't get back? What if it doesn't work? What if I don't learn whatever lesson I'm here to learn? What if I'm stuck here forever?

My phone dings. It's a text from Rita, and it's three paragraphs long with to-dos for this next week. I copy and paste it and send it to one of my assistants and then startle as I hear Liam coming through the door.

"Hey, Wren. I've got to go."

"Hang in there," she says.

"I'll try." I disconnect the call, stand, and nervously smooth my clothes as I move toward Liam. "Hey, you."

He bounds to the kitchen, pulls down two wine glasses, and pours each nearly to the brim before offering me one with a crooked smile on his face.

"I'm assuming it was a good meeting?" We head onto the balcony and sit, even though it's steamy.

He collapses in his chair, a bewildered look on his face. "The book just got picked up for *Good Morning America*'s book club." He's dazed as he says it. "They're sending me out on a bigger tour, Harper. Three months."

I practically choke on my own wine. "Three months? Aren't book tours usually, like, two weeks?"

"Apparently preorders have been through the roof and they want to ride this wave." He drags a shaky hand across his face. "It's happening. It's all really happening."

My brain works to catch up. "When do you leave?"

"At the end of the month. They want me to do some pre-tour stuff to bump up sales for the first book. They hope to hit all the bestseller lists."

221

"Wow, Liam. This is huge." I reach across and squeeze his arm, but the irony is not lost on me that he will be leaving right when I hopefully will too. "I'm so happy for you."

He turns, and there are tears in his eyes. "I wanted this, but I thought it would never happen. All the authors I know say it's just luck or timing or whatever when they hit it big. But I *felt* it with this book. I knew it was special when I was writing it." He sets the wine on the table and leans toward me. "Come with me."

My first thought is, *Who, me?* but I know I can't say that. Even in this imaginary place, I know going anywhere in the future isn't possible. In the immediate sense, I have a gallery to save, my own work to consider, a lesson to learn, and a hot man to stay as far away from as humanly possible. "Liam, this is such great news, but I have an insane deadline at the gallery for this upcoming show."

"Yeah, right. It's always about the gallery. I get it." He leans back in his chair, his eyes dull and flat.

I bristle. "What's that supposed to mean?"

"Do you remember that day ten years ago? After you brought your piece to Rita and then LaTasha showed up?"

"I remember." That night changed my entire life.

"You almost walked away, but you didn't. Do you remember what you said to me?"

I swallow, hoping he will fill in the gaps.

"You told me that you didn't care what happened in my past, or what Rita Clementine thought of your work. All you cared about was not letting what we experienced together that week slip away. You said you'd risk anything to keep it, anything to keep me."

I'd said that? I nod, my mouth suddenly dry.

"Well, you *said* those words, Harper, but ever since, it hasn't really been about me, or us. And I've been okay with that, mostly. Instead, it's been about your career. Your climb to the top. Your art. Rita. Your followers. Your gallery. I've been over here, supporting you and trying to make something of myself too, because I love you more than anything in this entire world, but you've never really extended me the same courtesy. There's always been room for just one true success in our relationship." He turns to look at me, his eyes a bit softer, pleading almost. "But now it's my turn, and I'd like you to support me the same way I've always supported you. So please come with me."

I don't know what to say, I'm so stunned. Is this true? Have I put my career above our relationship? I think about my marriage to Ben, how much I've sacrificed for the two of us, how much I've put our marriage and his health first. Some would say at the expense of my own dreams.

It seems in both realities I've never quite found the balance of prioritizing myself, my career, *and* my relationship. Is this the lesson I'm supposed to learn here? I fumble for words and land on an apology. "I'm so sorry you feel that way, Liam. I value you more than you can possibly know. And I fully support your dreams." I choose my next words carefully. "But I also care about saving the gallery. I'm going to lose it unless I can figure something out in the next three weeks. But once I do, I'd love to join you on some of the tour dates." I hear myself making an empty promise, and I hate myself a little for it. "Maybe not the whole time, but some of the time? Would that be a fair compromise?"

He blinks at me as if I am speaking another language, then finally nods. "Thank you. Yes." He deflates, closes his eyes, and sighs.

Finally, he opens them and looks at me. "I guess a little time apart might be good for us."

My heart suddenly slams in my chest. "Good how?"

He swirls his wine around and around, staring into it. "I appreciate you being willing to compromise now, Harper, but, I mean, come on." He offers me a sad smile. "It's been ten years." His voice is a whisper. "I'm tired of feeling like you're just out of reach, like I can't connect with you no matter how hard I try. I want a little part of you. A part that's reserved just for me. For us. But every time I get too close, you pull away, especially this last week. You've been treating me like a stranger." He stares deeply into his wine. "I feel like you're missing something, and I can't fill in the gaps no matter how hard I try."

Ben flashes through my mind again, so clearly that I nearly fall off my chair. Is this about Ben, or is this about me?

"I'm so sorry you feel that way." I grip his hand, but it's cool and loose in mine. It feels like whatever this fictitious world is that's been built between us is slipping away, and there's nothing I can do to stop it.

Perhaps my dream life is not such a dream after all . . . and if I want it to be different, then I have to fight for what matters, even if I lose it all in the end.

29

Before sunrise, I sit up in bed, but Liam isn't beside me.

I smooth my hands over the sheets, confused. *Where is he?* My eyes adjust, and I see him asleep on the couch in front of the main bank of windows.

Our last conversation comes rocketing back into focus, and my stomach plummets. He wants to take some time apart while he's on his book tour. And I have a gallery to save. I groan and heave myself out of bed, take a quick shower, and make the strongest pot of coffee I can. While I wait for it to brew, I scroll through my phone, once again trying to find intel on Ben but coming up blank. He isn't a composer anymore, apparently, and he has zero recent online presence, which, in this day and age, is both annoying and impressive. I've even searched obituaries to make sure he hasn't passed away.

Liam finally sits up, hair sticking up at adorable angles. I shove my phone into my pocket guiltily and pour him a cup of coffee.

He graciously accepts it and takes a long, sleepy sip. "Thanks."

I contemplate what to say as my phone begins to ding with incoming texts. I feel like Liam and I have so much to talk about, and yet if Rita and I want to pull off our big idea, we have to work around the clock until it's done. I gather my things and pour my coffee in a to-go mug. "Do you think we can talk when I get home?"

"I'm going out with my team tonight," he says, pulling on a T-shirt. "About the new tour dates."

I hate that I'm putting a damper on his exciting news, so I try to stay neutral. "Okay, maybe tomorrow?" I don't know how this will all end, but I do know that Liam cannot leave for his book tour with us at odds. I've done it once before—leaving him and our relationship—and I won't do it again, even in this fake world.

"We'll see. Good luck today." He adds another splash of cream to his cup before slinking out onto the balcony. I stare after him and almost cancel my day. This is way more important than an art gallery, or my career. This is Liam.

But part of me doesn't trust myself to spend all day with him. What if I let my guard down? What if I make a mistake? I choose to stay on safer territory and battle the foot traffic to the gallery because I'm not sure how to fix a relationship I can't fully lean into. Is this part of my lesson here? To choose between love and work? Before I can go too far down that rabbit hole, Rita is waiting for me outside, talking to someone on the phone. She ends the call and taps her watch with a pointy nude nail. "You're fifteen minutes late."

"Sorry." We rush inside, where, to my surprise, our idea is already underway. Rita has called in the biggest online art influencers to post about this upcoming show. For my big idea, we've nabbed the freshest talent to each bring in a half-finished piece. Attendees will be allowed to contribute to any piece they want, so that the art becomes "living art." Then we will have an auction, where a quarter of the proceeds will go to a charity I picked. I chose a pancreatic cancer charity as a way to honor Ben, even in this other world. The other two-thirds will go to the artists and the gallery.

After crunching the numbers, it could be enough to save the entire business and put us back on the map in terms of innovation. Rita already has interviews lined up with some of the largest trade publications.

"This is going to be a moment," Rita says, extending her arms in front of her. "Like before."

Though I wasn't around when Rita was at the peak of her career, I've read all about it. The parties. The intrigue. The mystery. There was no social media to tease an event. It was simply word of mouth, reporters, and the clout of being invited. We're creating a bit of mystery around this event too, and it feels different, purposeful even, despite it being a Hail Mary to save the gallery.

"I really think it's going to work," I say.

With less than three weeks to go, our list of to-dos is a mile long. After crossing off most of our tasks, Kendall stops me in the hall.

"Hey, lady. You got a visitor." She lifts her eyebrows suggestively and then motions toward the front door. Liam stands there and offers a wave.

"This is looking great," he says by way of greeting.

"Thanks. It's getting there."

"Got a sec?" He nods for me to follow him and pushes through the gallery doors and walks a few steps to the café next door. We grab a table outside and order two lattes.

"Everything okay?" I ask.

"Yeah, I just wanted to see you. I don't like how we left things."

There's so much I want to say but can't. I hate being a horrible girlfriend in this version of life. What's the point of a glimpse if I can't go all in? I silence my phone as it sounds with a new slew of incoming texts.

"Look, I know I said the tour might be good for us to take some time apart, but Harper, I don't want time apart. I just want you." He reaches out and interlaces his fingers through mine. The feel of him, after so many years, ricochets through my body like an electric spark. I can't pull away . . . and if I'm honest, I don't want to.

"I want you too," I hear myself say. It's not only the kind thing to say; if it were just the two of us in this life, then it would also be true.

Something releases from his shoulders—a visible weight that sloughs off like a second skin. "Do you mean that?"

"Yes, I mean that. Look, I know I've been a little off lately, and I'm sorry for that. Everything will be better once I can get through this show. But you matter to me, Liam. You've always mattered." It's the truth, at least.

He smiles and squeezes my hand tighter. A thousand images surge through his touch straight toward my heart. Memories of our week together all those years ago break through some of the barriers I've created.

"Can we spend some time together tonight? Alone?"

"I thought you were meeting with your team."

"I moved it," he explains.

I attempt to spin up some excuse in my head as to why that's a terrible idea and wonder if I can buy a chastity belt on the way home. Instead, I nod. "I'd love that."

"Okay, good." My phone vibrates again, and he chuckles. "I'll let you get back to it." He throws a few bills on the table, stands, and kisses the top of my head before disappearing down the street. I think through the details of this evening. I've managed to avoid kissing Liam or getting too close. But what if I can't tonight?

I finish my drink and take a quick walk around the block. Somehow I need to understand why I'm here, what lesson I'm supposed to learn. Because if I'm already in a relationship with Liam, is it really cheating to be affectionate with him? And though I'm helping Rita save her gallery, shouldn't I be focused more on my own art? Wasn't that my wish in the first place? After I've taken the time to process, I enter the bustling gallery and knock on Rita's door.

"Can we talk?"

She barely looks up. "If it's about this show, yes. If not, no."

"This will only take a minute."

I slide into the chair across from her desk, transported back to the very first time I came here. Rita sniffs, drops the pen, and glances at a painting on her wall.

"Do you remember the night I brought my piece to your gallery?" I ask.

"Well, of course I do, my dear," she says. "I saw something in you I hadn't seen in a long time. I was jealous of it, if I'm being honest. That you got to start fresh. That you were just beginning when I felt like I was on my way out."

The puzzle pieces continue to shift and fit together in my head. "But you weren't on your way out," I say. "And you're still not on your way out. You're right here."

She shrugs. "Oh, I don't know about that, Harper. Handing over the keys to the kingdom was a pretty big signal that I'm nearly done."

"Are you?"

She contemplates the question. "I'm not sure. I mean, if I'm honest, I do miss it. But it's a young person's game, and I'm no longer young."

"Who says it's a young person's game? Shouldn't it be a game for someone who knows how to play it best?"

She smirks and arranges her bracelets. "Touché."

"What happened to me wanting to focus on my art?"

She shrugs. "You know the answer to that better than I do. You've been stretched thin at certain points over the years, and that might have been my mistake in hiring you, my dear. An artist should be an artist, not a gallery owner. You've been caught between two worlds, and it's taken a toll on you. I'm sorry for that."

Her words have more impact than she can possibly know. I *have* been caught between two worlds, literally and figuratively. In my real life, I've been so focused on keeping Ben alive that I've let my dreams wane. And in this world, I've put work first. Though I can't possibly know the lesson I'm here to learn yet, I take a shaky breath and know at least one thing I have to do.

"You're right," I say. "I've always wanted to be an artist. It's been a dream my entire life, and I want to pour more effort into it." I rummage in my purse for the gallery keys. "After the opening, the gallery is yours. It's always been yours. You should give it a resurrection, but you don't need my help to do it."

Her lips part as the keys land in her hands. After a moment, she looks up at me. "But you said you wanted this."

Now it's my turn to shrug. "I did once, but I want art more." I wave as I turn, promising her I will continue to help with the show and that we can deal with the paperwork and contracts later. As I leave for the day, alerting my assistants to what's left to do, I feel a lightness in my body, a freedom. *Space.*

I rush home, an idea already festering in my mind, a piece I want to contribute for the gallery's big opening night. I barely get through the loft door and kick off my shoes before I'm putting on my smock, tying up my hair, and losing myself to the rhythm of my work. It's only when Liam comes through the door that I look up, bleary-eyed and content.

He smiles when he sees me. "Well, well. What do we have here?"

I take it from his surprise that I haven't had much time for my own art lately. I remove my smock and wash my hands before approaching him. "I quit the gallery today," I say. "I want to paint. I want to pay attention to my own life. To our life." A little ripple of pleasure flares in my body as I say it. It feels like testing the waters at doing something I shouldn't. But I remind myself I'm not. And what if going all in with Liam is part of the lesson I'm supposed to learn here? How will I know unless I try?

Liam stares down at me and that devastating smile sweeps over his face. "You really quit?"

I nod. "I did. I'm helping with the show, and then we'll see what's next."

"Harper." He walks slowly to me, and I can tell from the look in his eyes that I'm in trouble. He slides his hands across my chest and throat, and my body aches for him like a long-lost addiction. Finally, he rests his palms on my neck. "I love you so much."

My stomach drops. In our one week together, we never said those words to each other, though I wanted to. Before I can respond, he closes his eyes and tugs me toward him. Time suspends as his lips hover near mine. This is a line I would never dare cross in reality, but before I can logic my way out of what's happening, his lips crush mine, and I remember.

I remember our first kiss and our last. I remember how right I felt in Liam's arms. I remember that he was my first true love and that still means something. I remember that I was a fool to walk away and let pride get in the way of ever finding him again. I remember the way he tastes and smells and how he can play my body like a piano. I remember that I loved him . . . that I still love him somewhere deep inside. This kiss unlocks it, and I remember.

I remember everything.

His arms wrap tightly around me, and I moan into his open mouth. My pelvis presses into his. My skin is on fire. Our tongues entwine and I ache for him. For every inch. All reasoning goes out the window as we stumble back toward the bed. I can't think, can't peel myself away from him. I want this. I want him.

As I lose myself to this man I once loved, one refrain repeats itself over and over again:

This is not real.

This is not real.

This is not my real life.

30

The next day I see on the calendar that Liam has a book signing in the West Village.

I lock myself in my office at the gallery and speed-read his first novel, which had been sitting on my shelf. When I'm done, I close it and sigh. Liam Hale is one hell of a novelist.

By nightfall, I'm exhausted from work but take the quick cab ride to the cute independent bookstore, Three Lives & Company. I almost laugh at the irony of the name, since currently I can relate to having at least two lives. I get there a few minutes late, slip in, and hide near the back. Liam is in the middle of a sneak-peek reading from his new book, and I smile seeing him up there behind a podium. He's wearing his reading glasses, his tall frame hooked over his yet-to-be-released book. Watching him now, my body tingles with memories of last night. The tenderness. The intensity. The way his mouth felt on mine.

Though I did let myself kiss Liam, I did not allow myself to go further, making up an excuse about my cycle and pulling away just in time, though it was the last thing I wanted to do. Instead, we spent

233

all night talking and laughing until the early morning. It was like rewinding time and taking a peek at who I used to be.

This morning, the guilt came crashing in. I kissed another man. Though this is Liam, and I feel safe with Liam, he is not Ben. And I miss Ben. I want Ben. I need to find Ben.

The crowd laughs at something Liam said, and I struggle back to the present moment. It is odd witnessing Liam, in this strange reality, live out his dream. Even though I don't understand how it's happening, it's still happening. This moment exists.

When he's done, I clap the loudest and hang back as excitable fans wait in line for him to sign their books. I can't wait to read the new one, to hopefully witness him hit at least some of the goals he has for himself before I leave this life. Just as the last woman steps in line to get her book signed, I freeze.

I watch the shock on Liam's face, followed by one of his killer smiles. He rises from the signing table, and the two of them embrace. Though I have no right, a stab of jealousy pierces my heart as I recognize who it is: LaTasha, Liam's infamous ex-girlfriend. The woman partially responsible for me making a giant mistake.

She is just as stunning as I remember, somehow less boho chic and infinitely more sophisticated in a cool menswear suit and combat boots. She touches Liam on every available inch of skin, just as she did a decade ago: his arms, his chest, even his face. Heat rises to my cheeks. Immediately I am shuttled back to that painful night we broke up. Back then, I didn't stick around. Tonight I'm not going anywhere. As they talk, I wonder if this is the way Liam felt seeing Ben and me together when he first arrived at our door in Chattanooga. If so, how awful for him.

I attempt to turn around but bump into a chair that squeaks loudly across the floor. I mumble an apology to no one, and then both Liam and LaTasha turn to see who is making all the unnecessary noise.

"Harper?" Liam's voice sounds more shocked than happy to see me. And now I look like a jealous creep standing here watching the two of them.

"Surprise," I say, waving jazz hands. "Hi, LaTasha."

She smirks. "Hey, girl! Get over here." She crushes me in a hug. She smells like patchouli. "What are you doing, slinking around back there? Come! Celebrate your man before he leaves for his next big book tour. We're going to see his name up in bright lights pretty soon."

I clutch his book to my chest, my stomach momentarily dropping at the term *we*. I was going to ask him to sign this book, hoping he'd write something cute in it. As I'd flipped through the copy in my office, I was shocked to see that he hadn't signed it already. "I know," I say. "He's destined for it."

"That he is." She beams up at him again and presses her hand into his shoulder. "I'll see you in Detroit, yeah? Darcy can't wait!" She flashes her wedding band. "She's dying to meet the last man I was with before I came to my senses. Bye, love." She leans in to kiss his cheek, then does the same to me. "Bye, Harper." She waves to me, then leaves the two of us standing there. Her perfume lingers, that same musky, delicious scent I remember from ten years ago. I want to laugh. LaTasha is married to a woman? An immediate ease rushes through my body as she walks away.

"You came," he says.

"I came," I reply. I reach up to kiss him. "Even though you didn't mention it."

He rolls his eyes. "Harper, I've invited you to every signing I've had over the last year, and you've come to precisely two of them." He offers a simple shrug.

Two signings? I've only been to *two* signings? What is wrong with me? I step closer. "Well, I'm here now," I say. I hoist the book in the air. "I noticed that this copy hasn't been signed. Would you do me the honors?"

He looks from me to the book again. "You finally read it?"

I laugh, insulted. "Well, of course I read it. This isn't the first time." I only say it because it must be true. There's no way I wouldn't have read every draft and offered my feedback . . . right?

A hint of a grin quirks his top lip. "I'd be happy to." He rips off his readers and folds them into the collar of his shirt, then leans casually to sit on the edge of the table. "Let's see." He cracks open the book and pops the top off his Sharpie. He hesitates a moment, then scribbles a few lines and closes the book. "There you go, beautiful."

"Thanks." I stand there awkwardly, feeling more like a fan than his live-in girlfriend. "Want to go grab a drink?"

He gestures toward the register, where a few people from his editorial team are waiting. "I'd love to, but the team's taking me out. Want to join?"

"No, you go do your thing. See you at home?"

"Yes, you will. Want to wait up?" He looks at me suggestively, and my body responds.

"Oh, definitely."

He gives me a look that makes my knees weak and moves past me as his team claps and hollers for him. Liam tosses his arms wide and is engulfed by people who are sucking up to him now that he's about to make them all rich.

I leave the bookstore and take a car back, watching the magic of Manhattan, lively and loud, capped beneath the moon. Back in Dumbo and inside our apartment, I stare at the large space. Without Liam here, it feels blank, void of what makes it so special in the first place.

I crawl into our massive bed and balance his book on my lap, suddenly nervous. For some reason I feel like whatever he wrote will send me a message. Something I need to learn during my time here. I take a breath and open it. I can still smell the Sharpie on the page.

For Harper,

It has always been you.

Liam

The words cause unexpected emotion. I trace the words with my fingers. I tried to tell myself for so many years that a week isn't enough time to create anything substantial. But it *is* real, and in this time line, I have felt it with every fiber of my being. A sudden thought hits me, and I'm caught between two worlds: Are we supposed to be together someday? Is that what lesson I'm here to learn? Just the thought of it makes me ache for Ben. I love Ben. I am committed to Ben. But I am also seeing that in another reality, I might somehow belong with Liam too.

I stay awake until I hear Liam stumble back into the loft, trying to navigate his way through the dark. After he brushes his teeth, he crawls into bed beside me.

"Hello, you," he whispers, pulling me close.

"Hello, you." I stare into the inky darkness until his face comes into focus. I have so much I want to say, so much I want to know.

Instead, his lips are on mine in an instant, and everything I've been conflicted about goes out the window. It's like the ten-year gap has dissolved, and it is all so new again.

I know I can't stay in this make-believe world, but for tonight, I'm all in.

31

It is the night of the full moon, and I'm running late for the opening.

My phone buzzes, and I quickly check it as I slick on more lipstick.

Good luck tonight, beautiful. I'll see you soon.

I smile at the text, then at the mirror that hangs on the back of my office door in the gallery. I assess my vintage green dress, studded black heels, blood-red lipstick, and hair pinned up like a 1920s film star. *Is this the last night I will ever have with Liam?*

I shoot back a quick reply, put down my phone, and take a deep breath. The opening starts in thirty minutes, and there's already a line around the block. Excitement fills every square inch of this place. After tonight I know I will most likely leave this gallery and this alternate reality. And I'm excited to get back. I am. But the part of me that has truly let my walls down is a little torn. Even if it's not real, even if it's all been a dream, I want to get this final step just right.

Despite my best efforts, I still haven't been able to find Ben online, and I've been too paralyzed to analyze what that means. I can't face him not existing in this world, even if it isn't real. But I remind myself that after tonight, hopefully it won't matter.

I place my phone in my small clutch, square my shoulders, and give myself a pep talk. "You can do this," I tell myself. "After this, you get to go home."

I exit my office and walk through the halls, admiring all the half-finished canvases. The artists are already here, incredibly fashionable, perched at their stations with paintbrushes and graffiti pens so that patrons can dabble and add whatever they want to each piece. I'm nervous and hopeful that this will be a success. I scan the sparse crowd for Rita and see her talking to Kendall.

I approach them. "Everyone ready?" I clasp my hands and address mainly Rita, who looks sensational in a geometric black-and-white pantsuit.

She nods and excuses herself for a moment. I can tell she's nervous. She has everything riding on this. This is a true make-or-break evening, and if it fails, it will be because of me, not her.

"You ready for this?" Kendall asks.

I smile and give her arm a squeeze. "I am."

"Good luck. You got this, babe."

I decide to introduce myself to all of the artists before the doors officially open. When I get to the third artist, I'm hit with a jolt of satisfaction.

"Hi, Keisha."

Keisha turns and smiles at me. "Hey, Harper." She gestures to her half-filled canvas, marked with outstanding graffiti. It reminds me of some of Alejandro's work.

"This is exceptional." I still remember the day when Liam brought me to that underground gallery and she'd been so vocal about what she wanted. "I hope you have a great night tonight."

Before I move on, she stops me. "I just wanted to say thank you." I pause. "For?"

Her darkly lined eyes stare deeply into mine. "I can't think of a single other person in this industry who would do what you did for me. Hunt down some kid she'd met one time. Give her the opportunity of a lifetime. Support her every step of the way. You changed my life."

I am so moved, I can only hug her. "You deserve it," I whisper. In my mind, every artist deserves it, and tonight is a culmination of those beliefs. Standing here with Keisha reminds me of similar things my kids have said to me over the years. What if *this* is part of the lesson I'm here to learn? That I am always going to be the most fulfilled if I serve others in some meaningful way?

I move on to say hello to the other artists and approach the front doors just as they are thrust open. An electric buzz hums through my body as I greet people, hand them a pamphlet, and give them instructions on what to do. There are QR codes and hashtags to use, and within minutes, this "living art" idea has caught on like wildfire. There are influencers, photographers, artists, and TikTokers posing with all the various pieces.

It's a crush of bodies and creativity, artists from all walks of life, all over the world. It is an amalgamation of the type of art I love, celebrating big names and small, known and unknown, up-and-comers and veterans.

Even though I know he's not here yet, I search for Liam in the crowd. Last night shudders through my body. I tell myself it was nothing more than kissing, but I also know those tender moments are going to be forever seared into my body.

As I make the rounds, I check the time, realizing my grand finale will be unveiled soon. Just as I slip away to take a breath and grab a flute of champagne, I feel a tap on my shoulder. My heart lifts. *Liam.*

When I turn, however, I'm disappointed to find it's just our art curator, Greg. "The guy from the Pancreatic Cancer Foundation is about to make a speech. We've already raised $100,000," he whispers confidentially. "And the night is still young."

One hundred thousand dollars? I almost choke on the bubbles. "Great start," I respond. I make sure everything is running smoothly, and then the lights dim and the event host, Deandra, comes on the microphone to introduce tonight's sponsors and guests. My mind wanders as she makes the introductions, and everyone claps politely in the appropriate places. Before I can confirm everything is set for my own piece, I hear the crowd welcoming the representative from the Pancreatic Cancer Foundation and almost faint on the spot.

It's not some random guy; it's Ben. *My* Ben.

He waves to the crowd as he approaches the microphone, and I feel like I literally might keel over. He looks sensational: healthy, browned, a full head of hair, and all his weight back on. How is he here?

"Hi, everyone. I'm Ben Foster, and I'm a cancer survivor."

My world tilts, and I reach out to grab a table before I crash to the earth. *Survivor?*

"My story is like so many others you've heard. No serious symptoms, just a few little nagging issues. I went in for some tests and came out with cancer. Stage four. You know, because stages one through three clearly weren't enough." He waits as the crowd chuckles. "But then I discovered a workshop that literally saved my life. It wasn't a doctor. It wasn't a healer. In the end, it was me saving my own life."

Everyone is riveted by his story, but I am now hyperventilating. Is he talking about the same workshop he's at now in our other life? I want to scream, to run on stage and tackle him. He's here! He's cancer-free! My wish came true!

"Oh my God," I say. "This is exactly what I asked for."

Someone casts me a look, and I remember to keep my thoughts in my head as I work this all out. During the ritual, I asked for Ben to be cancer-free and me to be known for my art. I didn't specify *how* I would be known for my art, or that Ben and I would be together. My eyes find Ben's again. I swallow a potential painful truth. What if Ben's life is better off without me?

I turn my attention back to him as he continues to talk, so at ease behind the microphone. "When I entered this seven-day intensive workshop, I was terminal, given only months to live. When I walked out of it, I was completely cancer-free. And I'm still cancer-free."

I want to ask all the questions: When did he go? How long has he been in remission? Where has he been living this whole time? And why couldn't I find him online?

The crowd erupts into applause, and he smiles and waits until they've calmed to continue. "Now, I know what you're thinking. This sounds like a fluke, but it's not. After that workshop, I changed my whole life. I sold everything I own. I quit my job. I got rid of all the stuff that made me sick in the first place: the environmental stressors, the toxins, the tech, the bills, the lifestyle, the hustle. And now I devote my time to raising awareness for this disease but also showing people there's more than one way to fight it. Because there's always a way, even when the doctors tell you there isn't."

I try to hang on to every word Ben says, but my brain is spinning at an unsafe speed. Ben is here. Ben is cancer-free. Ben sold all his belongings and is a spokesperson for living a healthy life.

I press a hand over my heart to calm it. Am I too young to have a heart attack?

"Harper, you're up!" Greg hisses at me from his booth, and I give him a nod as if my husband from my other life isn't standing on stage right now, at my fictitious event. What are the chances?

I'm desperate to talk to Ben, to hold him, to study him, to stare into his eyes to see if there's even a modicum of recognition. But right now, this is my moment to wow Rita, to wrap this night up in the silver bow I promised her. As Ben walks off stage, I pass him, and he hands me the microphone. Our eyes lock, and I swear I stop breathing. He looks at me and something passes between us: the tiniest spark of recognition. He hesitates, but before he speaks, I butt in.

"Great speech," I say.

"Thanks." He turns to go but stops. "I know this sounds like a line, but have we met?"

Yes! "That's a bit complicated," I say instead. "Requiring a longer conversation and at least two drinks."

He tosses his head back and laughs, and I want to drink him in. It's been so long since I've seen him like this, light, able, healthy, filled out. The lines around his eyes crinkle just in the precise way I love. "Okay, deal. I'll wait for you?"

I'll wait for you. Those words send a ripple of pleasure through my entire body. I can only nod.

He offers a small wave and I take my place behind the podium, thank everyone for coming, and then stare right at Rita, wanting to get this over with so I can talk to Ben.

Here we go. I steady my voice while I assess the crowd. "Ten years ago, I received the opportunity of a lifetime." This part is true, at least. I did receive the opportunity of a lifetime, and in this warped sense of reality, I stayed. My piece was good enough. I was good enough.

I explain my very first assignment from Rita and how she must have seen something in my work. "Somewhere along the way, the gallery fell into my hands, but I've realized something very important: this gallery has always belonged to Rita Clementine, and so it shall remain in her name . . . and her hands. As my farewell gift, I've created a piece that I want Rita to finish. My career started because she saw something special. Tonight I want my work to sing because she adds something special to it."

Rita's eyes are full of emotion, and I nod at her before stepping over to the massive canvas that has been shrouded. The curtain drops, and the crowd whoops. I have created the shell of the gallery, but all the walls are empty. There is an outline of a woman in the center, but that is all. I make room for Rita, and everyone pushes in as she takes a step toward the paintbrushes, rolls up her sleeves, and gets to work.

A hush falls over the crowd while her hands expertly create something from nothing. Shapes become scenes; a simple sketch springs to life with oils. She loses herself as the DJ plays and people take videos I know will go viral. It's a moving tribute, a moment I will never forget. I know she said artists should be artists, not gallery owners, but she is the exception. She has always been the exception. I step back into the shadows and find Ben waiting there.

"I'd say this was a mild success," he jokes, clinking his champagne flute to mine.

"It is." I gaze into the crowd to soak it all in. Haven't I dreamed of scenarios just like this my whole life? But right now I don't care. I just want to absorb this version of Ben.

"So, tell me about this complicated way we know each other, Ms. Swanson." Ben grins.

So much of me wants to tell him the truth: what we are to each other, the life that we've lived, how desperate I am to get back to it, and him. But I can't.

"First, tell me where you live," I say. "Or are you still nomadic?"

He grins. "Still nomadic. I stop in a place for about three months, then move on. Do what I can with the cancer community there, then find the next group."

"And this workshop. What was it?" I'm trying to act light and interested, but inside, I'm desperate to know.

"Ever heard of a guy named Dr. Joe Dispenza?"

Holy shit. "I have," I say.

He breaks into a long-winded explanation about how it all works, but I don't care how it all works. I just want to know how long he's been cancer-free.

"So tell me, *have* we met before?" he asks. "I have the strangest sense, like I know you from somewhere."

I bob my head like an idiot. "I do too." It's partly the truth.

"Then what's so complicated about that?" His eyes roam my face, and I burst into a grin. I've missed him. I've missed our relationship, our conversations, and our easy understanding of each other.

"Can I hug you?" I realize this is an odd request, but I can think of nothing else except being in his arms again.

He smiles. "Sure." He opens his arms playfully. I take a shaky breath, then step into them and shiver as his hands encircle my waist and hold me tenderly. It's like stepping back in time and also straight to the future, all while in an alternate reality. I am not nearly drunk enough for this moment.

"You smell so good," he mumbles into my hair.

I'm wearing the perfume he loves. "So do you," I say. I hold on to him a beat too long and reluctantly release him.

"That was easily the best hug of my life," he says.

"I come from a long line of good huggers," I explain.

Ben reaches out a hand and swipes a tear that's on my cheek. "Hey, what's going on, Harper? Are you okay?"

I want to tell him the truth. That I'm not okay. That I haven't been okay in a really long time. Standing here, it's like time travel in reverse. Here is healthy Ben. Here is happy Ben. Here is cured Ben, with his whole life ahead of him. Would I be willing to stay in this life if only to let him live? Even if it's not with me?

Before I can explain what I'm feeling or why I'm crying, he motions toward the door. "I think someone's here for you." I drag my eyes away from him and back to the door. There, looking slightly confused, stands Liam. He looks from Ben to me and back again before walking over.

"Amazing speech," he says, kissing my cheek and looping an arm around my waist.

"Wasn't it?" Ben looks between us, and if I'm not mistaken, a flare of jealousy sparks in his eyes.

"And yours too. Incredible story, man. Liam Hale." He extends his hand.

"Ben Foster."

It's strange to watch, especially considering this introduction happened not too long ago in my real life.

"How do you two know each other?" Liam asks.

"We don't," Ben says.

I know Liam is probably wondering why in the world we were hugging so long if we don't even know each other. Is there a way to explain? I turn to Ben. "Will you excuse us for just a moment?"

"Oh, sure. Yeah, yeah. You guys do your thing. I'll be here." He lifts his champagne flute in a toast and wanders off.

"Nice guy," Liam says. "I used to cover stories like his. I miss it sometimes." He scratches his jaw. "Harp, are you okay?"

I feel like I've just seen a ghost. My eyes are glued to Ben's back as he weaves through the crowd. Part of me is afraid he's going to leave and I'll never see him like this again. I wish I could explain it to Liam, but I know I can't. How could I?

Before I can answer, Liam's phone buzzes and he sighs. "Oh, you've got to be kidding me."

"Everything okay?" My focus snaps back to him, even though it takes everything in me to tear my eyes away from Ben.

"A shipment of books didn't come in for my pre-launch event tomorrow. They need my author copies, and they need them now. I think I can still get them to the bookstore before they close." He glances at my watch. "Harper, I'm so sorry to do this on your big night."

I wave him away. "It's completely fine." I walk him outside and give him a hug. "I'll see you at home, okay?" I almost cry as I say it, because what if I don't see him tonight? What if I don't get to tell him goodbye? What if this moment is all we have left?

"Wait." I stop him before he goes with my hand on his arm. "I . . ." I what? I have so many things I want to convey, but I'm not sure how to verbalize what this fictitious month has meant to me without making him confused.

"Everything okay?" His genuine concern brings tears to my eyes.

"I just want you to know that I won't forget any of this." I gesture around me. "This. Us. All of it."

He moves to cradle my face in his hands and holds my gaze for a beat. "Are you going somewhere I don't know about?" Before I can answer, his lips curve into a slight smile as he kisses me softly, tenderly, and I hold steady, because I know, to the depths of my being, that this is it for us. For now. Maybe forever.

"See you at home," he says.

I watch him go, and part of my heart goes with him. *Home.* A thousand scenes, both imagined and real, appear like snapshots in my head. Our whole secret history unravels in reverse, like it's ten years ago, except now he's the one walking away, not me.

I want to go after him, but I don't.

Instead, I stand there until he is completely out of sight.

32

B efore I can head back in, Ben walks outside.

"Are you leaving?" I ask. Though I'm sad that Liam has left, I don't want this to be the last time I see Ben healthy. I'm not ready to tell this version of him goodbye either.

He shoves his hands in his pockets and rocks back on his heels. "I was, yeah." He glances behind him, then back at me. "Feel like taking a walk?" He raises his hands. "I promise I'm not a serial killer."

"Glad we cleared that up." My heart thumps wildly. I always wanted to take a trip with Ben to New York, but then he got sick and we couldn't. And now I realize that Liam is so entangled in this city, in all my favorite spots, in why I loved Brooklyn, that coming here would have been a stark reminder of a life not lived.

Ben falls easily into step beside me, and we walk and talk. I tell him everything I've ever wanted to tell him, pointing out my most sacred spots. We stop for a fat ice cream sundae, then walk along the water and down random streets. I know people at the gallery will be looking for me, but I don't care. Tonight it all ends anyway, and I want to hang on to this version of Ben as long as I possibly can.

Ben stops outside a playground and motions me inside. We slip onto the cold swings and push gently back and forth. The squeak of the chains fills the silence.

"So how long have you two been together?"

It's the first time he's brought up Liam. "Ten years."

He whistles. "Wow. Serious."

I nod. "It is."

"I was afraid of that," he says. "He seems like a great guy." In true Ben fashion, he's respectful.

I nod. "He is." I twist toward him on the swings. "Tell me about your life going forward," I say. "How you want to live it. Do you want to stay nomadic, or do you want to settle down?"

He's silent for a while, pushing off the rubber ground for a few beats before he speaks. "Well, cancer taught me a lot about myself, but mostly that I want to have a family someday. I love traveling, don't get me wrong, but now I want roots. A partner. Kids. A home."

He looks at me as he says the word *home*, and a montage of our life together plays back on a loop. I want to tell him everything: how many adventures we've had, how much of a home we've created in and for each other in just a few short years. "You should have that," I finally say. "You deserve it after everything you've been through."

"What about you? What do you want?"

I stare at the sky, smudged free of stars from all of the bright streetlights. "I want a home too," I say. "A family." As I say the words, I realize it's true. Ben and I haven't talked about kids since before he got sick, but the thought has rippled through my mind more than once.

We rock silently until it's late, and I tell him I need to get back to the gallery and help clean up. I know I'm going to get a mouthful from Rita about my disappearing act, but I know she no longer

251

needs me. Maybe she never did. Maybe it's always been the other way around.

When we get to the gallery doors, the crowd has thinned, though I can still hear music thumping inside. Ben stops me by lightly touching my arm. That simple touch sends heat pulsing through my entire body.

"Well." His fingers travel down my arm before he takes my hand. Electricity charges between us. "It was really nice meeting you, Harper."

I don't know what to say. I don't know what's real and what isn't. After a few moments, I find my voice. "It was really nice meeting you too, Ben."

He moves in until he is just inches away. My body charges to life again, but he bypasses my mouth and kisses me softly on the cheek. "If we're meant to find each other again, we will," he whispers in my ear. My body erupts into goose bumps as he steps back and flings his arms wide. "I've got all the time in the world." He lifts a hand in a wave, turns, and walks away, just as Liam did hours before.

I've got all the time in the world.

Those words press into the most vulnerable places. I almost run after him, almost tell him he doesn't have all the time in the world, that in fact we have such little time left. I don't know why I'm here instead of there, or what it means. Is it about Liam, or is it about Ben? Is this my ultimate lesson? That I am always destined to find Ben in every life?

As I approach the gallery doors and prepare to walk back inside, I pause. Maybe none of this is about who I choose or why. Maybe it's about *me*. Maybe it's about learning to be okay on my own, just as Ben has been saying all along.

Not picking a man. Not basing my decisions or my life on a partner.

My head spinning with what I'm possibly here to learn, I take a step inside. The gallery is a mess, with empty dishes, crumpled, paint-splattered tarps, and trashed tables. People file out, and I force a smile and say good night. After I help clean up, Rita walks me to the door. She is exhausted but happy, and there is a light in her eyes, a reclamation of sorts.

"Well, you did it, my dear," she says, squeezing my arm. "You really did it."

"*We* did it," I say. "But now you will." I give her a hug and take a step back to stare at the gallery. "Take care of her." I wink.

"Don't be a stranger, Harper."

On my way home, I replay the entire night. Liam leaving and Ben showing up. That has to mean something. I check the time and quicken my pace. I have to have the ritual completed before midnight, and my stomach churns just thinking of it.

When I get to the loft, it's dark. I let myself inside quietly, so as not to disturb Liam, using my phone light to navigate. Quickly I realize that he's not on the couch or in bed. "Liam?" I call. I check my phone to find a text he left a while ago.

Sorry, beautiful. I got caught up with the bookstore owner, and we're headed out for a quick drink. I'll be home shortly.

I type back a reply, pour myself a glass of water, and stare at the photo on the refrigerator. It's the one he took of the two of us on the Manhattan Bridge, happy and lovestruck. I pluck the photo free, change into pajamas, scrub my face, and climb into bed. I caress the photograph, remembering when things were easy. Finally, I toss it aside and close my eyes as my thoughts swirl and my heart breaks.

Right on time, my phone buzzes. I answer it. Wren's face pops onto FaceTime, just as it did a month ago.

"You ready?"

I nod, but I'm not sure. I want to go home, but part of me wants to stay. I want to tell her that Ben found me here, that I fell for Liam all over again, that I don't want to leave if it means Ben can stay healthy. Though I want to ask if that's an option, the deeper part of me simply wants both worlds . . . but I know I can't.

She instructs me to get a candle and then write down a new sentence: *I wish for the new to return to old but still have all that I behold.* I'm worried that this sentence is much too vague, that I might wake up in another dimension, but as a zebra or Republican.

"Are you sure this is going to work?" I ask.

"No," she says. "In order for the spell to work, you had to learn something, and I have no way of knowing if you did."

What have I learned? That I don't have to work so hard to prove myself? That I am allowed to change my mind? That career isn't everything? That I would do anything for my husband? That maybe you can love two people at the same time? That I've kept walls up, and when they come down anything is possible? My eyes are already growing heavy as she guides me through the ritual. I slow my breathing, tune into my body, and then I say the loaded sentence three times. "I wish for the new to return to old but still have all that I behold. I wish for the new to return to old but still have all that I behold. I wish for the new to return to old but still have all that I behold."

To my relief, the tingles come just as they did the first time, and I let that sensation spill over me as I complete the final sentence. "And so it is, and it is so."

"Good luck, Harper." Wren ends the call, and I blow out the candle, pull the covers up to my chin, and wait for sleep to come and take me home.

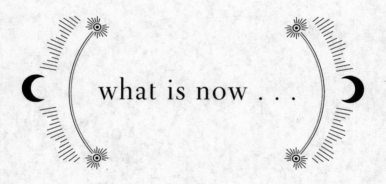

(what is now . . .)

33

I wake up panting.

I'm too afraid to open my eyes. What if the ritual didn't work and I'm stuck in Brooklyn forever, waiting to learn some invaluable lesson? After a few breaths, I say a silent prayer, peel one eyelid open, then the other. It's only when my eyes focus that I realize I am back home. In my bed. In Chattanooga. Quickly, I glance at my wrist. My tattoo is there, and I trace my fingers over it, letting out a giant exhale.

I glance at the bed next to me, but Ben's not here. "No, no, no." I rush to my phone and stab the side button to see what day it is. I gasp when I realize that no time has passed since the first full moon ritual. It's simply the next morning *after* the full moon. Not a month later, like in the other time line. I triple-check that this is possible, which would mean Ben is still at his workshop and that I am really home and no longer stuck in some insane alternate time warp.

My fingers shake as I look at the last text exchange from Ben, which simply said good night. I collapse back against the bed, reeling. There's no way all of that was a dream. Was it? Brooklyn. Liam. The gallery. Our relationship. Finding Ben again. I sit up. Am I just supposed to pretend I haven't seen such a strange, realistic glimpse into another life?

I check my phone again to find Liam has texted too, asking if I'm okay. I don't know how I can see him now. Not after what I just experienced and the emotional roller coaster we just went through together. I'm afraid to get too close, afraid to look into his eyes, because he will read everything there: my fears, my feelings, my uncertainty about what lesson I learned . . . all of it.

But then another thought rises to the surface. Last night Ben attributed his healing to the Joe Dispenza workshop. And here, in real life, Ben is at the *same* workshop. A blade of hope, as sharp as a dagger, pierces my heart. Maybe *this* is the lesson. Ben is at this workshop to get better, but I must give him the space he needs to heal. Could it really be one week away that saves his life?

Just as I am settling back into reality, Wren sends me a frantic text.

Where are you? You were supposed to open today. I'm off this morning, remember?

I stare at the text, perplexed. *Open what?* I respond.

Oh my God, Harper. Are you hungover? The gallery! We have people waiting to get in!

The gallery? A sickening feeling of déjà vu creeps over my skin as my fingers hover over the phone. Did I somehow promise her I'd open her gallery for her last night? I don't think I did. After a quick assessment that I *am* really here, and that I am not, in fact, still dreaming, I type out a quick reply.

I'll be right there.

It's all I can say until I know what's what. Before I make a cup of coffee or change clothes, I send Ben a text. I practically hold my breath as I see the text bubbles with his reply.

Going to be tied up most of today, but I feel great. Hope you slept well. Love you so much.

Placated for the moment that Ben still exists and is still at the workshop, I decide to take a quick shower but pause as I prepare to climb into our somewhat grimy tub and shower combo. It's been completely renovated, replete with a separate soaking tub. I blink in stunned surprise and open the glass shower door, sure I'm going to be sucked down the drain and spit out into the 1950s. How is this here?

There's no time to dwell on this change, however—how it got here or what exactly it means. All I know is that I am back in Chattanooga, and even though it already feels like the Twilight Zone, being home means I get to see Ben in a few days. That is my main focus. That is all that matters now.

After sucking down two cups of blistering coffee, I swipe my keys and rush out the door. A warm glow of sunshine greets me as I tip my face to the sky and take a moment to stand still. There are no angry car horns or heavy foot traffic here. It's still early and quiet, and a swift punch of both gratitude and grief hits me right in the heart. Even in such a short time, the city sounds became almost like a lullaby. It takes me a moment to reacclimate to *this* city, which is punctuated by mountains, not New Yorkers.

I've seen the other side—all the things I once wanted, all the things I once dreamed of—but at this moment, I'm grateful to be home. Wren's gallery isn't far, just a quick jaunt downtown. She snagged a killer corner space that gets a ton of foot traffic, and when I arrive, a few people sit on the curb, some scrolling through their phones, others smoking. As I approach the door, I realize I have no way to get in.

Once again, a strange sense of déjà vu nearly stops me in my tracks as I extract my keys and find that one is not like the others. Why would I have a key to Wren's gallery? I think back to my wish last night: *I wish for the new to return to old but still have all that I behold.* If what I just experienced was real, does that mean I could have possibly changed something in this time line?

Part of me must already know the answer is yes, considering I still live in the same place but have a brand-new bathroom. "Please make this stop," I say. A woman smoking a cigarette jerks her head my way as she hears me talking to myself. With a nearly trembling hand, I stick the key in the lock. It turns, and I give a shocked little gasp. I hold the door open for those who are waiting and step inside after them. I have to hold back an actual scream as I stare at these walls, walls that are partially covered with my art.

"What is happening?" I whisper as I move numbly to a section carved with my name on the wall. Just like in the other time line, it seems I am now a gallery owner. But instead of Rita, it's with Wren?

I definitely need more coffee.

I welcome the guests and then charge back to Wren's office, which is divided by two desks. I close the door, gulp a few deep breaths, and attempt to steady my quaking nerves. "It's okay. You're going to figure this out. There is no way you've entered yet *another* parallel universe. It's fine. You're fine. It's all going to be fine." What do I do first?

My phone buzzes. It's Liam again.

Hey, Harper. Really hope everything's okay after yesterday. We're scheduled for an interview this morning. Is that still good for you? I can come to you. You're at the gallery, right? I can bring coffee.

"What?" I drop the phone and scurry away from the desk as if I've just seen a spider the size of my hand. Why would Liam come here? How would he even know I'm supposed to be at the gallery? And what happened yesterday? I struggle to think back to my pre–time warp world and remember the picnic followed by the night at Wren and Jenna's and then our conversation before we went our separate ways. Did that still happen, or is there something else he's referring to? And how in the world do I find out without sounding completely insane?

"Think, Harper, think." I retrace my steps once again. In this life, in my *actual* existence, the last thing I remember is the full moon ritual that would send me on a monthlong head trip into that whole parallel universe thing. Yet now I'm back, which means I must have learned my lesson. But what have I changed? I think of my wish again: *I wish for the new to return to old, but still have all that I behold.*

Do I now behold being a gallery owner *and* a working artist? And having a nicer bathroom, apparently? I type out a frantic text to Wren.

Need to talk. I know it's your day off but it's an emergency! GET HERE NOW.

I respond to Liam and ask if we can push the interview until later today. With both of those things sorted, I pour myself another cup of coffee, even though the last thing I need is more caffeine, and frantically check every few seconds to make sure I'm really here.

A few minutes later, a very hungover Wren bursts through the office door. Her giant sunglasses, piled dreads, and visible neck tattoos give her the appearance of Zoë Kravitz or an edgy rockstar. "You rang?" She whips off her sunglasses, winces, and puts them back on before collapsing in her desk chair. "Jenna's still sleeping. Last night was too much."

"Yes, it *was* too much," I snap, trying to keep my emotions in check. "Can you walk me through what you remember?"

She tilts her head at me. "Why do I feel like this is a trick question?"

I tap my foot impatiently. "Well, here's what I remember. Liam and I came to your house. We left. You walked me through that insane full moon ritual, told me you'd see me on the other side, where I then woke up in *Brooklyn*, with Liam as my romantic partner and as a gallery owner for Rita Clementine! Then, when I managed to locate you there, you told me I had to wait an *entire month* until the next full moon and that I had to learn some sort of lesson before I could get back, which I guess I did, because now I'm here, but everything is different! I mean, not everything, but most things. Exhibit A: I work here now. And I have a renovated bathroom."

Wren massages her temples. "I'm sorry, I'm having trouble following. What full moon ritual? And where did you work before here?"

"What full moon . . . Are you serious right now?" I pace back and forth. "I was an art teacher at Jenna's school! You know this!"

She laughs. "You? A schoolteacher?" She crosses her tattooed arms. "Never happened."

I feel gobsmacked. My kids mean everything to me. Why would I have never been a teacher? It's why we moved to Chattanooga in the first place. "Are you telling me that because of whatever voodoo you pulled from that book, my life is now *completely* different?"

She pulls out some eye drops and dabs a few into her eyes. "Don't blame me for this, sis. I'm just as lost as you are."

Sheer panic. That's what I feel. These aren't some hypothetical things we're talking about. This is my life. "Tell me this. Ben is still a composer, right?"

"Okay, Harper, now I'm actually worried. You know he quit when he was first diagnosed."

"What?" What could have possibly happened in the other time line to have such a ripple effect on this one? "Humor me. What does he do instead?"

"He works with a bunch of organizations. Cancer research. That kind of thing. Wait—why am I answering these questions? You know all this already."

"Wren, I'm telling you, I *don't*." I stare deeply into her eyes, begging her to remember what she said to me, to remember our world before. Then something dawns on me. "Wait, if Ben's not a composer anymore, then why is Liam here?"

"Um, for you, dummy. Well, for us. He's covering the gallery, because the only paper I haven't gotten written up in is the *Times*, so they sent him to hype up your solo show. Obviously it was surprising that you two already knew each other, but honestly, your history gives us a bit of an advantage, which I'm not mad about."

Liam is here to write a story about *my* career, not Ben's? "Exactly how popular is this gallery, Wren?"

She smiles. "Very. Can I please go home now?"

I open my mouth to tell her no, she cannot go home, but really, what can she possibly do for me here? It's comforting that not everything is different; we still have our apartment, Ben is still at the workshop, and Liam is still here, but now the circumstances have changed as to why.

"Am I happy at least?" I finally ask. It seems like a silly question, but it's not. I assumed everything would be great in my grass-is-greener life, but it was more complicated than that. I know that Ben's diagnosis is not happy, of course, but if I'm a working artist and running a gallery, it has to be pretty good, right?

"I can't answer that for you," she says, then shrugs. "But I mean, I think so."

"I need to take a walk. Can you cover for a while?"

"Seriously?"

I don't wait for her to answer. I'm dazed as I leave the gallery, so many unanswered questions flowing through my head. No one knows what I've been through, and I have no way to explain it. Not even to Ben. I've never been at such a loss with what to do next. Maybe find a psychiatrist? Get a lobotomy?

I find myself gravitating toward my former students' warehouse gallery. I remember where to walk, and when I arrive, I steady myself before knocking lightly on the door. There's a commotion from inside, a bunch of hushed whispers, and then the door slides open a fraction. It's Alejandro.

"Oh, thank God. You're here."

He squints at me. "Can I help you?"

I can tell he doesn't recognize me, and of all the little deaths, this one cuts especially deep. I don't know why I'm here . . . I guess I just need confirmation that I have somehow shifted the fabric of my reality in innumerable ways.

"Sorry. Wrong address."

I walk away before he can question me, then make a right and head toward my studio. What if I don't rent it anymore? As I'm beginning to panic about all of these unwanted changes, I find that yes, I still have my studio. Once inside, I deflate, suddenly needing a nap. It's already eleven, and I panic as I realize I have to see Liam later.

I can't possibly answer questions or pretend that we are virtual strangers, because we aren't. Everything is spinning out of control, and I have no idea what to do next.

Spotting a blanket on my old couch, I curl up underneath it and close my eyes. Yes, I have a gallon of caffeine pumping through my veins, but I need my brain to stop working overtime for just a little while.

I need to figure out what is happening.

I need to understand this new version of my old life.

34

I t's almost two.

I groan, rub my eyes, and sit up, glancing around the space. For a moment, I forget where I am. I have about thirty texts from Wren, ranging from *Where are you?* to *Yo, you are so covering my next shift.* She then proceeds to ask how the solo show is coming, which, evidently, I am still supposed to create.

Despite the recent time travel, it's evident from glancing at the pieces scattered around the studio that I'm in the midst of creating something special for Ben, just like in my before world. There are more advanced themes here, however—more fully fleshed-out concepts than anything I previously had.

I study each idea as if I'm an observer instead of the one who apparently came up with them, and despite this strange situation and how confused I am, a spark of excitement travels up my spine. Here, it seems I'm playing off the famous "How Did Humans Evolve?" graphic and building Ben from the time he was a boy to a man to an athlete to a professional to a cancer patient and beyond. I consider the theme and find it to be simple, potent, and effective. I gnaw nervously on a cuticle and remember what every art teacher ever told me about emotions: It's important to use them, to channel them into your work. And as I throw on a smock, that is exactly what I prepare to do.

As a teacher, I've often talked about the concept of pain. Do we need it to create art? Do we always have to scrape the underbelly of our emotional core to artistically say what we need to say? Before now, I haven't really allowed myself to access the full well of my emotions about Ben. How deeply I love him. How I finally got my happily ever after and now it might be cut short. There's pain here—real, throbbing pain—and apparently I'm going to share it with the world via a solo show.

Though it doesn't seem like the most opportune time to create, I lose myself for a while anyway, in an attempt to let my thoughts settle until I figure out what I'm supposed to do next. Before I get too consumed, I text Liam that I'm at my studio and send him the address. I have no idea if he's already been here or not. I'm so confused as to what has happened and what hasn't, and why he would be here for me and not Ben. I wonder if this is how it's going to be now: constantly trying to figure out what's true and what isn't. How exhausting.

Tossing my phone to the side, I stare at the canvases. I smooth out my sketches and begin to build, music cranked, and lose myself to the thing I love doing most. I remember so many hours spent just like this through college and then during that fateful week in New York when I thought everything would turn out differently. When I thought I'd get my chance and my happy ending, all wrapped into one. But didn't I, in some ways? Isn't that what I'd just seen in that alternate reality? That I *did* stay, that I *did* turn my art into something beautiful, that I *did* build a life with Liam? That I chose not to walk away?

Even still, there were bumps and ridges, and a part of me had seemed to abandon what mattered most in order to climb my own career ladder. But I fixed that, didn't I? I gave Liam more time and attention. I quit the gallery to pursue art. I chose my art *and* my relationship.

I can only hope in this world that I'm not also sacrificing my relationship with Ben for my career. I won't know what's different between us until he returns. Even the thought of him coming back on the path to being healed makes my heart soar.

Just as I'm finding my rhythm, there's a knock. I stare down at myself, already paint-smeared and sticky with sweat, and open the door.

Liam looks handsome, as always, in a fitted T-shirt and jeans that hang just so on his hips. His hands are behind his back, and it dawns on me that in this life we are still two people who only knew each other once. What I've just experienced with him isn't real. Everything is either a memory or make-believe.

"Hi," I say. There are so many other things I could say, so many ways I could come undone. *I've just seen a different life. I've somehow changed my current reality. I'm so lost. I don't know where I am. I don't know what to do next. I don't know who to trust.*

"Hi." He produces a six-pack of beer and Thai takeout. "Hungry?"

I step aside so he can come in, suddenly realizing I'm famished.

He whistles as he takes in the large warehouse space. "So this is what a real artist's studio looks like, huh?"

I laugh as I rinse my brushes in the sink by the door. "Your space is beyond incredible, and we both know it."

It's the first time I've acknowledged that I took up such space in his home, if only for a short time, and his eyes flick to mine and hold my gaze for a beat too long before he turns back to the windows. "I don't know. This gives my loft a run for its money." He sets the food on the coffee table in front of my couch and studies my work so far. He's quiet while he moves from image to image, half-erected sketches and canvases of Ben the boy to Ben the man. Once he becomes a survivor, I want him to explode into stardust. I haven't figured out how I'll accomplish this yet, but I want it to be a visceral experience for the viewer.

"This is really moving, Harper. What a tribute."

"It's a start, at least." I motion for him to take a seat. We tap our beers in a quick cheers, and I suck down a healthy gulp, not realizing how thirsty I am. Liam divides the boxes of takeout between us. As I dive into one of the containers, he looks around the studio again.

"I think it's great you followed your passion, Harper. I know how much you always wanted all this."

I nod, because what can I say? *No, that's not true?* Apparently, somehow it is, even though I missed the actual ride to the top, as though this opportunity has just been handed over on a silver platter . . . and if I'm being honest, I'm not sure how I feel about that.

I pull my legs into a cross-legged position and nurse my beer. "Do you ever paint or take photos anymore?" I want to ask him if he's thought about writing a book, and if he hasn't, he should.

"Nah. No time, really."

We fall into a comfortable silence as we finish our food. I want to tell him what he's like in our other life, how he discovered a new dream and went after it. I scratch the label on my beer, some of the cold, gummy paper jamming under my nail. I think back to that first night at the Edwin Hotel, which already seems like a lifetime ago.

"I'm sorry about yesterday," I say, testing the waters to see if we did, in fact, have a picnic. "I wasn't expecting to feel such a rush of emotion."

"Harper, I get it. It's all right. Let's just focus on the story, okay?"

"Right." My heart snags. "The story." So the picnic did happen, though this version of Liam seems more professional, more emotionally detached than before.

"But you're still one of my favorite people," he adds lightly. "Don't forget that."

"Don't you mean *were*?" What I really mean is, *me too*. Even as I think those words, they feel like a betrayal to Ben. *Ben* is my favorite person. *Ben* is my life.

"No, I mean are," he says. "You don't have to know someone for years for them to make a lasting impression."

"Can you really know someone after only a week?" Seeing Liam here now and in that other life proves that yes, you *can* know someone in an instant if you're meant to. I'd felt that way about Ben too. As I stare at Liam, my thoughts are all tangled up between my fake world and this one. The lines blur between reality and fantasy.

"I think you can." He stretches his arms in front of him and rolls his neck, then hops up and begins to pace. "Want me to prove it?"

I laugh and motion to him. "By all means."

He turns and steadies himself, watching me. "Okay, here goes. The first thing you do in the morning is check that Ben is still breathing. You worry, like a mother worries about her newborn, that one day you will wake up and he won't be there."

This opening stuns me into absolute stillness, because it's true.

"You make coffee for the two of you, and while you love Ben's company, you prefer to drink it alone, outside, watching the sunrise. It's why you chose your condo—and why you still live there—because the balcony gives you an unobstructed view of the sunrise. That matters more to you than having an extra bathroom. You miss competing in obstacle course races and sometimes channel that competitive spirit in other ways: tracking your time home from work, speed walking, or getting in and out of the grocery store faster than last time. Though you present a tough exterior, if you let yourself, you would love a good cry at the end of every day. But you're afraid that if you fall apart, you might not be able to piece yourself back together. In the past, it was your MO to run when things got hard, but Ben's diagnosis has taught you that it's okay to stay." He takes a deep breath. "And even though you are wildly successful, you still feel like you have something to prove, though I'm not sure if it's to yourself or to the world. How am I doing so far?"

I am speechless. "How could you possibly know all of that?" It's like he's taken a deep look right into my soul. No one, not even Ben, has ever been able to do that.

"I see you, Harper."

I see you.

I glance down to make sure my tattoo is still really there, and it is. I run my fingers over the three simple words. His words, just like Ben's, create a physical ache inside me.

"Plus"—he laughs—"I've been interviewing you for days now, so I have a bit of an unfair advantage."

"About that," I say. "Remind me how you came to write this story."

"My boss told me to come to Chattanooga to cover the gallery. I may have known it was yours." He gives me a sheepish look. "I've followed your career these last few years. Not in a creepy way," he adds. "I'm just really proud of you."

"Thanks, Liam." I close my eyes and rest my head on the couch. "Look. I know you're here to interview me, but do you think we could take a rain check? I'm just not feeling very chatty."

"Of course." He gathers the takeout containers and heads to the door. "Want me to walk you home?"

I shake my head and tell him I want to keep working. When he's gone, I turn back to the pieces, Ben's pensive eyes staring out at me from each canvas. "What a mess," I say to this fictitious version of Ben. I almost expect him to respond, to tell me that this is all part of some master plan and one day I'll understand. But right now I don't. Right now I would do anything for life to be simple, without time travel and ex-boyfriends and portals and all of these infinite possibilities.

Though it's late, I get back to work, pouring everything I have—all the confusion, uncertainty, love, and despair—into making something great.

35

Finally, it's the day Ben comes home, and I am as excited as a child on Christmas.

I've been scrambling the last few days to figure out what is the same in this world and what I must have done to cause such ripple effects in my current reality. Once Ben bursts through that door, however, his voice bright as he calls for me, all I can think of is seeing him, holding him, kissing him.

I run inside from the balcony to jump into his arms, which feel sturdier than when I last saw him. Finally, I pull back to assess. He looks well-fed and rested. It's still jarring to see the physical differences from the Ben I glimpsed in Brooklyn, but I know that version of my husband was not real. *This* is real. I kiss his lips and tug him against me.

"Oh my God, I missed you so much," I say. "It feels like you've been gone a year."

"I know." He threads his fingers through my hair and finally pulls back and whistles as he studies the condo. "You've been stress-cleaning, I see."

I roll my eyes. "Guilty." I follow him into the bedroom as he unpacks, not wanting to pepper him with too many questions but still wanting to devour every detail. Mostly I want to know how he feels, if he's better, and what we are supposed to do next. When will we know if he's healed? I didn't ask the other version of Ben that question. How soon he'd known. If he'd gone to get testing to confirm and how he could be sure the cancer wouldn't come back.

To my surprise, Ben doesn't talk so much about himself as about what he witnessed at the workshop. People bound to wheelchairs walking for the first time. People who were blind suddenly able to see. People with multiple sclerosis running by the end of the week. He met and made so many new friends, and my heart swells listening to all of it. I cling to the hope that maybe he will be one of these miracles too—that he got his energy elevated to such a level that the cancer had nowhere to go but up and out. I know spontaneous recoveries can happen; I've just never allowed myself to think that Ben could be one of them. But after what I've experienced, I'm open to believing just about anything is possible. I'm living proof that there's more to this world than we think.

"How does it feel to be back?"

He looks around our bedroom and then sits on the bed. "Great to see you, obviously, but harder than I thought." He rubs a hand over his head. "If I'm being honest, it was nice to be somewhere else. I love our home, Harp, but I also associate it with being sick."

I nod, because I completely understand. My thoughts drift to the version of him who was nomadic for so long before deciding he wanted to settle down and start a family. "What if we sell?" I ask. It's not something we've really talked about since his treatment ended.

His eyes spark with interest. "Where would we go?"

"Anywhere we want."

He taps me on the knee. "Close your eyes."

I smile and do as I'm told.

"If you could move anywhere, where's the first place that comes to mind?"

I ponder the question. We've never talked about moving because he's never wanted to. In our original lives, we moved here because I got my teaching job. In this version, I'm not sure how we ended up here.

Brooklyn pulses through my head, almost like a heartbeat. "I don't know. New York, maybe?" As I say it, my mind surges with images of Liam: Liam in his loft, Liam in his bed, Liam's lips on mine. I don't know how to tell him that I've just been there, that I've seen this alternate reality that I'm still trying to interpret. I don't know if I like that New York version of me. I also don't know if I could ever leave this place, because it has so much of Ben in it. I don't know anything right now, except that I'm beyond relieved to see my husband. I open my eyes. "But I know you hate New York."

"Harper." He rests his warm hand on my thigh and squeezes. "You can't make decisions based on me anymore, okay? You have to start thinking about what you want for yourself. If New York is where you want to be, then that's where you should be."

My eyes fill with tears, and I shake my head, confused. "But I thought you went to this workshop to get better, Ben. Wasn't that the whole point?"

He shrugs. "I mean, there's the hope of getting better, but what I really took away from my time there was peace. I've been avoiding really, truly thinking about the end, and now I'm not running from it. I'm making peace with what comes next, whether that's now or in another fifty years."

"Let's go with another fifty years." I sigh and flop back on the bed.

"Hey, you. Don't be sad." He strokes my cheek and trails his hands down my neck and stomach. My body aches for him. "Three things," he whispers now.

I sit back up. I've missed our little game. "You, me, hope. Your turn."

He smiles. "Hope is a good one. I'd say you, the workshop, and coming home."

We're quiet for a moment as I gather my next thoughts. "Do you ever think about having a family?" The words are tentative coming out of my mouth, and I can tell I've caught him off guard.

His eyes darken momentarily, and he shakes his head. "The doctors are pretty sure the chemo wrecked me, Harp. You know that."

"Let's say it hadn't. Would you want a family?" I don't know what I'm saying. Ben just got back, and now we're talking about moving and starting a family? My mind is all mixed up, and the last thing I want to do is overwhelm him.

"I want a family. Especially with you." He leans in to kiss me, and I wrap my arms around his neck and pour everything I have into the moment.

"Then let's try." The words escape my lips, shocking us both. Even as I say it, I'm not sure that I really mean it, but Ben pulls back long enough to look at me.

He smooths the hair away from my face. "But what if I don't live to meet them?"

I kiss his lips, his hair, his cheeks. "But what if you do?"

We fall into each other, and it is slow and tender. Ben and I only briefly talked about kids before we got married. We assumed we'd have them after a few years, but in the beginning, we were mostly focused on having fun and enjoying each other. Then, when he got diagnosed, all future plans flew out the window. But this could be a way to keep him with me, to carry on his legacy, to give him another reason to live.

Afterward, I kiss him deeply, then curl into him, never wanting to let go. I feel guilty for what happened with Liam, even if it was all make-believe. As I cling to his chest, I remind myself that this is the man I love.

This is where I belong.

36

After another couple of days, it's time for Liam to head back to New York.

I am torn about his departure for many reasons, one of which is that I'm afraid I won't ever see him again—in this life or in my dreams. Plus, I have to keep my promise. The moment he leaves, I'm telling Ben the truth.

Liam stops by the condo to say goodbye and tells me when to expect the article. I tell Ben I'm going to walk him down to say good-bye, and we ride the elevator silently.

A thousand thoughts ravage my mind as we step onto the curb. His rental car is already there, his bags in the trunk. He unlocks the car and opens the driver's side door. The past and present mingle. My what-if life blends with this one. In both realities, there's so much regret, so much I feel is still unsaid. How can I let him go without really telling him how I feel? I know this is a door firmly closing, but I have to know at least one thing in order to put all of this to bed for good.

"What do you think would have happened if I hadn't left Brooklyn?" I ask. It's an unfair question, but I ask it anyway because I have to know.

He doesn't ask what I mean. He taps the keys into his open palm. "Do you really want me to answer that?" His eyes flick painfully over my face. But I only nod. "Okay," he sighs. "Well." He leans casually against the car and crosses his arms. "I think we would still be together. I think you'd be a successful artist. I think we'd be happy." He stares at his toes, not daring to lock eyes with mine.

It takes everything in me not to tell him that he's mostly right, that I've seen us and that I wish there was a parallel universe where both realities could exist. Before I can say anything else, Liam steps forward and gently cups my face in his free hand. His touch nearly takes my breath away. The heat of his palm ignites something like wildfire in my chest. I fold my hand over his, both of us gazing deeply into each other's eyes. I want to say so much. I want to tell him what he meant to me then and what he means to me now. I want to tell him all about our fictional life. But I can't, because it's fair to no one. Finally, I turn my head, kiss his hand, then drop it and take a step back. He's breathing hard, looking at his hand, then back at me like he could devour me, but I break the spell before he can do anything we'll both regret.

"I have a favor to ask."

"Anything," he responds, his voice husky.

"This feature. I know you're here for me and the gallery, but is there a way you could make it more about Ben instead?"

He considers my request, clearly confused. "What do you mean?"

To my surprise, Ben and Liam have become fast friends these last few days in this new, altered reality, too, and Ben has spent more time with him than I have. They've done brunch and taken walks and have had endless conversations. Liam even convinced Ben to take him to his music studio, which he rarely uses anymore. "I feel like his story is wildly more interesting than mine for obvious reasons," I explain. *Especially if he lives*, I almost add but don't. "Is that even remotely possible?"

"Do you mean like a tribute?"

"Yes," I say. "Exactly like that."

He considers the request, though I realize it's probably up to his boss, not him. Finally, he nods. "I spent some quality time with Ben, but I'd have to look through all my notes. I'll see what I can do."

"Thank you," I say.

He opens his rental car door and then offers me a slow smile. "Maybe I'll see you in the next life, Harper." He waves as he gets into the car. I stand there, my arms studded with gooseflesh as I contemplate his words. Was that a nod to our other life, or was that just a casual line? I stand there until the taillights snake right, and I try not to feel the black hole widening in my chest. In many ways, though, it feels like closure I've never gotten. Now I can finally, completely focus on the present.

Back in the apartment, Ben stands on the balcony, resting his forearms on the rail.

"He's gone." I freeze when I see the look on Ben's face as he turns. I realize, foolishly, that from this vantage point, he probably saw that entire exchange.

"Anything you want to tell me?" he asks.

I open my mouth, then close it. I knew this conversation was coming, but I still don't want to have it. Not when he's feeling better. Not when Liam is already gone and I feel like I finally have some closure. "I can explain."

He looks as if I've punched him. "Explain what?"

I motion to the chaise, and he sits carefully while I gather the words. "It's a bit complicated." Even as I say the words, I wonder if that's true. What's so complicated about falling in love and then being so afraid of those emotions that you screw it all up? I don't know how to describe what we were. But I try. I tell him about our time in Brooklyn, about all that happened in just seven days. "I was young and threw it all away before my career or a relationship could really begin. So it was a shock, seeing him here like this. It caught me completely off guard."

To my surprise, Ben begins to laugh, but it is a sad, hollow sound. "Harper, if that's not fate, then I don't know what is."

"What do you mean?"

He motions to our apartment. "I come up with this idea for you to fall in love with someone else and then the journalist who shows up to interview you is the one who got away? You can't write that." He drops his head in his hands and then lifts it again. "There's a reason this happened."

I massage my temples and sigh. Part of me hoped his stupid idea hadn't carried over to this version of our lives. That I'd changed that wish in the other time line. "This isn't some rom-com, Ben. This is my life. I am married to *you*. I love *you*. I choose *you* with my whole heart. That's just my past, and I'm sharing it with you now because it feels important, but it also has no bearing on our present or future."

His foot taps rapidly as he contemplates what to say. "Do you still have feelings for him?"

It's the one question I wish he wouldn't ask, because I can't lie. I'm silent long enough that he knows the answer must be complicated. He nods, crossing his arms. "Well, you're right. This sucks. My idea was stupid, I'm stupid, and I do want you all for myself. There. You win."

I smile, in spite of the situation. "See? I told you that you weren't that evolved."

"You should pursue it," he finally says, looking at me. "After I'm gone. He's a good guy." His voice cracks as he says it.

"I don't need to make plans for when you're gone," I reply. "Because you're going to be fine."

"You don't know that, Harp."

"I *do* know that, Ben." I can't tell him how I know, but I do. I've started to realize that this must be the lesson I am supposed to learn. That the reason I was thrust into that strange time warp was to show me that he is going to be okay. That miracles do happen. That in the end, he lives.

Instead of responding, Ben stands and lets himself back into the condo. I follow, but he's swiping his keys from the island and heading toward the front door.

"Where are you going?" I ask.

"Out," he says, shutting the door quickly behind him.

I stand there alone, staring after him, wondering how I've managed to so royally screw everything up.

37

I know Ben well enough to give him time alone.

But I am antsy, unsure of what to do with myself. I think about going to my studio to paint, but I don't feel inspired, only drained. Instead, I watch the sunset outside with a glass of wine, and by ten I'm ready for bed. Trying not to worry, I shoot Ben a quick text and then crawl under the covers.

I thumb through a book, but I can't focus. I can't believe I've mangled his homecoming this badly. Why didn't I tell him about Liam sooner? I try not to worry, try to tell myself that he has every reason to be upset. He's human, and he just found out his wife has a complicated past with someone else. I hate myself for doing this to him, for putting this on his shoulders when he should only be focused on his health. Wren was right. Maybe I should have kept my history with Liam to myself.

I toss and turn until I hear the key in the lock and wait for him to come into the bedroom. It has been so long since he's been out so late without me. I listen to the ordinary sounds of the keys hitting the island, the removal of his shoes, the suctioning of the fridge as he pours himself a glass of water. He hesitates at the bedroom door, but I see his shadow.

"Ben, can we talk?"

Instead of storming into the bathroom, he sits on the bed and faces me. I can barely make out his features in the dark. "I'm sorry," he says. "I had no right to just disappear like that."

"Of course you did," I say, scooting closer. "You should only be thinking about your health. This is the worst kind of distraction."

He takes my hand and squeezes. "No, you're wrong, Harper. It made me realize how much I do want our marriage, how much more life I want to experience with you." His voice falters, and he drops his head into his hands and begins to cry. Everything cracks open: his cancer journey, all the hope, stoicism, pain, and fear. He cries for his life because it's slipping through his fingers, even though today he feels fine. "But it also made me realize that one day you will move on. And if you do, I think you should reach out to Liam."

I shove down the frustration at his name being brought up *again*, but I know we need to talk about it. "I understand why you're talking about this, but my heart isn't with Liam, Ben. I promise. It's with you." I grip his hand and squeeze.

Is that completely true?

We say nothing as we sit in silence, until I finally wrap my arms around him. "This is all so unfair," I finally say. It's not something either of us has said much during this journey, though we've definitely thought it a million times. We took it as a challenge, one that Ben would overcome. "I don't want to lose you," I say. "I don't think I can survive it."

He pulls me to his heaving chest and grips me so hard I can barely breathe. "I'm sorry, Harper. I'm sorry that no matter what, you'll carry this with you. Because of me, you'll be in pain."

"It's not your fault." I'm so sick of speaking in hypotheticals, both of us dancing around and around what he assumes is coming. I'm not sure how to live for today but also *not* think about the end. I've never figured out quite how to balance the two. And part of me hopes that now I won't have to. "Maybe the workshop worked," I say. "Maybe we don't have to think about these things. Right?"

I need him to validate this feeling, to tell me he feels different, that he's going to be okay. But he doesn't.

"I'm tired, Harp. Let's go to bed. We can talk more tomorrow."

We get ready for bed. The silence fills the void as thoughts clash violently in my head. At least with Liam gone we can get back to some semblance of a normal life. I need to focus on the here and now: Ben. My show. The gallery. Possibly moving. A tiny voice in the back of my head whispers, *Brooklyn*, but I push it away. If I want to move to New York someday, I can, but not today.

After Ben is asleep, I position myself on my side and watch him, tracing my fingers over the blade of his nose, the perfect shape of his lips, the dip of his chin.

I wish I could get out of my head and focus on the moment. It's something I've never been good at, but it's never too late to start. After a while, I grip Ben's hand and tug it to my chest. I try to sync my breathing to his.

Finally, my eyes grow heavy and I drift, Ben's hand firmly over my heart.

38

I stand on the top of the hill and wait for Ben.

After following a cryptic text, I've left my studio to end up in Coolidge Park. It's only noon and crowds of people are studded below like cattle. A stack of cardboard sits next to me at the top of the hill. I shield my eyes from the stiff rays of the sun and search for Ben.

It's been a week since I've been "back" on this side of reality, and I think I've gotten a handle on most of the changes, both professionally and personally. With Liam gone and both of us settling back into a routine, I feel calmer and happier. The work at the gallery is intense, though in some ways I feel like all the work I did with Rita in my fake life helped prepare me for it.

After a few minutes, I spot Ben crossing a freshly mowed patch of grass. He is smartly dressed, and I break into a grin as he huffs his way to the top of the hill to greet me. It takes him a moment to catch his breath.

"Fancy meeting you here," I say.

"Happy anniversary, hot stuff." He kisses me softly.

"Happy anniversary." Was it really just a year ago that we were getting married? So much has happened these last twelve months. Before Ben, I wasn't much for anniversaries or birthdays. But now, each milestone feels like a gift, and though I don't care what we do today, it's nice that he feels good enough to plan something.

"So, why are we here?" I ask, gesturing around us.

"Don't you remember our second date?"

"I do." I smile in memory. After our initial obstacle course race meet-cute, we took a walk the next day and stumbled upon this hill, where kids were sledding to the bottom on pieces of wrinkled cardboard that townspeople leave at the top for anyone to use. Rather than walk by, we took turns racing each other to the bottom.

"That was such a fun day."

"It was. And today we are going to take a walk down memory lane, revisiting all of the fun, simple things we used to do together. Though we won't actually be *physically* doing all the things we used to do, because, you know, cancer," he jokes, "I thought we could at least do this." He takes my hand and leads me over to two giant pieces of cardboard. "Best out of ten wins?"

I am so charmed by this small, simple gesture that it takes me a moment to realize he's just issued a competitive challenge. "You're on, Foster."

For the next half hour, we race each other to the bottom, half the time getting stuck in well-worn dirt patches on the way down. I laugh until my body hurts, my cheeks stiff and shoulders sun happy. When we are exhausted from running up the hill, Ben meets me at the bottom.

"Still a winner," I declare.

He rolls his eyes, and I see that his hands are shaking slightly as he fishes a bottle of water from his backpack. "Still competitive."

"Always." I take a sip of the water he offers and study his body language, worried that running up and down that hill so many times was physically too much. "Want to take a break? Sit for a while?"

"No time."

To my delight, Ben recreates some of our best Chattanooga dates: we walk by the place we used to kayak and pose for a picture, peruse a few downtown art galleries, and then grab some street food. It is a perfect, meaningful day, and by sundown, I can tell Ben has overdone it. Instead of heading straight back to the condo, however, he steers me toward the water, where there are a thousand locks chained to the fence by lovers, friends, and strangers. It has always reminded me of the streets of Paris, and though Ben and I once talked about putting a lock here together, we never did.

When we step on the dock, he digs in his pocket.

"I think I know where this is going," I say.

He produces a lock, but to my surprise, he then lowers down to one knee. He takes my left hand in his, easily slipping my wedding band from my ring finger like a magic trick, and stares deeply into my eyes.

"What are you doing?"

"What you beat me to at that Oscars party," he says. He takes a moment to gather himself. "I know that when we met, we moved fast. We got engaged fast, we got married fast, and we have even moved through this diagnosis fast. But I also know there's no one on this earth I'd rather move faster with than you." He stares at my bare finger. "Now I'm the one moving fast into uncharted territory. I'm the one forging ahead." He takes a breath. "But no matter where I am, I will always be with you, Harper." He slips my band back on my ring finger. "Would you do me the honor of becoming my wife again?"

I'm so touched I can barely utter the word *yes*. I bend down to throw my arms around him, and we share one long, emotional kiss. "Are we really getting married again?"

He laughs. "Oh my God, no. I don't have the energy for another wedding. I just needed to ask you. It's something I always wanted to do, and now I have." As he stands, his right knee buckles, and he lowers back down suddenly.

"Hey. You okay?"

He tries to shake it off as he pulls himself to his feet, but I can see his legs are trembling, and so are his hands. "Fine, fine. Just got a little lightheaded."

I offer him water, and he drinks it. We wait for a beat as he gathers himself. I know we need to get home, but I don't want to ruin this part of his surprise. When he's steady, he takes my hand and guides me to the fence to find a spare square inch to place our lock. He uncaps a Sharpie and holds it over the lock.

"What should we write?" I ask.

He stares at the moonlit water, and I am so grateful for this day. I'll never forget it. "How about, 'Ben and Harper: in every life.'"

My body erupts into chills with those words. I'm instantly transported back to healthy Ben, leaning in to whisper that if we're meant to find each other again, we will. "In every life," I whisper now. "It's perfect."

He nods and scribbles it on the lock. We clamp it closed around the metal bars of the dock, and once again, I lace my fingers through his. He leans forward to kiss me, but I notice he's broken into a cold sweat. I peck him lightly, suddenly worried, and sensing I'm about to ask, he insists he's fine.

"Good anniversary?" he asks on the slow walk back to our condo.

"The best." I wrap my arm around his waist and lightly squeeze. He sags against me, and I keep my arm firmly in place to guide him home. I try to keep my thoughts in positive territory, but it's nearly impossible. But I'm also still clinging to the hope I've seen from that other life. Our happy ending has to be coming. I just know it.

When we are in front of our building, my phone dings, and I stop to read the text before stuffing it back into my pocket.

"Everything good?"

I offer a smile. "Yeah, fine. That was Liam."

His body stiffens slightly. "Oh?"

"He's just letting me know the feature comes out tomorrow."

With everything that's been happening, I completely forgot not only about the article but about what I asked Liam to do. I know that he got approval to make the article more about Ben, but that's all I know. We stop on the sidewalk in front of our building. "Look, I need to tell you something."

"Okay." He rubs the back of his neck. "Do I want to hear this?"

"No, no, it's nothing like that," I reassure him. "Before Liam left, I asked if he'd make some changes to the article."

"Like what?"

"Like make it about you instead of me?"

"Is that a question?" A flicker of annoyance passes over Ben's face. "Why would you ask him to do that?"

We stare at each other silently until I find my voice. "Because your story is so much more interesting than mine. Because you deserve to have a piece written about you. Because I love you." I take his hand and kiss it.

"Have you read it?"

"Not yet."

"And you didn't think to check with me? Neither of you did?"

I feel like icy water has been splashed in my face. "I'm sorry, Ben. I thought you'd be happy about it."

He extracts his hand and takes a step back. "Harper, if I wanted the whole world to know my story, I would have set something up myself. I've been private about my struggles for a reason."

"But why?" I ask, genuinely confused. "Imagine how much light you could shed on pancreatic cancer or even alternative therapies for patients who are terminal. It could help so many people."

"That's not your decision to make," he says quietly.

I can't remind him that in our before world he was more than happy to have an article written about his life. Ben was open to it, hungry for it even. What's changed in this time line to make him so hesitant?

I can't put my finger on why there are all these subtle differences; why he isn't a composer anymore; why he wants to stay hidden; why his motivations have shifted. It's not the Ben I know . . . and yet it is. Even though this version of my husband seems more introspective and private, he still has the same good intentions. He's still the man I love. The man I want to honor, which is why I wanted Liam to write the article in the first place.

I stand there, worried that I've done the wrong thing, and text Liam to send me the draft. I give him my email address, then forward it to Ben. "Just read it," I say. "If you don't want him to run it, I'll ask him not to."

"Okay, thank you."

We walk inside. The mood has shifted, and I worry I've ruined our special day. While Ben gets ready for bed, I hunt for my laptop under a pile of clothes on the bed. When I see Liam's name in my inbox, a pang of emotion rips through my body like a current, but I block everything out. After a few minutes, Ben emerges from the bathroom.

"I sent it to you."

He nods, thumbs through his phone, and begins to read, just as I do. When I see the draft title, I pause: "The Last Song." My eyes are already teary before I even dive in. Just like when I read his novel, I'm pulled in by his words.

The Last Song
by Liam Hale

Ben Foster doesn't look like someone who's dying of terminal cancer. In fact, an obstacle course racer turned professional composer turned cancer research advocate, his office is stuffed with awards and gold medals, and he has an easy way of making you believe almost anything. During our first interview, when I asked him how he was faring with his terminal bout of cancer over the last twelve months, he shrugged.

"I mean, we're all dying, right? I'm so competitive, maybe I'm just trying to get there first."

I devour the rest of the article, which contains touching sentiments from so many of his colleagues and friends. I'm beyond impressed he was able to cobble this much information together about Ben in such a short time. Near the end, I hesitate. My breath halts again, circulating like angry hornets in my chest.

Though not the original reason I flew out to do this article, like all good journalists, I decided to follow the real story here: A well-known composer dying of cancer wishes for his wife to fall in love before he's gone. A romantic myself, I was floored by the sentiment and realized I could never do what Ben is doing. I could never trust the world like that, could never release what I hold so tightly to, especially when it comes to those I love.

But upon knocking on their door, my world came crashing down. Because, you see, Ben's wife, Harper Swanson Foster, isn't just some stranger. She is the woman I spent one sacred week with ten years ago and never saw again. A woman I fell madly in love with in only seven days. And now she was standing in front of me, married to a man who wanted her to find happiness before it was too late.

This story does not end with me and Harper running off into the sunset, however. Because this is real life, and the moral of the story is simple: love. Love your people while you still have them. Love your partners while they're still here. Love the ups and downs, the good and the bad. Love the fights and the trivial nonsense. Love it all.

It is so clear the love Ben has for his people. The love Harper has for Ben. The love Harper and I once shared so long ago, even when we were young and free and thought we had all the time in the world.

As I left the two of them to head back to my real world, I realized that I have made a lot of choices in my life to avoid getting hurt. In contrast, Ben and Harper are facing life head-on. They are feeling their way through, not around. To illustrate this sentiment, I asked Ben what the theme song to his life would be.

He took me to his studio he rarely uses anymore, since his work revolves mostly around cancer research. However, as we stood there, he launched into one of the most haunting ballads I've ever heard. I asked him what he might call it when he finishes.

"The Last Song," he said. "Because it is."

Today we don't yet know where Ben's story will end, or Harper's, but I know one thing: my life is better for knowing both of them, and I will be rooting for them and loving them and remembering them until the very end.

I slam my computer closed. By asking Liam to make the article about Ben, it somehow now includes all three of us *and* resurrects Ben's original Master Plan. While it is undoubtedly beautiful, it still crosses a personal line for me. A line we did not discuss first. I groan. This is exactly how Ben must feel. Writing the article about Ben is one thing; sharing our personal history is another. Ben finishes a few minutes after me and sits on the bed.

"Well, it's good," he says. "I'll give him that."

I shift to look at him in the dark. "This article is supposed to be about you. I didn't think he'd write about our past."

He rotates and clutches my hand. "Harper, it's about all of us. And I know you've shut down this whole idea of being with anyone else, especially while I'm here, but please promise me that after I'm gone, you'll reach out to him. He came back into your life for a reason. This has to be it." He rubs his thumb over my wedding ring again and again. "Right?"

I want to snatch my hand free but don't. I can't possibly predict the future, but the last thing on my mind is moving on with Liam. Why can't he just let it go?

"I'm going to go take a shower." I sever the moment and leave him staring after me. I crank the shower and take a few deep breaths. Am I mad because Ben won't let this whole idea of me and Liam go, or because, deep down, I fear he's right?

I glance at my wedding ring and replay what a lovely day we had. Now it feels tainted. I fish my phone from my pocket again to find that Liam has texted me.

Did you get it?

Why didn't you tell me our story was going to be part of it? I hastily type back.

I guess I should have, Harper. I'm sorry.

I don't want the whole world knowing about us. I realize I might be overreacting, but the thought of every New Yorker opening the paper to read about this complicated love story makes my skin crawl. After a few minutes, he replies.

I won't run it if you don't want me to. Just say the word.

I know it's not that easy. It's the *New York Times*, not some local paper. *It's fine*, I type back. *Do whatever.*

I don't want to say more, don't want to give this situation any more energy than I already have.

What did you think of what I wrote about Ben?

What do I think? I think I want to scream. I think I want to undo all the little changes in this new world. I think I don't want to be in the middle of this love triangle anymore. I think I never want to time-hop or explore what-if scenarios again. I think I want a healthy husband and a normal life. But I can't have any of those things, as long as this tether to my past-future-time-warp self still exists.

I think we shouldn't talk anymore, Liam. I'm so sorry. Take care of yourself.

I don't want to cut Liam out of my life because I'm overreacting to some story. That's not it. The truth is, as long as he keeps showing up, especially after what I've seen in that other glimpse, I can't separate then from now. I can't be fully present to this life. To my home. To my marriage. To Ben.

Before I can change my mind, I send the text and then let my fingers hover over his contact info. Without another thought, I swiftly block his number. The irony isn't lost on me that with a click of my finger, I've erased someone I was once so desperate to find.

Someone who found me here after all these years. Someone I conjured in my dreams. Someone who is still inserting himself into my marriage and life.

When the water is scalding, I undress, step into the shower, and let the steam wash the anger away.

Well, not anymore. Now I want exactly what I have.

Nothing more, nothing less.

39

Ben and I drive the short distance to Lookout Mountain, Georgia, which contains endless waterfalls and miles of challenging, breathtaking hiking trails.

When we park, Ben exits the car, stretches his arms, and gazes over the top of the bluff. "Man, I've missed this."

"Me too." Prep work for my show has been so all-consuming, I've barely stopped to take breaks. Wren has been taking over some of my shifts so I can focus. Still, I'm not confident I can finish in time, and it reminds me eerily of my time in Brooklyn. I've been neglecting time with Ben, and today I'm making more of an effort to connect with him.

I turn my attention back to why we're both here: to get some fresh air. I need this as much as he does. Staring at the vast expanse of trees, I remember so many afternoons just like this before he got sick, when Ben and I would drive to nearby trails and spend the entire day hiking. We'd pack a picnic lunch, plenty of water, and trek the hardest trails, expertly navigating our way back before sunset. Today we are doing a simple three-mile loop, which used to be our warm-up.

I lightly stretch my legs, realizing I haven't prioritized exercise this last year. I grab a backpack stuffed with food and water, and we set out to the top of the ridge that overlooks a waterfall. The path descends down to the bottom and then winds its way back up to the parking lot.

"Ready?" I ask.

"Born ready." He offers me a goofy grin as he fits a ball cap on.

I lead the way and let these odd few weeks slough from my shoulders as the sweet sounds of nature take over. Nothing but birdsong, fresh air, and the crunch of twigs beneath our boots. In a matter of minutes, we are both in the zone, and I am floored at how winded I am by the time we make it to the bottom.

Ben is breathing heavily as well and sits on a rock. The spray from the water is powerful, and the violent hiss drowns out any chance of conversation. He closes his eyes, whips off his ball cap, and aims his face right toward the spray. I do the same, thrusting my arms wide and allowing the cool mist to lower my body temperature. After a few minutes, we move away from the strong spray and find a giant boulder to spread out on. I unpack our bagged lunches, and we munch thoughtfully, taking it all in.

"I've really missed this," Ben says. "It's the little things, you know?"

I swallow a hunk of sandwich and ball the wax paper in my fist. "Me too." I gesture to the winding path back to the top. "I also miss being in better shape. That incline is going to be a beast."

He squeezes my knee. "You've sacrificed so much for me, Harper. I never wanted you to give up the things you love because of me."

"I haven't," I say all too quickly. But is that true? In this new reality, I work nonstop, especially since Ben is no longer collecting a hefty salary. I've stopped seeing my friends as much, and Ben and I are sometimes like two ships passing in the night, just as I was with Liam in my other life. It wasn't really like that with us before the full moon ritual. "I want to be here," I say. "You'd do the same for me." I also know it's only temporary, but the fact that I won't always be here like this, as Ben's caretaker, shakes me in its relentless fist. Yes, I will get my life back . . . but will it be at the cost of his? Or will it be because he regains his health?

He snorts. "Likely story."

I shove him playfully because we both know he'd drop everything in a heartbeat to take care of me. It's been so strange that in all this time, with all this stress, my health has stayed intact, as if the universe wouldn't possibly throw us too many curveballs to handle. Though lately, I've been more tired than usual.

I search for what to say. I hate keeping things from Ben, and it's been hard for me to separate my before world from this altered after, especially since Ben can't possibly understand what happened to me with that full moon ritual. His not knowing bothers me more than I thought it would. If I've learned anything, it's that I don't want there to be anything left unsaid between us.

"So I had this dream recently," I say. I'm not even sure how I'm going to frame this when I start talking, but I take it one sentence at a time. "Which seemed very real. In it, I was still me, but I was living in Brooklyn, as a working artist and gallery owner. It's like I'd never left New York."

A muscle in Ben's jaw flexes, but he waits for me to continue.

"And though we didn't know each other, you still found me."

His eyes flash to mine.

"In this dream, you were totally healthy. You had beaten cancer, all because of the Dr. Joe Dispenza workshop. You showed up to a big opening I had, and we had an instant connection. You and I went for a walk, and do you know what you said to me when you left?"

Ben only shakes his head, a hint of emotion in his eyes.

"You said, 'I've got all the time in the world.'" I swallow and stare at the gushing waterfall. "I watched you walk away, and I began to wonder if I'd ever see you healthy like that again." I could stop the story right there, but I continue. "And ever since then, I've been wondering if what I experienced could come true. If you could actually be completely healed. If the cancer could be gone." I haven't dared say it out loud until now. "I just can't let it go. I got to see you healthy and happy, and it's stuck with me ever since."

He reaches for my hand.

"Do you think that maybe, when we dream, we're actually living out some alternate version of reality? And that maybe there's another version of you out there somewhere living a healthy life? Even if it's without me?"

"I'm right where I'm supposed to be," he finally says, squeezing my fingers.

"Me too," I say, and I mean it. Still, the question I've been dying to ask lingers, and I know I have to ask it. "Do you think it's possible, though? That you're better?"

He's quiet as he contemplates my question. "Yes," he finally says. "I'm not banking on anything, but I'd be lying if a part of me wasn't hopeful."

That's all I need to hear. And the proof is there. He *has* been feeling better. Since our anniversary, he's been able to do more on his own without my help. That has to mean something. We stare at each other for a few unspoken moments, then gather our trash and stuff it back into my backpack.

"You ready, old man?"

He smirks. "I have a confession," he says as he stands. "This whole cancer thing has just been a ruse so you don't feel so bad when I beat you. I know how competitive you are." This time he blows past me, and I laugh as I try to catch up. Though there are a ton of switchbacks and divots, I tame the impulse to tell him to be careful as we surge upward, my breath becoming thinner with the rising altitude.

Just as we settle into a steadier pace, my heart and brain feeling so much better for having told him some version of my dream, Ben staggers ahead of me and pitches forward on the path.

My heart leaps into my throat. When he doesn't initially jump up, I rush forward and see that his palms are bloody. His nose is gushing blood, and his face is a sickening shade of gray.

"Oh my God." I search around for a nearby hiker, removing my backpack and grabbing a spare T-shirt to help staunch the bleeding. Did he hit his face, or is this just a nosebleed? Ben has never had a nosebleed, and though nosebleeds for the most part aren't dangerous, I know in his case, it could mean something more serious. I remind myself of what is coming, however. Ben is going to get better. Ben is going to beat cancer. This is just a blip. He sits up, and I have him pinch his nose and lean forward to help a clot form. With bloody hands, I find my phone, but my fingers are too slick to make contact. I scream in frustration and tell Siri to dial 911, but there's no service.

I attempt to stay calm and calculate how far we have to go to get to the top. Another half mile, maybe? There's no way he can make it up, but there's also no way I can leave him here. I move him to a rock on the side of the path, though the blood is not slowing. I try to stay calm, though Ben appears on the verge of passing out. Even though he insists he can make it to the top, I know he can't.

Panicked, I'm relieved when a few hikers spring into view. They are laughing and chatting happily as they meander their way toward us, and I rush down the path. They all startle as they take in my bloody appearance. I explain the situation and ask if any of them have reception. They don't. I beg one of them to sit with Ben while I race to the top to try to get service. A young man, Craig, volunteers to do it, and I give Ben a quick kiss and take off toward the parking lot. My legs burn, my lungs are on fire, and I berate myself for bringing him here. What was I thinking? Though Ben has been feeling better, what if he isn't?

Near the top, I finally get a signal and dial 911. I tell them they are going to have to send paramedics about halfway down the path. After a series of back-and-forths about the exact location, which I have no idea of, they promise to send someone. I stay on the line until the ambulance arrives what seems like hours later. Ben is finally fastened on a stretcher and hoisted in the air.

By this time, there's a crowd, and a hush of concern falls among all the hikers. I follow helplessly, not knowing what any of this means. He seemed good today, strong. But I know how good someone can seem and still be sick on the inside.

I tamp down my worries and crawl into the back of the ambulance. I'll have to get my car later. Taking Ben's hand in mine, I find him almost unconscious. I want to scream at the paramedics to tell me what's happening, but no one utters a word.

I have a terrible feeling that something bad is looming, that what I've seen in that other life might not apply here.

What if Ben doesn't get better? What if it *was* all just a dream?

I grip his hand as we careen around corners and bump over potholes. I stare at his bloody face and try to keep hope alive.

But I can feel it slipping through my fingers like sand.

40

Though I fear it's coming, I am still shocked when I hear the words from his oncologist's mouth.

The best thing to do at this point is to make him comfortable, Harper.

I stare into Dr. Abdi's face. I can't make sense of her words, can't understand what she's trying to tell me. As I gaze into her dark, sympathetic eyes, I want to scream that I don't understand. Because, since his workshop, Ben has been doing better, *feeling* better, able to dive into things he hasn't since his initial diagnosis. I want to tell her that I've seen him cured, that I know a miracle is waiting for us. It has to be. Instead, I simply explain that for the most part he's been feeling great.

"I know, Harper, and that's wonderful," she says. "But the truth is, he still has terminal cancer, and when you're in stage four, like Ben, things can turn on a dime. It's just spread too far at this point. I'm so sorry."

She squeezes my shoulder and rushes off to another emergency. *I'm so sorry. I'm so sorry your husband is dying. I'm so sorry your world is about to upend. I'm so sorry miracles aren't reserved for people like you. I'm so sorry you're going to be a widow.* Such ordinary words for what is happening.

I peek into the hospital room and shiver. I've never liked hospitals, but being here reminds me of how far we've come, how much normalcy we have regained since he left this place. Now, as I look at him, weak and resting, I wonder if that was the right decision. Could they have done more for him if we hadn't walked away?

I call Wren and Jenna and ask them to bring me a bag from home. Ben has been asked to stay the night for monitoring, and he's barely been awake long enough to acknowledge where he is.

Inside the room, I watch the whir and beep of machines and then curl up on the window seat, studying the vibrant trees below. I know immediately that things are going to be different this time when we leave the hospital; he's going to need more full-time care. I wonder if I should call hospice.

I drop my head into my hands and cry, softly enough so as not to rouse Ben. When I feel drained of tears, there's a tiny knock on the door, and Jenna and Wren stick their heads in.

"You two just can't stay away from this place, huh?" Wren jokes. They stare at Ben, and I notice Jenna's eyes cloud with emotion. She sets the overnight bag by my feet, and Wren pushes in beside me, Jenna on my other side. They each place a hand on my knee.

I don't say anything. I can't. It's too hard. How could Ben be cured in one world and not in this one? This is the reality that matters, so he has to survive. He must. Too overwhelmed to speak, I lean my head against Jenna's shoulder and cry all over again. It seems my tears are all I've got.

As they hold space for me, my brain buzzes with one awful refrain: *The end is coming; the end is coming; the end is coming.* And I know without a doubt that I'm not ready.

"What can we do for you?" Jenna finally asks.

I wipe my eyes, which feel almost swollen shut. My MO would be to say that there's nothing to be done. This whole time I've hoarded Ben mostly to myself, tucking all the emotions in like sheets on a bed. I've taken care of everything. But I can't do it anymore. It doesn't help either of us. "I need to figure out what we need at home to make him comfortable. He's just been so much better lately . . ." My voice fades in disbelief as I stare at his slight frame in the hospital bed.

Just hours ago, he was ready for a hike. Now the doctors have once again confirmed there's literally nothing else to be done. Is this when a miracle will happen? Is this when everything changes?

"We're here for whatever you need," Wren says. "I know you have a lot on your plate with the show."

I blink at her dumbly. "The show?" I scoff. "There's not going to *be* a show, clearly." I gesture to Ben. "Look at him, Wren. He is the most important thing in the world to me, not some ridiculous solo show."

Wren opens her mouth to speak, but Jenna silences her with a look. "You don't have to do anything you don't want to, okay? Let's just focus on what we need to do next."

I nod and feel the anger drain from my body in one lonely whoosh. "I need to call Ben's mom. Excuse me." I grab my phone and step outside the hospital room, tapping the phone against my blood-stained palm. I have so many people to call, but I am not in the headspace to talk to anyone. With shaking hands, I open the

WhatsApp group we started for Ben with some of his nearest and dearest during his journey. We didn't want to have to constantly keep people up to date via separate texts, so we figured this would be the easiest way. What started as an informational update chain quickly flooded into endless back-and-forth conversations, memes, and inspirational platitudes that would make both of us roll our eyes or laugh hysterically.

I tap out a quick update and then text his mom. She lives in Connecticut and hates to fly. Though I don't want to alarm her, I have no way of knowing how Ben will feel once he's awake. I tell her not to panic and that I will let her know if she needs to fly in after I talk to Ben. Suddenly feeling claustrophobic, I hurry outside, texting Wren and Jenna that I need some air and to let me know if he wakes up.

Night has fallen, and the air is cool. I'm still in my hiking clothes, smeared with Ben's blood. I can smell the tang of pennies mixed with my own sweat. I collapse on a bench and stare at the sky, which, due to the bright hospital lights, is devoid of stars.

I feel wrung out from the inside, unable to reclaim even an ounce of positive thinking. I think of Ben again in that other life, how confident he seemed in his health and recovery.

"I've got all the time in the world."

But it's clear he doesn't have all the time in the world, does he? Despite his positive attitude. Despite the workshop. Despite what I witnessed in Brooklyn. Despite being the picture of health his whole life. Sometimes things just don't work out. Suddenly I open my mouth and let out a frustrated scream, startling a few passersby who jump and worriedly clutch their chests. I don't care. All the rage, grief, and uncertainty pour out of me in one loud, messy rush, and once I start, I fear I can't stop.

It's only when my phone buzzes and my throat is raw that I quiet down, glassy-eyed and almost comatose from exhaustion. It's from Wren.

He's awake.

Darting back inside, a spike of adrenaline clears my brain, like an ice bath. I burst into his room to find Ben sitting up, a lopsided grin on his face.

"Fancy meeting you here," Ben jokes as he adjusts with a tiny grimace.

"Thank God you're awake."

"What happened?" He swallows, and beneath a bit of that bravado, I sense fear lurking.

I glance at Wren. She looks at Jenna and motions toward the door. "We're just going to go grab something to drink. Ben, want a cocktail?"

"Yeah, whiskey, neat," he jokes.

"Coming right up." Wren winks at him, and once they are out of earshot, I let him know what the doctors said.

He nods, silent, and then I grip his hand, which is cold and pale. "Maybe it's time to bring in an at-home nurse."

Ben snatches his hand away. "No. I don't want a nurse."

"But Ben . . ." I'm not sure how to drive home the fact that his organs might stop working, that he could be in excruciating pain, that he could eventually be bedridden.

"I just had a bad day," he says. "That's all." I notice his fingers tremble as he raises one hand to vigorously rub his head. The IV line slithers up his forearm like a snake.

"Okay," I say softly. "I texted your mom. Just to let her know you're here."

He nods, his jaw twitching. "When can I leave?"

"Tomorrow. They just want to keep an eye on your vitals tonight."

Resting his head against the stiff pillow, he sighs. "I really hate it here, Harp."

"I know." I rest my hand on his again, knowing that if I could, I would trade places with him in a second. "We'll go home tomorrow."

"And what if tomorrow never comes?" he asks at last, his eyes sliding lifelessly back to mine. He motions around him. "I don't want to die here."

"No one's dying here. Don't say that."

"Harper, come on." His voice is quiet as he rubs his hand over the back of mine, such a familiar gesture that sends chills through my body. "We both know it's almost time."

My heart cracks wide open, and I simply shake my head through my veil of tears. "You don't know that. We just had a conversation about you feeling better."

"But I'm not better," he says, motioning to the machines. "Clearly." He sighs. "Even so, I don't want to sleep here tonight."

I sit silently for a moment, biting my tongue until I taste the sharp tang of blood. "Okay, let me see what I can do." I pat his knee and go find Dr. Abdi to see if we can discharge him tonight, but the moment I walk into the hall, I burst into a fresh round of tears. Wren and Jenna are coming back with paper cups of water and rush over, fearing the worst. I cling to them like literal lifelines.

All this time, Ben never even hinted once at giving up.

If he's telling me he's running out of time, then I have to believe him.

41

I find myself on my daily walk while Ben takes his afternoon nap.

It's been three weeks, and the turn he's taken is enough to make me heartsick. But if I sit inside, biding my time, I will start to resent everything about my situation and feel unreasonably sorry for myself. Or find ways to get back to that other world, where he was healthy and happy. But I know I can't do that. So I walk.

Wren insists that instead of walking, I should be painting, but I can't bring myself to finish the show. I know I need to; time has never been more of the essence, because this isn't just any random show anymore. It's a show for Ben. It's a show *about* Ben. And yet, at its core, I feel it's still missing something, though I'm not quite sure what.

At the crosswalk, I hesitate, seeing the clump of warehouses ahead where my students are creating. Well, my once-upon-a-time-in-another-life students. Before I did the full moon ritual, Wren was considering a youth show. I may not have been their teacher in this new warped reality, but I can still help them, and I don't have to wait on Wren because I'm part owner of the gallery too. I am able to give back to these kids I've come to know and love in some small way.

After a moment of consideration, I march across the street. I don't even know what day of the week it is, as each day blends into the next, but I cross my fingers that someone is here. I knock on the door, wait anxiously, and finally Kayla appears.

"Can I help you?"

My heart gives a little tug. Always so polite, even to strangers, though I feel like anything but.

"Hi. My name is Harper Swanson Foster, and I am the co-owner of the Terrington gallery." I offer her a card, then peer behind her, but it's dark. "I got wind that you and some students are doing some art here."

She narrows her eyes as she reads my card, but I see the flare of interest at the mention of the Terrington name. "Are we in trouble?"

I laugh. "Far from it. If you're open to it, I'd like to take a look at some of your pieces. I was thinking of doing a youth show, and I'd love to see how we might be able to help you get your art in front of collectors." I don't even know what I'm saying. I'm in no condition to make promises to anyone, but I need to channel some of this helpless energy into doing something good.

She slides the door open, and I'm surprised to find it's only her here today. She wipes a brush dry and walks me around the space. When we get over to a corner, I notice a multimedia display.

"What's all this?" I ask.

"Oh, this is dope. Let me show you." She projects an abstract painting on the wall, hits some buttons, and music gives the effect of causing the painting to undulate in waves. The effect is dreamy, almost like floating beneath an ocean.

Suddenly an idea clicks.

"How would you like to help me with something?" I fill her in on my tribute to Ben—a tribute I'm not even confident I can finish in time—and her face softens.

"I'll talk to the crew," she says. "See what we can do."

I scribble down my info and studio address and ask her and her friends to meet me there in a few days. I can only hope that Leilani and Alejandro will come too. I know that I need to finish what I started, but I'm certain I can't do it alone. I need some inspiration and a wow factor that only these kids can provide.

"Hey, thanks for the opportunity, Mrs. Foster," Kayla says on the way out. "We won't let you down."

"Call me Harper," I say. "And I know you won't. This is your shot, so take it." I wave goodbye and feel marginally better at having connected with one of my former students in some small way. I cannot believe how much I miss being their teacher, being able to help shape their lives and choices.

Every day that passes I wonder what has happened in this life and what hasn't; it makes me feel like I'm on a steady decline to dementia. I second-guess everything. That uncertainty, coupled with Ben's physical deterioration, is enough to do me in. Maybe having these bright, passionate kids involved will infuse me with the necessary energy to finish the show. I can only hope Wren will be on board too.

I check the time and know I need to get back to Ben, but I stop by Wren's first.

"Everything okay?" she asks when she sees me.

"I have a proposition for you." She ushers me inside. I tell her about the underground gallery and how the kids might be able to help with the show.

"I like this," she finally says. "A youth show. I'm not sure why we haven't done that before." She pats my knee. "This is good, Harper. Good work."

I close my eyes and rest my head against her couch. Ben hasn't texted yet, which tells me he's still resting. Part of me dreads going back to the condo. It's so sad and quiet there, especially these last few weeks.

"Another full moon tonight," Wren finally offers. "Sure you don't want to do another ritual?" She's joking, but something she says pricks a deep longing to get back to Brooklyn. Yes, my life was complicated, but I'd found Ben. Healthy Ben. Happy Ben. Very much alive Ben. Suddenly I sit up.

"Wait. Would that be possible? To go back there and just . . . stay?" My heart pounds uncontrollably as I think it. Part of me knows that I can't bypass grief—that it could find me even there, that the cancer could come back, that it could all fall apart. But would I give up this life so Ben could be healthy in another?

Yes. The answer is one thousand percent yes.

Wren scratches her head. "I mean . . . I'm not sure. Technically, maybe? You're not really considering that, are you? I was joking."

I open my mouth to tell her of course not, but the urge is there. I hate seeing Ben so sick, so small, so frail. I hate knowing that he's going to waste away in his bed if a miracle doesn't happen, and soon. I hate that the Dr. Joe Dispenza workshop didn't seem to work in this time line, but I have no idea why. I hate that I'm not a teacher. I hate that I'm an artist and gallery owner and yet I *still* long for something more.

I drop my head into my hands and sigh. "I don't know what I'm doing, Wren. Everything feels so mixed up, and I'm just so exhausted all the time." Tears well in my eyes as I say it. There hasn't really been room for my emotions, especially since the doctor told me that all I could do was make Ben comfortable. Here I am, once again trying to keep it together for both of us. I'm not sure how much longer I can pretend that I'm not falling apart too.

My phone dings, and it's Ben. "I need to go," I say. "Time for Ben's afternoon walk." It kills both of us that he's moved to a wheel-chair because it tires him too much to walk. I don't know how we got here, but we're here, and for the sake of my sanity, I'm trying to adapt and adjust.

Wren walks me to the door. "Harper, you're not really going to do another ritual tonight, are you?" Her eyes are pensive. This version of her hasn't seen what's possible. She doesn't know how powerful those "spells" really are, that by saying a few sentences and setting an intention, I can just disappear somewhere else. And the desire to vanish is so strong, it nearly knocks me over, but I take a deep breath and steady myself before I answer.

"Nah," I say. I wave to her and walk quickly back to my condo. Even as I cast the ridiculous idea aside, when I get inside our apartment and glimpse Ben struggling to get himself into his wheelchair, I truly consider it.

What would Ben want me to do?

Who would Ben want me to save?

"Ready?" I ask too brightly, once again burying my pain.

"Only if you can keep up," he jokes as he slides himself into the chair and grunts with this tiny accomplishment.

I move into place behind him, tears leaking silently down my face.

42

"H old your horses there, Foster," I call to Ben as he wheels himself across the pedestrian bridge.

Normally I'm the one to guide him, but today he has a surge of energy post-nap and wants to lead. I give him these small victories, still glimpsing a bit of the competitor in there.

"Gotta keep up, Swanson. No excuses," he calls breathlessly over his shoulder. His bony arms tremble with the effort.

I jog to catch up. He finally slows as he bumps across the wooden planks. I point to a bench at the end. "Want to stop for a sec?" I have to talk to him about the show, and today seems like a good day.

Ben does not want a nurse at home, but he has been open to pain medication and a wheelchair. As the weeks have passed, his symptoms have worsened, his appetite has all but vanished, and yet he's still managing to take it all in stride the best he can. He still has dark days, and I feel like, deep down, he is waiting for something, some sign, some sense of permission, to let go. And selfishly, I just can't tell him it's okay yet.

When we are situated, we take a moment to soak in the sun before I launch in. "So now that we have found our rhythm with this whole 'Ben on wheels thing,' I wanted to see if you're okay with me still doing my show in August." I'm nervous as I say it, because part of me feels selfish for even thinking about doing the show, but the other part recognizes it's all for him. I need to do this; I need him to see it.

"Harper." He rotates to look completely at me, his hands resting comfortably on the chair rails. I can see the bones in his face, his skin almost translucent in the sun. "I would literally pay you at this point just to get you out of the condo. Yes, please do the show."

"Okay." I laugh. "But who will change your bedpan?"

He gives me a look. We've set up a separate bed with a bedpan, because sometimes he can't make it to the toilet. The jokes have been endless, and Jenna and Wren delight in bringing him bulk boxes of adult diapers. Though we are lighthearted, it's a fact that Ben's identity has been entirely stripped: his strength, his weight, his movement, his energy, even his work with the cancer foundations has slowed to a crawl. It amazes me how he's coping. I glance at the water, tamping down my emotion.

"So," Ben says, "after all the dust settles, what are you going to do first?"

I know what he means by *dust*. The dust is the aftermath: after his passing, after the grief has lessened its hold on me, after I'm supposedly "back to normal," whatever that means. I shrug. "A threesome, maybe?"

"Good one." He bursts into a laugh, which causes him to cough. He waits until it subsides and sighs. "Seriously. Have you thought about it?"

I cock a shoulder, then let it drop. "I'll probably sell the condo, like we talked about. I don't think I can be there . . ." *After you're gone.*

The condo has now transformed into its own version of a hospital, and every time I step through the door, I feel physically ill, which I've learned is quite normal with caretakers. But lately my appetite seems as lackluster as his, and I can't seem to shake this exhaustion.

"And what about this show of yours? Going to take it on the road, you think?"

"If Wren thinks it's ready, then who knows?" Ben doesn't know the show is a tribute to him. I already know I'm not selling any of the originals. Wren has discussed doing reprints so I can make some extra money besides the original ticketed price, but I can't imagine people, beyond Ben's friends, family, and fans, wanting to purchase anything, even though, thanks to Liam's article, Ben has become internet famous. We both have. However it goes, perhaps it can still be a launching pad to something new.

"What about a cat?"

I scrunch my nose. "Too conditional."

"Dog?"

"Too much work."

He laughs again. "Goldfish?"

"Typical life span?"

"Like a day if you forget to feed it."

I smile. "Perfect."

Truthfully, I can't imagine taking care of anything else, not even a home. Part of me has thought about traveling for a while, just selling everything I own and hitting the road, kind of like Ben did in that other life. But that sounds exhausting too, and I know I can't simply outrun the pain. I need to sit with it, feel it, go through it, even if I don't want to.

We fall into amicable silence, and for some reason, my heart begins to pound. I can feel myself emotionally preparing for the end. Until recently, deep down I still held out hope for a miracle. That image of him in Brooklyn is forever seared in my memory. I still remember the weight of him when we hugged, the mischief in his eyes. Watching him decline in front of me has been the most brutal part of this entire experience.

"I've got all the time in the world."

After a few more minutes, we continue on and sit in the park. I'm reminded of the day we got tattoos and rode the carousel. Was that only a couple of months ago? It seems like years. I thought that had been the worst of it, that we were facing something hard, but I had no idea how hard it would get.

Ben perches on the edge of the grass and tips his face to the sun. He closes his eyes, and I watch his shallow breathing. He doesn't know that I watch him sleep most nights, absolutely terrified that he will go and I will miss it. I memorize him now, as my heart leaps wildly in my chest. The silence stretches between us, its own private conversation.

It's okay to let go.
Please hang on.
Don't leave me.
Find your peace.

The sentiments clash for space in my tired brain, battling for top position. I close my eyes too, attempting to regulate my breathing, even though I constantly feel drained yet wired, always hovering on the edge of sleep. I know I need to take better care of myself, but I can't. I am so tethered to this situation, I don't know where Ben ends and I begin.

Before I know it, Ben is fast asleep. This happens a lot, though rarely when we are out. I situate myself in the grass beside him and lie back, staring at the bright blue sky. I close my eyes and listen to the children squeal and play, their heavy footsteps ripping through the grass. I think about my suggestion that we should have a baby and what that would mean for both of us, especially now. When I broached the topic, Ben hadn't yet taken a turn for the worse. Has he forgotten about it?

Regardless, life thrums all around, a beautiful melody. A few tears drain from my eyes onto the ground beneath me. I roll my head to check on Ben, but he is fast asleep. I know I will need to get him out of the sun soon so he doesn't get burned, but he's not getting enough fresh air lately, unless it's on our balcony. Sometimes he sits there for hours, staring at nothing.

The deepest edges of grief burrow their way in, filling my heart, body, and mind until there's no more space. I hold my breath, suck it all in, and then swallow it down because I have to. Before I can stop myself, my mind slips back to the ritual. I could easily concoct a new dream or a new wish. That Ben and I are together. That he is perfectly healthy. That we live happily ever after. Could it be that easy? My heart begins to beat even faster as I consider such a simple wish. If I get the wording just right, then maybe it could all work out for everyone in the end?

After a little longer, I wake him, and we move silently back to the apartment. That burst of energy has leaked out of him like a deflated balloon. I can already tell he will sleep for the rest of the day. We've made more than a few jokes about him sleeping as much as a cat, except that he can't clean himself. Today is not a day for jokes.

Once I tuck him into his bed, kiss his cheek, and turn on his white noise machine, I busy myself with chores. I do a load of laundry, scrub the countertops and floors. I put a chicken in the Crock-Pot. I stand out on the balcony until nightfall, thinking of nothing and everything; then I eat alone at our dining room table as tears mix with my food. I cry as I chew, trying to muffle my anguish so Ben won't hear me in the other room.

My appetite gone, I attempt watching a movie to take my mind off the fact that tonight is the full moon and that I could probably make all this go away if I really wanted to.

When it's after eleven and I am still wide-awake, my phone buzzes. It's Wren.

Harp, you're not going to do that ritual tonight, right?

I sigh as more tears leak down my cheeks. I want to be able to tell her no. I understand that I can't just escape into another world when things get hard. But what if that is the ultimate lesson I'm here to learn? That there is another way out where everyone can be happy?

I just need more time with him, Wren, I type back. *I can't lose him. I'm not ready.*

The text bubbles appear, then disappear before one simple sentence steals my breath.

You're never going to be ready, Harper.

I know she's right, but before I can stop myself, I find a scrap piece of paper and write down my new wish.

I want to be happy with Ben. I want Ben to be healthy. I want to have as many years with him as I can.

I consider the language, wondering if the universe could interpret this in some strange way where it won't give me exactly what I want, just like the first time. I have to be precise with my words, this I know. I scribble out those sentences and try again. Before I get anything new written down, Wren is calling. I sigh but pick up.

"You're writing down a new wish, aren't you?"

"Maybe."

"Harper, listen. If this is what you really want to do, I'll support you. I'll go grab the book, we can wait until midnight, and you can disappear again. But I think you should stay."

I scoff. "Why?"

She's so quiet, I fear I've lost the connection. "Because *this* Ben needs you. *This* life needs you. *This* is where you belong, Harper. You said so yourself: you went away, and when you came back, you changed things somehow. What if this is the place you need to be, right here, right now?"

I want to tell her that it was so much easier in the other life. No real life-threatening dramas to attend to, no emergencies—just a relationship to maintain and a gallery to save. After a year of hardship, I want it to be easy. For me. For Ben. Don't we both deserve that?

"I don't want to be here anymore," I say. "It's too painful."

"It won't always be this hard," she says.

I sigh. "How do you know that?"

"Because grief doesn't last forever. Because time really does help. Because you can't outrun pain. Or avoid it. I'm telling you, Harper. The braver thing to do is to stay. Face it. Face it all the best you can."

"I just want it to stop," I finally whisper. "I can't keep pretending it's all okay. I just can't."

"So stop pretending," she says. "No one is asking you not to feel your feelings. Channel them. Use them. Paint them."

I roll my eyes, because leave it to Wren to always turn it back to painting somehow. "I'm not sure I can this time."

"Well, I know you can. You are Harper Swanson Foster. You can do anything, even time-hop."

Despite the sadness, I laugh. "This is true," I sniff.

"But just because you can doesn't mean you should, okay? Look, you've seen a glimpse of what your future could have been. You're back now, and you have most of what you wanted, right? But no one gets their happily ever after, Harper. Life isn't a fairy tale, no matter how much you want it to be."

"I don't want a fairy tale," I whisper. "I just don't want my husband to die."

"I know, babe," she says. "I know."

She stays on the phone with me as I watch the living room clock inch closer to midnight. When it's five until twelve, she clears her throat.

"So what's the verdict, sis?"

I stare at the blank piece of paper. I could write down three new sentences, grab a candle, and convince her to take me through the ritual. I know I could. Instead, I stand and walk to the edge of the bedroom to check on Ben. I can hear the shallow whoosh of air moving in and out of his lungs, mixing with the noise machine. I move closer to him, stroke his angular cheek, and move a hand through his hair that has grown back long enough to style. Here, in this bed, is my whole world. My whole heart, as if beating outside my chest, hangs by a thread, and there's a very tangible way I could help him. There's an *actual* solution to make this all go away.

"I want him to stop hurting," I whisper now into the phone.

"Him or you?"

I know she's right. I want us both to stop hurting. Right now. I stand there, on the precipice of making it all better or sticking it out. I don't know what to do.

"It's midnight," Wren finally whispers. I can hear the relief in her voice. "Get some rest, Harper. I love you both." The call disconnects, and I begin to cry all over again, smothering the sound behind my fist.

I don't want to stay here, but it seems I've made my choice. This man, this version of Ben, needs me. I can't walk away. I can't take the easy way out.

Maybe that means there's still a miracle in store. Or maybe not.

Either way, it seems I'm destined to find out.

43

It's the night of my solo show, and I'm a nervous wreck.

  I'm running late to the gallery, though Wren and I have checked and triple-checked that everything is perfectly in place. Thanks to Alejandro, Leilani, Kayla, and the rest of the art crew, they have added some incredible effects I never could have achieved on my own, and even built a wheelchair ramp to boot. Ben has no idea what the show is about; nor does he know I've invited all of his closest friends and family to be here, some who have flown a long way to see him.

  Once Ben is out of the car and in his wheelchair, I push him up to the entrance. I am worried that by inviting all of his friends and family, it will signify something: not just a gathering, but an ending. Ben is down to a hundred and forty pounds, though he still looks sharp in a suit and a checkered bowtie. I'm wearing a long jumpsuit with the same pattern, my hair wavy and wild, and he has told me no less than five times how beautiful I look tonight. I'm on edge for so many reasons, but mainly I just want this night to be perfect for him. For us.

  When we approach the gallery, I stop. There is no large production tonight like at Rita Clementine's gallery, no line of influencers out the door. This is a private event, and everyone is already inside. This whole night, this whole show, is about him.

"I just want you to know how much I appreciate your support around this show the last couple of months," I say. "I know it's taken up a lot of my time."

"Harper." He grips my hand and stares deeply into my eyes. "You are doing what you love. I support you completely. You know that." He squeezes my fingers. "I'm so proud of you." He releases me and gestures toward the door. "And I can't wait to see what you've created that you've been so hush-hush about."

"Famous last words, Foster." I yank open the door and wheel him inside. As he crosses the threshold, a chorus of "Surprise!" echoes off the stark white walls.

I move beside him to clock the look on his face, which is awash with shock. Everyone he truly cares about is here in one space. Ben barely has time to register what's happening before his loved ones rush him, crouching down to enclose him in tight hugs and clap him on the back. His face is wrecked from raw emotion, and I hope I haven't done the wrong thing by inviting so many people here. Yes, this is a celebration, but it could also be viewed as a goodbye party, cementing his inevitable departure from us all. Even though I know that, I'm not giving up hope. Not yet.

He finds me in the crowd and reaches back for my hand. "Harper. I don't understand. Why is everyone here for me? Tonight is about you."

"No," I say, steering him toward the main gallery floor, where my pieces are positioned to tell his story. "Tonight is about you."

Alejandro hits the lights and the music. Kayla and Leilani helped orchestrate the audio production, which has taken this show to a new level. They stand back, excited to see their work in real time.

This is the moment I will remember: watching Ben's face as he registers the content of my show, how the story starts when he is young and blossoms through hormones, health, success, love, heartbreak, and sickness. There is a projected image of him as a boy that dances all around us, singing a sweet song his mom recorded when he was five years old. In the middle, he forgets the lyrics, then makes up his own before bursting into giggles. It plays on a loop, synced with the musical piece he composed for his own departure, "The Last Song." The sounds blend and crash into each other, creating a truly powerful effect.

Ben presses a trembling hand over his mouth. The image of him distorts and drifts across the walls, then explodes into stardust. And then he begins again, reborn, repurposed. It is a living, breathing installation of his complete infiniteness. No beginning and no end. In this place, in this moment, he lives forever.

The crowd falls completely silent as he rolls himself forward and gingerly reaches out to touch each piece, to read their descriptions. He marvels, soaking it all in, and then he openly begins to cry.

My heart breaks for him as I step forward and lightly touch his back. He rotates and clings to me until the tears subside. "I can't believe you did this for me," he says, finally pulling back to stare at the pieces again. "I just can't believe it."

"Believe it," I say. "You make a pretty great muse, Foster."

He kisses me softly.

"Now you get to listen." I steer him to a spot near the makeshift stage at the front.

For the next hour, people tell stories about Ben, their greatest adventures, the tender moments, the hilarious tomes about this man who is so deeply loved. Then it's my turn, and I move toward the stage and the bright lights, unsteady and emotional. Wren hands me the microphone, and I soak in the crowd, proud of what I've put together.

"First of all, thank you all for coming. Ben hates crowds, but this one I know he loves." I wink at him and then gather my words. "As all of you were talking, it dawned on me that almost everyone in this room has known Ben much longer than I have. Your history cuts deeper. You've known different versions of him, but at the same time, I feel like I know him best of all. I mean, it *is* a competition, after all." I'm grateful for the laughs as I turn to Ben and vow to keep my voice in check. "I have loved you ever since the moment I beat you at that obstacle race," I say to another chorus of laughter. "It's like we both knew we would begin a different race . . . also against the clock; in so many ways, we have moved at warp speed, but I am so grateful that we did." I walk everyone through our early adventures and travels. "When Ben was diagnosed, we were obviously shocked, but we thought, 'Okay, challenge accepted.' And despite doing everything humanly possible, here we are." A somber hush falls across the gallery, until I find the right words to continue. "Though I can't possibly know how our story ends, I do know that this situation has taught us to stay present for each and every moment. It has taught us what's important, *who's* important, and that we need to love our people as fiercely as we can. While we can." Liam's article pops to mind, as he wrote something similar. A few tears slip down my cheeks, but I stare right at Ben. "No matter what happens, it has been a privilege to journey with you, Benjamin Adam Foster. Today, tomorrow, and for as long as we have left."

Before I can move off stage, Ben wheels up the ramp and I move to embrace him as the crowd watches. A few sniffles break the spell as he gently takes the microphone.

"Well, let's not think for a second I'm going to let Harper have the last word," he says, looking up at me. "This competitive streak runs deep, y'all. Even if I am in a wheelchair." I playfully poke him and move to the front of the crowd as he wheels himself to center stage. "Tonight is an absolute gift," he begins, clearing the emotion from his voice. "My lovely wife has been with me through this cancer journey from the start, as you all know. But what you may not know is that she has never wavered, never complained, and has made me feel loved, protected, and seen the entire time. That is the real gift."

I smile at him and nod in a silent salute.

"But this . . ." He gestures around him. "This is a reminder of the life I *have* lived. The people I *have* loved. The amazing things I *have* done. It has been a short life, much shorter than I would like, but it has been a good one. A full one. A meaningful one." There are a few more sniffles from the audience before he continues. "Facing the end is not something any of us can rationalize. We all know it's coming for each and every one of us." He points into the crowd. "Especially you, Josh. Maybe sooner rather than later, if you keep jumping out of planes. Heed my warning." He gestures to his wheelchair.

Josh hoots from the crowd.

"But to really sit with that, to come to terms with your own transition . . . It is a big moment, and in its own right, it is also a gift." He sighs. "I don't want to leave this life. I don't want to leave all of my most beloved friends and family. I don't want to think about not waking up every day next to my beautiful wife, or going on a bike ride or a run, or helping others in a similar position, or composing something truly amazing. These are the things I love, but they are also the things I must let go."

Everyone is crying. I stand between his mom, his sister, and my parents, who drove here from Ohio.

"I just want each and every one of you to know how much you've meant to me along the way. Whether I see you frequently or just once in a while, you matter to me." Ben stops talking and takes time to make eye contact with each and every one of us. "You matter. And you matter. And you matter." When he gets to me, his voice breaks. "And to my beautiful bride, I know we are short on time, but it has been the best time of my life. Even when it was the worst. You make everything better. You have made me better, and I will miss you most of all."

The tears flow freely, and I don't even bother to wipe them away. He wheels himself back down the ramp and is once again embraced by countless individuals.

"Now, let's see some art!" Wren cues the music, and the show resumes as people mingle and sample some of Ben's favorite foods I had made by a local chef. Wren shows people how to move through each exhibit, and after Ben has seen all of the pieces, I seize the opportunity to steal him away.

I push him to a separate part of the gallery. As a surprise, I'm going to show him the final piece, which is one of my favorites. Everyone signed their names in a particular way, so that when you step back, it composes a silhouette of his body. It is a wildly creative piece, one he will hopefully cherish.

"I didn't think I had this much salt left in my system," he whispers, wiping away more tears. "Where are you taking me, woman?"

"I have a surprise that's just for you," I say, leading him toward the art.

"Wait. I have something for you first." He wheels himself to face me and fishes in his pocket for something. He pulls out a long, flat box. I squint to see what it is and laugh in shock.

"A pregnancy test?"

He looks at me with tears still in his eyes. "Yes, Harper. You haven't been eating. You're exhausted and nauseous all the time. I know it's been a lot since I've, you know, taken a turn, but I really think you should take this."

My heart slams around wickedly in my chest. Could I really be pregnant? I know we talked about starting a family, but that feels like ages ago. I try to remind him that I haven't skipped a period, but as I think back, I can't remember if I had one last month or not. I do some quick calculations in my head and look at him. "Oh shit," I say.

"Go." He hands me the box and points to the women's bathroom.

My hands are shaking as I let myself into the single stall. The watch Ben gave me slides up and down my wrist as I open the box. My hands find my stomach and press lightly. Could there be life in here? Surely not . . .

As I take the test and set a timer on my watch, I think about what Ben said he wanted in that other life: a family, a home. Could we both actually get what we want, even if it's only temporary?

Ben knocks on the door. "You're really going to make me wait out here?"

"Give me a second," I call.

I feel like I'm going to be sick. What will I do if I'm actually pregnant? I know the probability is small, infinitesimal even. The timer goes off. I take a deep breath and grab the stick but don't look at the results yet. When I open the door, Ben is practically jumping out of his skin to know.

"Well?"

"Here. You look first. I can't." I thrust the stick in his hands and then bend forward at the waist. "Why am I so nervous?" I stand back up and shake out my hands. I watch his face as he reads the results.

"Harper . . ." He says my voice so softly, it's barely a whisper. And I know. I know before he turns it around to show me. I know from the look on his face.

"I'm pregnant," I say out loud for the very first time.

"You're pregnant," he confirms.

Suddenly it all makes sense. He's right. How could I have missed the signs? My hands drop to my stomach again, where new life has begun. Part me and part Ben. *This* has to be the ultimate lesson in faith.

After the initial shock, Ben erupts into the biggest grin I've ever seen. "You're really pregnant? With *my* baby?"

I roll my eyes. "Yes, with your baby." I lean in to kiss him and step forward so he can gingerly cradle my stomach.

"I can't believe I'm getting my wish," he says now, ogling my belly.

"What do you mean?" I ask.

"I wanted you to love someone new before I left." He smiles up at me. "Maybe this is the person I was waiting for all along."

I smile at the sentiment. "Maybe you're right."

His face shifts and tears slide freely down his cheeks. "I have to be here," he says as he presses his lips to my stomach, then stares up at me again. "I have to see this baby come into the world."

"So do it," I say, a mischievous grin on my face. "You have a reason to live, Foster. So live."

Slowly, he pulls away and stares at me with more intensity than I've ever seen. "Challenge accepted," he says. "I'm all in."

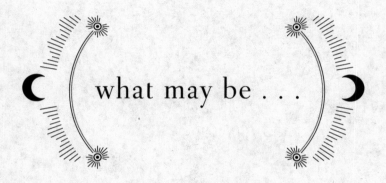

what may be . . .

Epilogue

A few years later . . .

Tonight is a big night.

Benjamin Jr. is taking a nap, though he has been a trouper while I get ready for my final *The Last Song* show. Our nanny, Gertrude, makes him an early dinner and will bring him by the gallery later, once the initial rush dies down.

Our apartment in Dumbo isn't anything fancy, but I love it more than I've ever loved another home. Ben helped me pick it out online before he passed away. Despite all the doctors' predictions, he made it all the way until Benjamin's birth. He could barely speak at the end, but he got to hold his son. He looked into his eyes. He witnessed the miracle of his legacy, living and breathing. And for him, that was enough.

When Benjamin turned one month old, Ben looked at me in bed and scribbled a few lines on his small whiteboard he carried around his neck.

> *I'm tired, Harp. I've hung on for as long as I can. I've met my son. I've loved you with all of my heart. And I know you are both going to have a spectacular life. I'll see you in the next life.*

He kissed me once, went to sleep, and never woke up.

The emotion of that day still takes my breath away sometimes, but I am also grateful. I received so much more time with him than I ever thought possible. I am lucky. Benjamin Jr. is lucky. We are all lucky.

Little did I know that my private show of Ben would blow up to sizable proportions and be shown across the country, largely thanks to Liam's article and Wren's connections on every coast.

Once I moved to Dumbo, I marched right to Rita Clementine's gallery and all but demanded a second chance. Luckily, she'd already caught wind of the show and dedicated half of her gallery to it, and now, after a year of showing it around the country and three months at Rita's gallery, I am retiring Ben's work and moving on to something new. I've been doing guest teaching gigs at galleries nationwide, and I'm thrilled I've found my way back to teaching in some capacity, even if it's not in a classroom.

Tonight is the last night that these pieces will be displayed, and it is a bittersweet moment for us all. I take my time getting dressed, creep into Benjamin's room, and smooth the hair from his sweet face while I watch him sleep.

Memories flood my system: my surprisingly easy pregnancy, the way Ben came alive at being able to help massage my feet or satisfy my wicked cravings, then holding my hand from his wheelchair while I pushed his son into the world. But he missed other things: Benjamin's first smile, his first cuddle, his first steps, his first word (*baba*). Being a mother has rocked me to my core and given me purpose in a way I've never known. And getting to raise Ben's son . . . Well, it's a privilege I don't take lightly.

I lean forward to stroke his soft cheek. The watch Ben gave me catches the light. I think about the engraving: *You're the only woman who makes me forget about time*. The concept of time has changed, stretched, warped, and created some seemingly impossible outcomes, but here I am anyway. I have survived.

After confirming that Gertrude will bring Benjamin by shortly after the show starts, I walk the short distance to Rita's gallery. I pass by Liam's loft and stop, as I often do, to think about what happened in those sacred dreams of mine. We haven't kept in touch, mainly because I blocked his number, though he did fly in for the memorial after Ben's passing. He offered his condolences, but that was that. Opening that door again felt too dangerous, though as time has trekked on, I have thought of him often, hoping he's well.

Being on my own these last three years has been necessary. I needed to learn to be by myself again. I've lived for my art and my son, and allowed myself ample time to grieve.

Rita is waiting outside for me, and I get the strangest sense of déjà vu as we both step inside. I smile, as I always do, when I get to see every version of my husband mounted on these walls.

"Excited?" she asks.

"Extremely," I say. Though we have become friendly these last few months, I still have never asked her what I wanted to ask her about that night so long ago. I place a hand on her arm, because this is the end of the line for us, and if I don't ask now, I probably never will. "Rita," I say. "I want to ask you something."

She turns, and I can see the flicker of impatience in her eyes. Rita is nothing if not focused, and I know her mind is on other things. But this is important. This question has haunted me for such a huge chunk of my life, and regardless of the answer, I am ready to know.

"That day I dropped off the painting at your apartment," I say.

"You mean the day you disappeared," she corrects.

I open my mouth, then close it. "Well, sure. Technically, yes." I take a deep breath. "I just need to know. Why wasn't it good enough?" *Why wasn't I good enough?* Despite how hard I've worked on myself, and how far I've come, that doubt still lingers, like a fading scar.

To my surprise, Rita scoffs. "My dear Harper, it *was* good enough. But you left."

My brain scrambles to think back. The only communication I ever received from Rita was a terse email asking if I had a preferred address to return the piece to. "But you emailed me," I explain. "And you said it was a shame it didn't work out."

She crosses her arms and really looks at me. "Yes, it was a shame it didn't work out because *you* left, Harper. After I told you I'd be in touch, which *means*," she emphasizes, "that you stay and you wait. But then Kendall told me you scurried back to Chicago because of some boy. And I figured if you left before you even knew what I thought about your work, then you weren't really serious about the opportunity in the first place. So." She flicks her fingers, her heavy rings catching the gallery lights. The explosion of color reminds me of how the sea glass had caught the light through her window, how much I'd loved that unexpected effect. Yet I never asked for the piece to be returned because it was too painful a reminder of how I'd let my dreams slip away. Sensing the conversation is over, she takes a step in the opposite direction, but I stop her.

"But I was serious," I say now.

"Harper." She steadies me with her steely gaze and tents her fingers around narrow hips. "I decided long ago that I have a knack for finding talent. But I'm not going to chase someone who isn't ready for the opportunity." She motions behind her to the show. "You clearly weren't ready for it then. But you are now."

Her words ring in my ears, and though I don't want to beat a dead horse, I still have to know. "Does that mean you *were* going to give me a shot?"

It's the one question I haven't asked, because I always assumed it was a blatant no. The quick dismissal, never hearing anything beyond that email, just like I never heard from Liam. I always thought it was a rejection . . . but now I'm wondering, what if it wasn't?

Rita's blood-red lips curl into the slightest hint of a smile. "Do you know what I thought when I walked into my gallery that day? When I first saw your piece?"

I've waited almost fifteen years for this answer, nearly fifteen years of wanting to know this single piece of feedback. "What?" My voice comes out a whisper.

"I literally thought, 'She's going to be a star.' You surprised me. I was expecting a simple portrait or some piece of pottery, but you brought that bridge to life. You brought the girl in it to life. It was magic. I still have it displayed in my home gallery, in fact."

"You do not." The fact that I left Liam and his loft and that painting has never been lost on me. It always felt as though pieces of me, just like the sea glass, were still here, waiting to be reclaimed.

"I do. And I think you should show it. You should create the show that you intended to back then, but from your perspective now.

Because, my dear, you're not just a visitor here anymore, are you?" She grips my elbow and then disappears as someone calls to her.

I am floored. It seems I wasted years of my life thinking I wasn't good enough professionally, when really I'd sabotaged my own success. But perhaps she's right. Perhaps I wasn't ready for it then. If my dream had come true, as I saw in that other life, I might never have married Ben. I never would have had his son. I never would have created this show, which means so much more to me than any other. Maybe it all worked out just as it should. Maybe now *is* the right time.

As I contemplate my life with all its twists and turns, I attempt to get myself in the zone. I have a ritual of taking a moment to talk to Ben before every show. I grip his wedding band, which hangs on a chain around my neck, coupled with mine. I issue him a quick hello, kiss it once, then step onto the gallery floor.

The show goes off without a hitch. I greet people and answer questions, and I am tired and ready to go home by 8:00 p.m., but I know it's going to be a late night because it's the last. I wave as Gertrude and Benjamin Jr. rush inside, and I scoop him up, depositing kisses all over his face.

"Mama, stop!" He giggles. "Listick." His sweet, husky lisp warms my heart.

"Oh, so sorry, big man," I say, smearing some of it away. He grips my hand, and I walk him through the show as I always do, regaling him with stories about his father. Each piece has a particular story. He is only three, but I want to reinforce these details of his father's life, keeping him with us, alive in our thoughts and conversation.

As we snake back to the front, Benjamin yawns. I release his hand, and he runs back to Gertrude.

"You two can go on home. No need to stay."

"But it's the last show," she says. "You sure?"

"This little one needs to go to bed, don't you?" I say, dropping down to tickle Benjamin. He looks so much like Ben as a boy, and in my deepest moments of grief, I look into his eyes and remember that Ben is still here. He lives on in his son.

I kiss Benjamin goodbye and continue on until the very last person has left the building. Rita and her staff gather around as we make a final toast, which includes Kendall. It's odd seeing her again, but it's been nice to reconnect. As I'm getting ready to leave, I pull Rita aside. The exhaustion is evident on her face, but I can tell she is proud, satisfied even.

"Thank you for giving me another shot," I say, shrugging into my coat. "I've waited for this a very long time."

"I know you have. And I believe you're ready for it this time, yes?"

I consider her question, really take it in. After a beat, I nod. "Yes, I am."

"Come by anytime, Harper Swanson," she says. "My door is always open to you."

For some reason, that hits me in the most vulnerable place, and I clear the emotion from my voice as I tell her goodbye. Outside, the cool fall air reminds me of my first week here. It still fills me with joy, this place. This moment. I stare up at Rita's gallery one more time and begin walking west. I will collect the pieces in the coming days and have to decide where they will live. But for tonight, I lose myself to my thoughts and take a moment to feel proud of how far I've come. I am living in the place I love, doing what I love, surrounded by love.

I grip Ben's wedding band again and stop on the street corner. With a small start, I realize I've walked toward Liam's loft. Memories flood my brain faster than I can catch them. My first week here. All that promise. The way I sabotaged my happiness by walking away. My dream life. Sometimes I struggle to remember which parts are real and which aren't. I glance up to where Liam's loft is and see soft light pouring in through the window. Does he still live here?

Before I can contemplate what I'm doing, I cross the street and approach his buzzer. I search for his last name, the dingy scrap of paper that says *Hale*. It is still there, written in a sloppy, cursive rush. Relief washes through me as I stab the button with nervous hands. While I wait for his voice on the other end, I wonder if it will be someone else who answers.

During those uncertain few seconds, I think about turning around and running home. But I've done so much running in my life. I'm ready to stand still, to face my life and choices. I'm ready to take this step, to move beyond the what-ifs, to finally know what we are, even if it hurts, even if it doesn't work out between us.

"Hello?"

Liam's voice fills the most defenseless spaces, at once so familiar and also completely new. He is a reminder . . . of this place, of what we once were, of what we could have been. Am I really ready to open that door? I close my eyes, open them, and take a deep breath. Yes, I'm ready. Ready for it all. No matter what it costs.

"It's Harper."

Stand in Your Power Full Moon Ritual

Created by Leslie Garbis
Singingishealing.com/ IG: @singingishealing

Stand in your power, fully seen and illuminated
by the full moon and say goodbye to that which is not in
perfect alignment, making room for what is.

The full moon is tied to our inner emotions. It can reveal what is
hidden and bring it to light. Think of your emotions like water, and
how the moon leads the tides and rules the waters. Remember that
the energy of the full moon helps show you in your fullness and also
shines a bright light on things that could be released.

For this simple ritual, you will need:
intentional time and space
a pen
a small piece of paper
a burning bowl, firepit, bonfire, or a bowl of water
a lighter
your intention of release

The Ritual

Create spaciousness in your schedule. Set a sacred space with candles and beautiful things that please you. Get comfortable and tune into the present moment. Breathe deeply. Feel yourself truly *seen* and bathed in the glow of the full moon. Now ask yourself:

What may be standing in the way of my most expansive self?
What could be lovingly and intentionally released?

Write it on a slip of paper. Speak or sing out loud: "I release __ with pure love and consciousness. And so it is."

Burn the paper and drop it into the burning bowl/firepit /bonfire/bowl of water. Breathe deeply and know that it is so. Give gratitude to yourself and to the full moon. Go make notes in your journal of what you released and why it no longer serves you. Jot down anything else that comes up.

Other Thoughts:

A full moon bath can be a great idea, connecting you to powerful lunar energies.

Cleanse and recharge your crystals under the full moon to release any negative energy they may have picked up during the month. Simply place them outside on the ground or on a windowsill to be fully exposed to the moonlight overnight.

Go outside and bathe in the moon's glow. Make yourself comfortable outside on the ground or on a deck or patio . . . and let the moonglow wash over you. Pay attention to your breath and feel yourself in your most expanded form under the powerful witnessing and illumination of the moon.

Acknowledgments

This was a very special book to write, and it couldn't have happened without the following people:

Rachel Beck, literary agent: You have been my literary agent since 2016, and you are the best partner I could ask for on this wild, unpredictable journey. You have let me shine, ask questions, be hopeful, sit in disappointment, pivot, rest, try new things, and say yes to what feels good and no to everything else. Thank you for all you have done for me and for never losing your enthusiasm for me or my work. You are such a champion, and I appreciate you more than you can possibly know.

Kimberly Carlton, editor: You are such a gift in my life. Your sharp eye, insight, understanding, compassion, enthusiasm, and belief in me and my work mean so very much. You really understand and hear what I am saying as both a writer and a human, and I could not be luckier to have you as my editor. I hope we can continue to take this journey together!

Julie Breihan, copyeditor: Once again, you have taken my words and made them into something better. Your insights are so specific and bring a level of magic to every line. Thank you a thousand times.

Amanda Bostic, publisher: It is so rare that you get to know your *actual* publisher. A publisher who shows up to your events, who champions your work, who fights for her authors. I respect and admire all that you do for writers, and I consider myself so lucky to be part of the Harper family.

Nekasha Pratt, head of marketing: Nekasha, you are one of the kindest, most positive, professional women in publishing. You make everyone feel so seen, welcome, and excited, and I am over the moon I get to work with you.

Kerri Potts, marketing director: You are so phenomenal at what you do, and I just genuinely enjoy spending time with you. From every social media panel you drag me onto, to our random, real conversations, I love that you are part of my world. Also, get your damn phone out of your bedroom and go get some sun. Pretty please.

Taylor Ward and Caitlin Halsted, publicity and editing: I appreciate everything that goes on both publicly and behind the scenes to make a book come to life, and you two work so tirelessly to make it all happen. Thank you.

Margaret Kercher, publicity director: Even though we don't live in the same town, I feel how hard you work for your authors. Your excitement and enthusiasm mean the world to me. I feel good things await us for this book, and I know you have a lot to do with what happens, so thank you.

Tanya Farrell and Emily Afifi, Wunderkind PR: I feel so lucky to work with such smart, capable women who lift up authors, keep us organized, and send us to the right events. The work you do can literally make the difference between a book's success or flying under the radar. I feel your efforts, and I thank you for them.

Micah Kandros, cover designer: When I saw the cover of this book, I literally gasped. Of all my book covers, this is my absolute favorite. Thank you for making the magic of this book come to life.

Jackie Hritz, freelance editor: You have pored over my early drafts for so many books, and I'm always thrilled to receive your feedback, because your insights always make my work so much better. Thank you for all you do for writers everywhere.

Court Stevens, author + friend: You are such an inspiration to me, as both an author and a human. I feel like we met when I was on the cusp of figuring out where I wanted to go with this whole author thing, and you've reminded me to let go, have fun, and play by my own rules. I love you. Let's please write our queer vampire trilogy.

Jennifer Moorman, author + friend: What a gift you are in my life. We have not only become great friends but we are simply blowing shit up . . . together. If that's not magic, I don't know what is. This is just the beginning for us, friend. Buckle up and get ready to cash those checks.

Joe and Anna Tower, muses and friends: You inspired so much of this book, not just because of your journey but for how deeply you have loved each other through it all and how resilient, honest, and dedicated you both have been. I miss you, I love you, and I'm rooting for you both. Always.

Janina Lawrence, Susannah Harris, Casey LeVasseur, Alyssa Rosenheck, Lauren Lowery, Sara Goodman Confino, Asia Mathis, Leslie Garbis, Vanessa Lillie, Melissa Collings, Christy Lynn, friends: Thank you for the support. Thank you for the conversations. Thank you for showing up. Thank you for your genuine friendship. I love you all.

Leslie Conliffe, film agent, IPG: I am so grateful to be part of the IPG family and see where these books can end up! (Fingers crossed that we will see one of these babies on screen someday.)

Dr. Joe Dispenza, Dr. Paul Saladino, Wayne Dyer, Abraham Hicks, Michael Beckwith, Dr. Shefali Tsabury, and Lacey Phillips,

healers, teachers, mentors: You have all changed my life. You have all changed the way I relate to my body, the way I view sickness and *disease*, the way I view healing, the way I view the world. The work you do matters. Your voices matter. It is all about believing in a new potential, and I can believe in those things because of your teachings, which help pave the way.

Ami McConnell and Fleet Abston, friends: You two have been so supportive throughout my entire author journey. I trust you, I look up to you both, and I appreciate you so much.

Rob Rufus, author, friend, and total badass: You are a goddamn rock star, a phenomenal writer, and an all-around amazing human. I'm so lucky to know you and am excited to watch you take over the literary world.

All the amazing authors who blurbed this book: Not only do I look up to each of you as authors, but I also LOVE your work and am a total fangirl of you all. Thank you for taking the time to read and review this book. It means the world to me.

The bloggers: You all are superheroes. Every post, every photo, every review matters. Thank you so much.

The librarians: You are the unsung heroes of the writing community, and I am so grateful we live in a world where people like you share books.

The bookstore owners: Thank you to every bookstore owner who has had me for an event or sold my book.

Nikki, best friend: This past year, we have been on such a learning and healing journey. I love you, I root for you, and I love our twenty-minute voice memos and two-hour walk-and-talks. Best thirty-plus-year friendship ever.

Emily, Randy, and Jereme Frey, family: Though we are a small family, we are a mighty bunch. We are creative. We are close. I am so grateful to have had parents who let me dream my big dreams, who have supported and encouraged me every step of the way, but also help keep me grounded. Having a brother who is also a musician and has created such amazing work (and let's face it, has also been married twice, too, just like me!) reminds me that this journey is unfolding just as it should. You are my people, and I love my people. Thank you for it all.

Sophie, my dear daughter: With every book, you cheer me on, lift me up, and give me amazing plot ideas. You inspire me on every level with your free spirit and innate wisdom and remind me every single day what matters: *to be yourself and live life by your own rules.*

Alex, partner, best friend, dreamer: You inspired both Ben and Liam in this book. Thanks to you, I don't have any "what-ifs" in my life, especially when it comes to love. I hope you know I could not do this crazy author life without you. You so tirelessly provide everything I need without me having to ask. Every nourishing meal, every hot bath drawn, every massage, every morning coffee conversation, every hug, every bit of support . . . It fills me up and reminds me that we are on this journey together. My success is yours, and vice versa. I love you. I'm so proud of us.

Lastly to YOU, the reader: If you're still reading this, thank YOU. You, who picked up this book. You, who took the time to spend with my words. I am forever grateful.

What I'm manifesting: *I would like to sell a million copies of this book. Like, today. Or maybe tomorrow. But mostly today. And so it is, and it is so.*

What are you manifesting?

Discussion Questions

1. When Ben presents his Master Plan, Harper immediately dismisses it. If you were in the same position, how would you respond?

2. In one life, Ben is healthy, and in the other, he isn't. Why do you think that is? Circumstances? A different environment?

3. Do you believe in parallel timelines? Why or why not?

4. For Harper, her biggest fear when she is younger is not living up to her potential and settling for an ordinary life. She wants to be an artist and live in New York, but her life swerves in another direction. Does she settle by becoming a teacher and letting her art dreams die? Or does she make the right decision?

5. Harper comes face-to-face with the one man who "got away." Have you ever had a big what-if when it comes to love?

6. If you were in Harper's position, how would you have handled Liam showing up? Is it a sign or a test?

7. Do you think it's possible to heal yourself without medical intervention, even if given a terminal diagnosis? Why or why not?

8. Have you ever given up a passion to follow a more stable path? Did you regret that choice?

9. Have you ever had to say goodbye to someone who was still living?

10. Have you ever felt like you were waiting for your "real" life to begin?

11. Do you believe that our minds have the ability to heal our bodies? Why or why not?

12. In the book, Harper has made excuses why she hasn't followed her passions. Can you relate? Why or why not?

13. Harper is very torn between staying loyal to Ben and admitting that she still has unresolved feelings for Liam. Do you think she handled that inner conflict well? Were there times you were uncomfortable with her choices, or did you empathize with her struggle?

14. If you could spend time in your "grass is greener" life, what would that look like? Where would you live? What would you be doing? Describe it.

15. At the end of the book, Ben makes a comment that maybe his unborn child is the "new" person Harper was meant to love. Do you agree? Is it her child, or is it Liam?

16. In the end, what do you think Harper learned? How did she change?

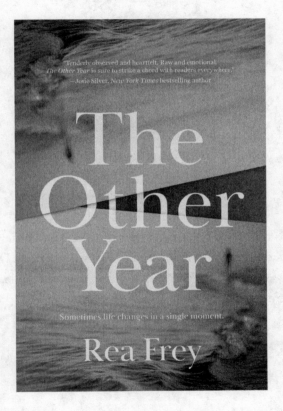

About the Author

Photo by Kate Gallaher

Rea Frey is the award-winning author of several domestic suspense, women's fiction, and nonfiction books. Known as a Book Doula, she helps other authors birth their books into the world. To learn more, visit www.reafrey.com.